Advance Praise for *White Sand, Blue Sea*

"Let Anita Hughes whisk you away to the glamorous island of St. Barts. . . . A love story filled with amazing adventures, exotic settings, and of course, romance, Hughes's latest novel is sure to delight." —Brenda Janowitz, author of *The Dinner Party*

"Family intrigue, romance, and yet another luscious setting from Anita Hughes. For any reader who hopes to kick back and escape into sun, sand, and drama, look no further."
—Jamie Brenner, author of *The Forever Summer*

Praise for Anita Hughes

"Anita Hughes combines a lush setting, family mystery, love, and longing in one enchanting story of three beautiful women who are tested and who endure." —Patti Callahan Henry, *New York Times* bestselling author of *Coming Up for Air,* on *French Coast*

"Gorgeously festive and evocative, this is a compelling story filled with characters you truly care about. I adored it."
—Melissa Hill, *USA Today* bestselling author of *The Charm Bracelet,* on *Christmas in Paris*

Also by Anita Hughes

Christmas in Paris

Santorini Sunsets

Island in the Sea

Rome in Love

French Coast

Lake Como

Market Street

Monarch Beach

WHITE SAND, BLUE SEA

ANITA HUGHES

St. Martin's Griffin ⚞ New York

WHITE SAND, BLUE SEA. Copyright © 2017 by Anita Hughes. All rights reserved. Printed in the United States of America. For information, address St. Martin's Press, 175 Fifth Avenue, New York, N.Y. 10010.

www.stmartins.com

The Library of Congress Cataloging-in-Publication Data is available upon request.

ISBN 978-1-250-11709-0 (trade paperback)
ISBN 978-1-250-11710-6 (e-book)

Our books may be purchased in bulk for promotional, educational, or business use. Please contact your local bookseller or the Macmillan Corporate and Premium Sales Department at 1-800-221-7945, extension 5442, or by e-mail at Macmillan SpecialMarkets@macmillan.com.

First Edition: April 2017

10 9 8 7 6 5 4 3 2 1

To my mother

WHITE SAND,
BLUE SEA

Chapter One

IT WAS LATE MORNING AND the sky was bright blue and the sun was the color of honey.

Olivia stood on the porch of her mother and stepfather's plantation-style villa and thought the view reminded her of a Gauguin painting. The ocean was a sheet of glass and the hills were dotted with palm trees and the horseshoe-shaped bay of Gustavia was filled with white sailboats. She slipped on her sunglasses and was glad to be back in St. Barts.

No matter how many years she had been coming, she was thrilled when the tiny plane landed at Gustaf airport. The customs officer greeted her in French and the taxi drivers lined up in their floral shirts and leather sandals. She scanned the brightly painted Volkswagen buses until she found Jean-Claude because he had the best gossip on the island.

He drove too quickly along the coast and she admired the white sand of Grand Cul de Sac and the chaise longues at St. Jean Beach. Whenever she tried describing St. Barts to her friends in New York, they could never understand how an island smaller than Manhattan had endless green coves and fourteen beaches.

Then Jean-Claude climbed the winding road to the villa and Olivia felt her shoulders relax. The gray New York spring dissolved like the final scene of a movie she'd watched on the plane, and all she could think about was snorkeling and eating coconut sorbet and stuffed crab.

Now she smoothed her blond hair and thought of the wonderful things they were going to do this week. Her twenty-fifth birthday was in four days and they would celebrate with an intimate dinner at Maya's. The maître d' would bring out the same banana soufflé she'd ordered since she was five years old and her mother and stepfather would give her a diamond tennis bracelet or ruby earrings.

And she was almost certain her boyfriend, Finn, was going to propose. He had been so nervous going through customs, Olivia thought he was going to fish out a diamond ring and drop to his knee on the linoleum floor. Finally he'd whispered to the customs officer and they'd disappeared into a private room. When they emerged, his blue eyes sparkled and his smile was as bright as the sun.

Finn was so traditional; he was probably on the tennis court now asking Felix, her stepfather, for her hand in marriage. She wondered if he would book a table at Eden Rock and propose over Caribbean lobster and chocolate cake with mango ice cream. Or perhaps they would take a moonlight stroll to see the turtles and he would draw her close and kiss her.

Only one person wasn't here to celebrate her birthday and she tried not to think about him. Her father had walked out of their Morningside Heights apartment twenty years ago, and she hadn't seen him since.

Hadley, her mother, would laugh and say, *Being Sebastian, he didn't simply walk out.* He left a bouquet of sunflowers and a list of things to ship when he had a forwarding address: his collection of Kipling's poems and Lawrence Durrell's travel writings and the alpaca jacket they'd bought in Peru.

For the first five years, Olivia had helped her mother mail his birthday invitation. Every April she expected him to bound up the stone steps of the villa and swing her in his arms, like a sitcom father on television.

Often the invitations were returned "address unknown" and sometimes she received a letter with details of his latest adventure. He spent three months painting in Tanzania and he wished he could show her the wide plains and amber light. He was on a barge on the Nile and was sorry he missed the piñata and vanilla custard birthday cake.

Most years he sent exotic presents: a tea set when he lived in Kyoto, jade earrings from a jeweler in Guiyang, a bolt of fabric from Marrakesh with the colors of the rainbow. But lately the presents had dried up and were replaced by cards that were late.

Felix had been the most wonderful stepfather, paying for her education at the Brearley School and Vassar and taking her to the Guggenheim and the Metropolitan on the weekends. And how could she miss something she never had? The only thing she remembered about Sebastian was his musk cologne and the occasional stubble on his chin.

A taxi stopped in front of the villa and a man stepped out. He wore blue slacks, a white shirt, and a straw hat. His suit jacket was slung over his shoulder and he carried a leather bag.

Olivia leaned over the balcony and wondered whether her mother and Felix had invited a guest and forgot to tell her. Sundial was always open to friends and often the bedrooms were filled with artists that Hadley represented or members of Felix's club. Esther was happy to set extra place settings at the glass dining room table and make pots of fish stew.

The doorbell rang and Olivia walked inside and hurried down the wooden staircase. She opened the door and saw the man standing on the porch, smoking a cigarette. His eyes widened and he dropped the cigarette.

"Hello, Olivia! God, it's been a long time. You shouldn't answer the door dressed like that, what if I were a complete stranger?" He glanced at her yellow swimsuit. "You should never dress like that at all, what was your mother thinking?" He handed her his jacket. "At least put this on, you're going to give the taxi driver a stroke."

"I don't remember you, but I don't seem to be in any danger," Olivia laughed. "And it's too hot to wear anything but the thinnest fabric. If you'll follow me, I'm sure your room is ready. My mother loves to keep the villa filled with guests and there are fresh towels next to the swimming pool. We only arrived yesterday and Esther is out buying papayas and caramboles. Wait until you try the fruit on the island, it's the best you've ever tasted."

"What sounds good right now is bourbon over ice." He loosened his collar. "I haven't had a chance to convert my yen to euros; could you pay the taxi driver? And there's another bag in the trunk. My back is terrible and I can't lug it up the stairs.

"This is some place!" he exclaimed and whistled when Olivia had paid the taxi driver and carried his bag into the marble foyer. He entered the living room and studied the parquet floor and yellow plaster walls and French doors leading onto the porch. Silk sofas were covered with floral throws and a marble bar was lined with brightly colored bottles.

He filled a glass with ice and poured a shot of bourbon. "If I had known the bar was stocked with Hennessy and there was a view of the whole island, I might have visited sooner."

"What did you say your name was?" Olivia asked, perching on a leather stool. "My mother must have forgotten to mention that you were coming. Though it is odd she asked someone outside of the immediate family; you see, we're celebrating my birthday. But it's always nice to have company and Esther will bake her buba rhum cake."

"I didn't say my name." He twirled his straw hat and looked at Olivia. "But you may have heard of it, it's the same as yours. I'm Sebastian, your father."

Olivia felt almost dizzy. Of course he was her father; why hadn't she seen it before! His eyes were the same green as in the old photograph on her bedside table. But his hair was salt and pepper and there were lines on his forehead.

She turned away and thought she mustn't cry. She flashed on all the years she'd imagined this moment: Sebastian appearing on the doorstep of her mother and stepfather's Central Park duplex and Olivia showing him her princess bedroom. Sebastian showing up at awards day at the Brearley School and clapping when she received the history prize. Sebastian coming to parents' day at Vassar and taking her out for a cheeseburger and a chocolate shake.

She was a grown woman and soon she'd be engaged; she didn't need her father. But he was exactly how she'd imagined him: with slicked-back hair and sparkling eyes and a small dimple on his cheek. How could she turn him away when he was finally here?

"We've been talking for ten minutes." Olivia glared at Sebastian. "Why didn't you tell me who you are?"

"It's an old trick I learned from a Serengeti tribesman." He refilled his glass. "I was trying to paint a herd of elk. He said the best way to capture their essence was to not let them know you were there."

"I'm not an elk, I'm your daughter," Olivia continued. "I've been waiting twenty years for you to show up. The least you could have done was tell me your name."

"Feisty like your mother . . . you have every reason to be angry with me. Where is Hadley? The last time I saw her, her hair was the color of flax and her eyes were like cornflowers." He fiddled with his glass. "Does she still do that thing when she is nervous, a slight cough that became a laugh?"

"I hadn't noticed." Olivia flushed. "She went to the post office but she'll be back in a minute. No one told me you were coming. I don't know anything about you: where you've been, where you're going, why you are here at all."

"I'm here for your birthday, of course," he explained, taking a silver cigarette case out of his pocket. "Do you mind? Your generation is so politically correct, lighting a cigarette is worse than reading a copy of *Playboy*." He lit the cigarette with a pearl lighter. "I don't want to talk about me right now. I want to hear all about you. Start by telling me what you do for fun."

"Finn and I like to visit the Frick on the weekends," she replied. "And sometimes we go to the Strand and I buy the latest paperback books. Finn loves biographies and anything on war and history."

"Museums and bookstores?" He raised his eyebrow. "Can't you do better than that? When I was your age I ate yak with a snake charmer in Tibet and drank ouzo with a cliff diver on Corfu."

"I spent a semester in Florence when I was at Vassar," she sighed. "It was wonderful to stroll along the Arno and imagine Raphael and Tintoretto crossing the same bridge." Her eyes were bright.

"The first time I saw Michelangelo's *David* I thought I was finally alive."

"Michelangelo did know his way around the human body," he murmured. "But that's not traveling, that's reading newspapers in different languages. In my day it was a rite of passage to see the places you read about in *National Geographic*: Senegal and Salamanca. Now the criteria for going somewhere is whether it has Wi-Fi and bottled water."

"We don't have time for twenty-four-hour flights and long layovers." Olivia shrugged. "Finn is an associate at his family's law firm and I manage my mother's art gallery. We come to St. Barts twice a year and spend a week in Nantucket during the summer." She stopped and a smile lit up her face. "But next year we might take a longer vacation. I'd like to go somewhere fabulous like Tahiti or Fiji."

He looked at Olivia and inhaled deeply on his cigarette. "A longer vacation? Do you mean a honeymoon?"

She nodded. "I'm not supposed to know but I think Finn is going to propose. He asked for my ring size and he's always busy on Thursday evenings. I'm sure he's designing the engagement ring."

"Are you sure he isn't doing what normal young men do?" Sebastian asked. "Going to a nightclub or playing poker in a friend's basement?"

"Finn's friends only have penthouses," Olivia laughed, "and he hates crowds, he'd never go to a nightclub. We've been dating for four years and his mother is making noises about grandchildren." She paused. "I'm not ready for children, but I wouldn't mind buying an apartment on the Upper West Side and maybe a weekend cottage in Montauk."

"I certainly hope you're not ready for children, you're not yet twenty-five," he spluttered. "When you have a baby, you'll think it's the loveliest thing in the world: a tiny perfect being that loves you unconditionally.

"But then they get older and you can't throw diapers and sterilized bottles into a bag and catch the next flight to Nairobi. All sorts of things get in the way: the dentist and ballet lessons and kindergarten. You may as well write out your will, your life is over."

"You still haven't told me why you're here. You've missed my birthday for twenty years, why show up now?" she asked and her lips trembled. "I can't believe my mother would keep it a secret but she must know, or you wouldn't be here at all."

He was about to answer when the front door opened. Olivia turned and saw her mother carrying a stack of envelopes. She wore a floral dress and her blond hair touched her shoulders.

"I asked Esther to pick up the mail but it always seems to collect at the post office." Hadley put her purse on the side table, then looked up. She gasped and the envelopes scattered over the wood floor.

Sebastian picked them up and handed them to Hadley. He studied her small waist and long legs and whistled.

"Hadley Miller," he said. "You don't look a day older than the last time I saw you."

"It hasn't been Hadley Miller in twenty years," she snapped. "What are you doing here and why didn't you tell anyone you were coming?"

"You sent me an invitation." He fiddled with his collar. "I thought I was welcome."

"I stopped sending you invitations to Olivia's birthday when she was ten years old." Hadley moved to the bar and filled a glass with tonic water and took a long sip. "Have you explained to your daughter why you never came?"

"St. Barts isn't the most convenient location for a birthday party." He turned to Olivia. "But there was not one night in the past two decades that I didn't think about you before I fell asleep." He walked over to the balcony. "I'm just a better father in my mind than in person. I wasn't cut out for watching Thanksgiving plays full of kindergartners with runny noses."

"How dare you waltz in unannounced," Hadley interjected. "This is not the time for a Sebastian pity party. I need to talk to Olivia in private."

"Your mother thought I was too self-centered to have a baby, but she was wrong," Sebastian continued. "I spent the first six months after you were born studying your plump body. You had a way of lying on your back and kicking your legs. And the first time you smiled, I felt like I won a prize." He paused. "But I'm an artist, I have to create. And you can't create if you spend all your time looking at the greatest creation of all."

"I'm sure I read that in a Hallmark card," Hadley retorted. "If you'll excuse us, I need Olivia in the pool house."

"Don't leave now, we're just getting reacquainted. Speaking of cards, I brought you a present," Sebastian said to Hadley and reached into his bag. "I was painting poppies near Tokyo and a farmer's wife wore these red slippers. I remember how your feet were always cold and thought they'd be perfect."

"My feet don't get cold in St. Barts." Hadley unwrapped the paper and discovered a pair of satin slippers with gold tassels. She handed them back to Sebastian. "Keep them. I'm sure they'll come in handy when you're sleeping in a tent in the Himalayas."

"Your mother always insisted I give her her birthday presents early because she wanted your birthday to be special," Sebastian explained to Olivia.

Olivia turned to her mother. "I thought you like that we share the same birthday."

"Of course I do." Hadley flushed. "But for a child a birthday is like Christmas but better. The whole world exists just for you." She paused. "Anyway, Felix likes me to pick out my own presents. Every year I go to Bloomingdale's the week before my birthday."

"How romantic," Sebastian murmured. "The best part about receiving a gift is being surprised when you unwrap the tissue paper."

"Felix is very practical," Hadley explained. "I've never returned a present, and every Christmas I get my favorite L'Occitane face cream."

"You do have the same peaches and cream complexion as when I painted you in Bombay." He paused. "My skin looks like it weathered ice storms in Greenland and desert winds in the Sahara."

"It's called age, Sebastian." Hadley smoothed her skirt. "But I do always celebrate April twenty-fifth. It is my and Olivia's birthday, and it's the day our divorce was final."

"I was sitting in a bar in the Australian outback and received the papers in a manila envelope," he sighed. "Those damn bush pilots can deliver mail anywhere."

"I'm enjoying your version of Jules Verne's *Around the World in Eighty Days* but you must be tired after a long flight." She handed Olivia her car keys. "Olivia can drive you to your hotel and you can return for dinner."

Felix put his shot glass on the counter. "I don't have a hotel room."

"You have to stay somewhere." Hadley frowned. "Since you're

here, you must attend Olivia's birthday party. We reserved a table at Maya's and the chef is making mahimahi in carpaccio and black potato truffles."

"God, that reminds me: I'm starving," Sebastian groaned. "Maybe Esther could rustle up a turkey sandwich. Of course I was planning on staying for Olivia's party. I have to drop off a painting with a client in Anguilla on Friday." He paused. "Frankly, I can't afford a hotel. St. Barts is worse than Portofino or Cannes."

Hadley's eyes flickered. "Where were you expecting to stay?"

"I was hoping to stay here." He hesitated. "Olivia and I have so much to catch up on. I brought a whole bag of photos, I almost broke my back dragging them through the airport."

"Felix would never allow it," Hadley stated. "And Esther doesn't have time to make up another room."

"I'll make up the room," Olivia said.

She should be furious at her father and insist he stay at a bed-and-breakfast in St. Jean or a hotel near the airport. But she couldn't remember her parents saying two words to each other and now they'd had a whole conversation. Didn't she deserve four days with the two people who created her?

"It's the twenty-first century and you and Felix are married," Sebastian commented. "It's your house too."

"It is spring break and I'm sure the hotels are full," Hadley sighed. "Every New York hedge fund manager has a private jet parked on the runway. I suppose you could have the guest suite in the pool house."

"I sleepwalk at night, you wouldn't want me to fall into the pool." He walked into the hallway. "You must have a den with a comfy leather sofa."

Sebastian strode past the dining room with its high-backed

velvet chairs and bright geometric rug. He entered a room with paneled walls and an antique desk.

He glanced at a gold-framed painting and gasped. "There it is! I knew it didn't belong in a stuffy living room on Central Park."

"When we got married Felix wasn't keen on displaying a painting by my ex-husband," Hadley said, following him. "But he has come to appreciate it; it is a fine piece of art."

"*The Miller Girls*," Sebastian breathed. His eyes gleamed and he looked twenty years younger. "Do you remember a collector who offered me one hundred thousand dollars and I wouldn't part with it? I was twenty-six and thought I was going to be the next Van Gogh or Cezanne."

He turned to Olivia.

"We were staying at a game preserve in Kenya. You were three years old and you spent your days chasing zebras and looking through a pair of binoculars.

"Hadley wanted to go back to Nairobi; the nights were cold and you only had one jacket. But then we reached the foot of Mount Elgon and we had to stay. All I needed was three days to get the color right." He pointed at the painting. "See how the sun is reflected on your hair. And look at the shawl your mother was wearing. It probably cost five Kenyan shillings, but she looked like a queen.

"For the next year we carried it everywhere. It was our good-luck charm; I sold every canvas. God, we saw amazing places: underwater caves in Vietnam and mountain villages in China." His eyes dimmed. "Until we got to Thailand and everything went wrong."

"I have to go," Hadley said suddenly. "I'm meeting Felix at the tennis club for lunch."

"I can sleep here." Sebastian waved at the brown sofa. "All I need is a blanket and a bottle of scotch."

"I don't think that's a good idea, Felix likes to come down for a cigar." Hadley shook her head. "I just remembered Esther made up the room at the end of the upstairs hall. It only has a shower but there's a view of the bay."

"Olivia will show me and then we can go to the beach together." Sebastian put his arm through Olivia's. "Does Felix have an extra pair of swim trunks? In Japan you can only buy Speedos, and I'm not going to the beach in a pair of men's underwear."

Olivia entered her room and picked up her sunglasses. Sebastian was getting settled and she said she had to grab a paperback book and a tube of suntan lotion. But really she needed a few moments to herself. Her father was in St. Barts to celebrate her birthday! If she left her door open she could hear him humming a song.

Her bedroom had a wood floor and gauze curtains and orange plaster walls. She usually loved curling up in a chintz armchair and gazing at the white sand beach and grand palm trees. But now her heart raced and she couldn't sit still.

She wanted to know so many things about him: What were his favorite movies, did he like chocolate ice cream, was he afraid of spiders? And she wanted to tell him about herself: She was allergic to pineapple but loved melon. She twisted her ankle ice skating when she was nine and convinced her mother to get a black Labrador for her eleventh birthday. It didn't last long. Felix was allergic and they had to give it away.

It was almost like they were pen pals meeting for the first time. They *had* been pen pals of sorts. She wrote Sebastian dozens of letters over the years and her most cherished possession was the wooden box containing his replies.

She opened the bedside drawer and took out a square box. She picked up the first letter and began to read.

Giza, Egypt
My darling Olivia,
I am sitting at the foot of the Great Pyramids and wishing one of these camels could fly. I would hoist myself on its hump and soar all the way to your sixth birthday party.

Do you remember when I used to read you The Swiss Family Robinson *and* The Jungle Book? *You didn't understand a word; you were barely five. But I hoped if I read out loud about jungles and waterfalls the desire to see the world would creep under your skin. Like when your mother sang to you while you were in the womb.*

This is the first time we won't celebrate your birthday together and I am terribly sad. But I gaze up at the pyramids and know what we have will survive. All the sand and wind could never erode my love for you.

I'm sure Hadley is reading this to you and wondering why I don't deliver the sentiment in person. One day when you're older I will explain it to you. For now, just know I love you more than anything and wish you the happiest birthday full of cake and presents.

Your loving father,
Sebastian

Olivia folded the letter and put it back in the box. Sebastian was her father and no matter what excuses he made, he'd spent twenty years traipsing around the planet without seeing her. Could she really forgive him because he appeared with a bag of photos and a smile that could light up Times Square?

But if she sulked around all week, she'd spoil her birthday and possibly Finn's proposal. Suddenly she thought of Finn and gulped. What would Sebastian think of Finn?

She searched her closet for a hat and thought it was impossible not to like Finn. He had short blond hair and blue eyes and strong shoulders from years of doing crew. He grew up in a leafy suburb of New Jersey where the houses had English gardens and tennis courts and a chauffeur. He graduated from Princeton and one day he'd be a partner at the family law firm.

But she thought of the way Finn packed a tuna salad sandwich for lunch because restaurants in Midtown charged twenty dollars for a Caesar salad. He wore his grandfather's Bulova watch because he didn't trust anything else to tell the exact time, and in four years he had never picked her up a minute late.

She slipped on her sandals and stood on the balcony. White clouds drifted across the sky and the air smelled of frangipani and hibiscus. She shielded her eyes from the sun and wondered what Finn would think of her father.

Chapter Two

HADLEY PEERED OUT THE DOOR of the pool house and heard her car peel away. She grabbed an apple from the fruit bowl and turned back to the ironing board.

She didn't really have a lunch date with Felix but when she'd stood in the library with Sebastian and Olivia she suddenly realized she needed to be alone. Now she touched the iron to see if it was hot and had to laugh.

She was incapable of telling Felix the orange juice was fresh squeezed when she forgot to buy oranges, even though juice from the carton tasted exactly the same. She could never change her birth date on her passport like some of her friends and if she couldn't sell an artist's work she fixed him a martini and gave him the bad news. But Sebastian had been in St. Barts for an hour and she was already telling a little white lie.

Esther would be angry with her for ironing the pillowcases; she had her own method of doing things. But Hadley found ironing so relaxing: the hot iron crisscrossed the fabric and you had time to think.

And she had so much to think about. She should be happy

Sebastian was here; she had been the one who invited him. Even if she'd stopped walking the invitation to the post office fifteen years ago, had anything really changed? Olivia was still his little girl and he was still her father.

But Sebastian was like the most expensive cognac. It went down so smoothly, you thought it didn't have any effect at all. You ended up dancing all night and thinking the stars were a string of pearls and the sky was black velvet. Then you woke up in the morning with a parched throat and a pounding headache.

She wasn't worried about herself. Being around Sebastian was like having the chicken pox: once you were exposed, you became immune. But Olivia barely remembered him; she was as susceptible as a baby who hadn't yet received its shots.

She turned over the pillowcase and thought about the year after Sebastian left. Olivia drew pictures in a sketchbook to show him when he returned. She checked the mailbox every day and Hadley watched her stand on tiptoes and something caught in her throat.

Then Felix entered their lives and attended Olivia's school plays and ballet recitals. They all drove up to the Hudson Valley to see the leaves change, and Olivia wore a satin flower girl dress and a coral bracelet to their wedding.

Felix and Olivia developed a genuine respect for each other and they both loved French movies and Renaissance art. Nothing made Hadley happier than sitting at the glass dining room table and having a lively conversation about books and music.

But nobody was like Sebastian. The moment he entered a room the whole world lit up, and when he turned to you, his smile felt brighter than the sun.

Did she really believe he'd missed the first quarter century of Olivia's life and had suddenly appeared to make amends?

She remembered when Olivia was two and they visited the floating markets in Bangkok. Sebastian carried Olivia on his shoulders and they sampled sliced coconut and water chestnuts. Olivia saw a red bolt of fabric and pulled at it with her fists.

Sebastian approached the salesgirl and complimented her on her stall. He hadn't seen such gorgeous fabrics anywhere in Bangkok. Did she make her shawl herself, where did she learn to sew?

Sebastian showed her his empty pockets and said he would come back and buy a scarf and maybe a shirt. The woman insisted he take something now and cut a piece of fabric from the red bolt.

What could he possibly want? She knew from gossip in the art circles that he hadn't painted an important piece in years. But there was always an industrialist in Brussels or a polo player in Palm Beach who wanted a Sebastian Miller on his wall.

Sebastian used to laugh that it was the collector who never traveled anywhere that didn't have five-star hotels or designer boutiques who wanted a street scene in Guangzhou hanging in his Fifth Avenue penthouse.

She suddenly thought about Felix and felt a little faint. What would he say when he discovered Sebastian's jacket on the coatrack and his slippers in the upstairs hallway?

And they really didn't need Sebastian delving into their marriage. Sometimes she thought Sebastian should have been a forensic accountant or a psychiatrist; he had a way of asking questions that made you squirm.

She folded the pillowcase and was sure she was worrying for nothing. Sebastian was in St. Barts because he wanted to celebrate Olivia's twenty-fifth birthday.

She had watched him drink in Olivia's slender cheekbones and dazzling smile and remembered Sebastian when he was in love.

He invested everything in a single emotion and you felt bigger than the entire coast of Africa.

Hadley leaned against the ironing board and remembered when they met, at a guesthouse in Cape Town during the rainiest week of the year.

Hadley fiddled with the phone cord and gazed out the window of the guesthouse. The bed-and-breakfast in Cape Town belonged to a friend's parents and it was everything she could imagine. There was a white picket fence and a bright red front door and stone walls covered in ivy. The guests ate buttermilk rusks and drank muddy coffee in the tile kitchen and at night the dining room table was set with platters of tomato bredie and pots of vegetable stew.

And the garden! When Hadley inhaled the sweet aroma, she thought it was worth the grueling flights and endless bus rides to get from Connecticut to South Africa. There were African lilies and honeysuckle and purple daisies. A willow tree shaded an iron bench tucked among beds of roses and orchids.

She had slept for sixteen hours and then showered in the communal bathroom. She slipped on khakis and a red sweater and grabbed her guidebook. There were so many things she wanted to do: see the African penguins at Boulders Beach and drive up Chapman's Peak to watch the sunset. Explore the fishing boats at Gordon's Bay and visit the Kristenbosch Botanical Gardens.

But then it started raining and she decided to curl up with a book in front of the fireplace. Everyone said the weather in Cape Town in August was as unpredictable as a teenage girl. One minute the northwest winds made it impossible to wear a skirt, the next the sun came out and you wore the thinnest cotton dress.

But for two days, the rain played on the gray slate roof. When she peered outside the air was misty, with a biting chill. Then she discovered the airline had lost her bag with her rubber rain boots and nylon jacket.

Now she put the phone down and sighed. She had been hopeful her suitcase would arrive, but it seemed as likely to be in Amsterdam or Istanbul. If she spent money on rain gear she wouldn't be able to browse in the shops on the Victoria & Albert Waterfront, but if she stayed in the guesthouse she wouldn't see Cape Town at all.

"You've been sitting in that spot for two days." A man her age entered the living room. He wore a gray rain jacket and held a ceramic mug. "Some people come to the guesthouse to relax and enjoy the food. The bunny chow is delicious and the bobotie is like my mother's meatloaf topped with a baked egg. But you're missing out. We're only a few blocks from the Martin Melck House and they have an exhibition about Nelson Mandela."

"Don't you think I want to go outside," Hadley demanded. "I waited for six hours on the tarmac in Greenland because I booked the cheapest flight. I rode a bus from the airport that bumped so badly, I looked like I tumbled down a staircase. And I spent twenty grand on a taxi from the bus terminal because I had no idea the guesthouse was only a fifteen-minute walk." She paused. "And then it started raining and the airline lost my luggage. I can hardly climb Lion's Head in a cotton sweater and a pair of Keds."

"They call winter the 'secret season' because you never know what the weather will be like." The man pulled out a chair.

"It doesn't seem like a secret to me." Hadley frowned. "It hasn't stopped raining since I arrived."

"It has to rain or the colors wouldn't be so vibrant." He pointed to the garden. "Have you seen such bright oranges and sunny yellows? Yesterday I hiked to the top of Table Mountain. The hills belong in Ireland and the ocean is like Tahiti and the waterfalls make you think you're in Polynesia."

"I haven't seen anything, I may as well go home," she sighed.

"It can't be that bad." He set his mug on the table. "Go to the market and buy a pair of boots and a raincoat."

"I'm staying here for free because the guesthouse belongs to the parents of a friend," she explained. "I've made out a daily budget for entrance fees and bus tickets and braised sausage with chutney. If I spend the money on clothes I won't be able to buy a milk tart."

"You wouldn't be missing out," he said and his face broke into a smile. "Milk tarts are so sweet, they make Dunkin' Donuts seem like health food.

"The great thing about traveling is talking to strangers. You've never met them before and you won't see them again. It's like going to a psychiatrist without the lumpy sofa and plastic plant." He held out his hand. "Sebastian Miller, it's a pleasure to meet you."

"Hadley Stevens," she said and noticed his eyes were as green as the hills behind the guesthouse.

"Let's play a game," he suggested. "It will help pass the time until it stops raining."

"No, thank you, I'm terrible at backgammon and I always lose at Monopoly."

"I wasn't thinking of a board game." He looked at Hadley.

She flushed. "Just because I'm traveling alone doesn't mean I'm that kind of girl."

"I didn't think you were." He glanced at her high-necked sweater and white sneakers. "I mean a word game. Tell me three facts about you, the more outrageous the better."

"Why would I do that?" she asked, studying the way his dark hair touched his collar.

"Because the only magazines are *Ladies' Home Journal* and I happen to have read the Robert Ludlums on the bookshelf."

Hadley curled her hair around her fingers and shrugged. It wasn't going to stop raining soon and she'd finished the paperback she brought on the plane.

"I'll go first," he suggested. "I grew up on the north shore of Chicago and we had a house with a rose garden. When I was eleven, I asked my mother if I could give her roses to the girl next door. She told all her friends at the country club how mature her son was . . . until she discovered I gave them to Sally's mother in exchange for homemade chocolate chip cookies."

"That doesn't sound too outrageous," Hadley laughed.

"I attended a Jesuit school and when I was fourteen the boys brought in *Playboy*s and hid them in their desks. I was more interested in my father's stack of *National Geographic*s. Then my class took a trip to Florence to see Botticelli's *Venus*." He sipped his coffee. "I realized there was nothing more miraculous than a beautiful woman and if you could spend your life sketching her glossy hair and luscious thighs you walked with the gods."

Hadley wrapped her arms around her chest and felt oddly naked. "And the third?"

"I believe in three things. That without Michelangelo we'd still be living in the dark ages, that the best men in history were the ones who drafted the American Constitution. And the greatest mystery isn't how the pyramids were built or whether the Loch Ness monster exists." He paused and looked at Hadley. "It's why we fall in love."

Hadley turned to the window and studied the bright birds of paradise and pink jacaranda.

"I'm the only person I know who doesn't like vanilla ice cream," she said finally.

He laughed. "You have to do better than that."

Hadley felt slightly dangerous. As if she were an international spy and had landed behind enemy lines.

"In the summer I sleep completely naked," she said. "I can't stand anything against my skin except freshly ironed sheets."

"That's much better." He leaned forward. "What's number three?"

"My mother was the black sheep of her family. My father teaches geography at Miss Porter's School in Connecticut and my mother was his student. It wasn't as scandalous as it sounds. She was eighteen and they didn't have their first date until after graduation but her family cut her off." She paused. "He still teaches there, and when I was a student I thought the other teachers expected me to follow in her footsteps and run off with the Latin teacher."

"Did you?" Sebastian asked.

"I'm only twenty-two and want to see the world." She shook her head. "Love isn't as interesting as taking the cable car to the top of Table Mountain or seeing the great white sharks in Simon's Town."

"That's where you're wrong," he said and drained his coffee cup. "Love is the greatest adventure of all."

Sebastian said he was starving and they moved into the kitchen and ate lamb skewers and chakalaka. Sebastian had been there for a week and knew which curry was spicy and which jam was too sweet.

"Are you an artist?" Hadley asked, eating a spoonful of malva pudding.

"I'm supposed to start law school next month. I admire my parents; my father built a prosperous law firm and my mother is a respected psychiatrist." He drummed his fingers on the tile counter. "But I suppose I'm a terrible egoist. I don't want to help others, all I want to do is paint."

"If you admire the great artists, why aren't you at the Louvre in Paris or the Uffizi in Florence?"

"I couldn't replicate the *Mona Lisa* or sculpt Michelangelo's *David*." He waved out the window. "But here everything is vast and wild and full of color. I want to paint sunsets with the sky on fire and cliffs that fall into the sea. I'm going to be one of the greatest artists of my generation."

Sebastian said he had to run an errand and Hadley took a rusk and a cup of tea into the living room. It had been fun to talk to an American her own age, but the rain kept coming down and she was no closer to seeing Cape Town.

She wondered if she should have been like the other girls at Mount Holyoke who fled to Italy or the French Riviera after college graduation. They all packed their Kate Spade sweaters and Gucci pumps and promised to meet in Rome or Cannes.

But she was a scholarship student and couldn't afford the designer boutiques on the Via Condotti or the cafés on the Boulevard Croisette. But in Cannes the sun shone three hundred days a year and in Rome she could have stayed in her roommate's seventeenth-century *palazzo*.

The front door opened and Hadley inhaled the scent of wet grass.

"You're still here, I thought you might have gone upstairs to take a nap," Sebastian said. He carried a brown box and his wet hair was plastered to his head.

Other guests mingled near the fireplace and Hadley flushed. They shouldn't have shared secrets. The last thing she needed was to get involved with someone when she might have to give up and go home.

"I'm not the least bit tired," she said. "I feel like a lion cooped up in its cage."

"Good, then you'll like these." He handed her the box.

She opened it and pulled out a yellow rain jacket and a pair of boots. There were thick gloves and a purple scarf.

"They're lovely but I can't accept them." She handed him the box. "I'm sure you'll find another American girl who wants to sleep with you; give it to her."

"Did you think I spent half an hour bartering in the rain just so I could kiss you?" he spluttered.

"Why else would you give a present to a complete stranger?"

Sebastian studied her shoulder-length blond hair and blue eyes and small nose. He shook the water out of his hair and smiled. "Because I want to paint you."

Hadley touched the iron and thought they had been so young, younger than Olivia and Finn. And Sebastian had been arrogant even then: certain that she would fall in love with him and that his paintings would be a success.

Why had she let him drink Felix's bourbon and stay at the villa? That was the problem with Sebastian. You said yes to everything and it was only when he was out of sight that you realized you'd had every intention of turning him down.

But then she remembered the way Olivia's face had lit up when she looked at her father. Surely he must have learned to behave himself, and he wasn't any longer the green-eyed boy who was more persuasive than a snake charmer.

She would just make him follow the rules. Drinks and dinner were at 6:00 p.m., and then Olivia and Finn would go out for an aperitif in Gustavia. He was welcome to join them if Olivia asked or he could stay with her and Felix and watch an old movie. Felix liked the lights off by midnight and Esther would be furious if Sebastian smoked in his room.

A car pulled into the driveway and Hadley's shoulders tensed. They'd had plenty of houseguests over the years, what was one more? She entered the living room and saw Sebastian's empty shot glass and suit jacket folded over an armchair. The difference with other houseguests was that Felix knew they were coming.

The car door opened and Felix stepped out. Hadley gasped and wondered what he was doing home. He usually spent all day on the tennis courts and arrived at the villa in time to shower and dress for dinner.

He slung his tennis bag over his shoulder and Hadley thought he'd grown more attractive with age. His gray hair suited him and he had a lean stomach and muscular legs. When Felix was around everything flowed smoothly: the fridge was stocked with limes and the butcher sent the best cuts of beef and Esther kept the vases filled with calla lilies.

Hadley remembered when they started dating and he always

opened her car door and gave her lilacs and boxes of chocolate truffles. It had been wonderful to slip out of the black slacks and blouses she wore at the gallery and put on sleek cocktail dresses and silver sandals and head out with Felix.

And the places they went! Chateaubriand and chestnut soufflé at La Grenouille and Bloody Marys and French onion soup at the St. Regis. She sat at the King Cole Bar and listened to jazz and felt young and pretty.

Sometimes she would lie in bed at night, her head buzzing from Kahlúa and cream and her skin smelling like cinnamon and vanilla, and feel a pang in her chest. But it was lovely to be with someone who took Olivia to the puppet show in Central Park and the tree lighting in Times Square and surprised them with tickets to *The Lion King* on Broadway. She remembered Olivia whispering to Felix she had seen a real lion in Africa and had to laugh.

Why was she thinking about this now? If only Sebastian hadn't shown up out of the blue. Felix would be furious that she asked Sebastian to stay without consulting him.

The front door opened and she wished she had time to mix a pitcher of martinis and refresh her makeup. Felix would be easier to deal with if he were stirring a toothpick-speared olive and her cheeks were brushed with powder.

"Felix, you're home." She met him in the foyer. "I wasn't expecting you for hours."

"I had a surprise visitor." He walked to the bar and filled a glass with ice. "You'll never guess who showed up at the club."

Hadley thought it couldn't have been Sebastian; that would have been low even for him. She was glad Felix had come home early. She could tell him about Sebastian's arrival and they could form a plan together.

"Finn appeared on the tennis court." He poured a shot of vermouth and laughed. "He was lucky I just beat Peter Gordon in straight sets or I wouldn't have appreciated the interruption."

"I thought he was going to Lorient to buy lobster for the barbecue." Hadley frowned.

"He wanted to discuss something first. He swore me to secrecy, but I said whatever he told me I would share with you." He paused. "Nothing is more important in a relationship than honesty. There isn't a thing I've done that I couldn't tell you."

Hadley noticed Sebastian's straw hat lying on the sofa and flinched. She tossed it under the sofa and smoothed her skirt.

"That's what marriage is all about," she agreed, suddenly longing for a gin and tonic.

"He asked me for Olivia's hand in marriage. Of course, I said we were thrilled. He wondered if they could have the ceremony here at Christmas. St. Barts is so important to Olivia and they could keep it intimate." He sipped his drink. "I gather Finn isn't one for sixteen-piece orchestras and ten-tier wedding cakes."

Hadley flashed on her wedding to Felix in the ballroom of the Carlyle. She hadn't known a single person besides her parents but it was important to Felix's family to have a five-course sit-down dinner and a bar stocked with Château Lafite Rothschild.

And it had been lovely! Wearing her Vera Wang gown and pearl necklace and watching Olivia scatter rose petals on the red runner.

When you were very young you thought you could get married on a barge on the Congo and true love would keep you together. But marriage needed traditions and love had to be very hardy to survive childhood croup and a steady diet of rice and beans.

"Having the wedding on St. Barts is a wonderful idea." Hadley pulled her mind back to the present. "We'll have the ceremony on the beach and the reception in our garden. Esther and I will make lobster ravioli and squash and kiwi meringue."

"There's only one problem." Felix fiddled with his glass. "We would have to invite Sebastian."

"Sebastian?" Hadley looked up.

"He is her father, he should have the option to give her away," he said thoughtfully. "I'll never understand how he chose to miss out on the most precious gift in the world."

"There is something I have to tell you." Hadley shifted on the sofa. Felix would understand Sebastian appearing unannounced; she had nothing to worry about.

"Tell me in a minute." Felix walked to the staircase. "I have a terrible headache, I need some aspirin."

A car screeched to a halt in the driveway. Hadley walked to the front door and saw Sebastian in the driver's seat. His cheeks were flushed and his forehead was covered in sweat.

She ran outside. "What happened? Where's Olivia?"

"It's nothing." Sebastian stepped out of the car and took off his sunglasses. He wore Felix's navy board shorts and his foot was covered in a bandage. "I went swimming at Gouverneur Beach. The water was magnificent, like taking a warm bath. Then I felt a sharp pain and was sure I was stung by a jellyfish."

"A jellyfish!" Hadley exclaimed. "I haven't seen one in years."

"The three lifeguards said it was a false alarm," he continued. "But they were very helpful. One even offered me a glass of coconut milk, she said drinking it neutralized the sting." He paused. "I told her it would be more effective spiked with rum and drunk in a dark nightclub."

"Three lifeguards?" Hadley crossed her arms over her chest.

"I've never been stung before, I didn't want to take any chances," he explained. "The other guard said I probably just brushed my foot against some coral. He bandaged me up and sent me home."

"Why didn't Olivia drive you?" Hadley asked.

"She offered but I insisted she wait for Finn," he mused. "Thank god I made her change out of that yellow bikini. Even in a one-piece every male under the age of fifty was staring at her." He looked at Hadley. "She has your small waist and long legs."

"She's taller than me and in much better shape." Hadley blushed. "You better come inside and get some ice."

"A shot of that bourbon sounds perfect but Olivia said drinks weren't until six." Sebastian's green eyes sparkled.

"I was talking about your foot," Hadley said, and suddenly saw Felix standing at the bar in the living room.

Felix! What would he say when Sebastian hobbled in wearing his swim trunks? And if she opened the bottle of bourbon he would see that it was half empty.

Felix was right; they weren't the kind of couple who had superficial flirtations or semi-innocent texts on their cell phones. Neither of them had secrets; it was one of the things she cherished about their marriage.

She would have just have to introduce them and explain why Sebastian's toothbrush was already in the upstairs bathroom.

"Where is the lucky bridegroom?" Sebastian limped into the living room. "I saw the write-up in *Town & Country* years ago. I was stranded at Mumbai airport and it was the only English-language magazine. What a surprise to see you wearing an ivory satin wedding dress. I was quite jealous." He looked at Hadley. "I'd been sleeping in a hut and eating chickpeas for breakfast. I would have given anything for the sautéed scallops and crème brûlée you served at the reception.

"I did send a gift, a set of terra-cotta pots I found in a mountain village." He paused. "I don't think I ever received a thank-you. Though another shot of that marvelous bourbon will do nicely."

Felix, standing motionless at the bar, looked at Sebastian.

"Have we met?" He held out his hand. "I'm Felix London and you are . . ."

Sebastian clasped Felix's hand. "Sebastian Miller, Olivia's father."

"Olivia's father!" Felix jumped back. He looked at Hadley and his cheeks paled. "What are you doing in St. Barts?"

"Didn't Hadley tell you I arrived? Good communication is so important in a marriage." Sebastian smiled. "I'm sure you two had more important things to discuss. If you like I can go back to the beach and join Olivia. Give you two some time alone in the villa."

"I was just about to explain to Felix . . ." Hadley flushed. She turned to Felix and smoothed her hair. "Sebastian arrived this morning."

"He just showed up at the front door?"

"It wasn't hard to find, the villa is quite well known on the island." Sebastian walked to the balcony. "What a splendid location, I would love to paint the white sand and vibrant hibiscus."

"But why are you here?" Felix poured a shot of vermouth.

"To celebrate Olivia's twenty-fifth birthday, of course." Sebastian turned to Felix. "Could I have a shot of that? I banged up my foot and it could use a little numbing."

"I have to tell you what a wonderful job you've done with my daughter. She's poised and elegant and appreciates art. I couldn't have raised her better myself." His eyes were moist. "Though she does seem a little . . . sheltered. She's only traveled to places that have a Starbucks at the airport."

"Hadley didn't tell me she invited you." Felix poured a second shot of vermouth and handed it to Sebastian.

"Not recently." Sebastian shrugged. "But invitations aren't like lawsuits, they don't have a statute of limitations." He gulped the vermouth. "I had some business in Anguilla and thought I'd stop by. The airport could be upgraded. All those private jets and the landing strip is no wider than a bike path.

"It was so kind of Hadley to lend me her car. I've already explored Gouverneur Beach," he said, finishing his drink. "And you mustn't apologize for the size of my room, I'm used to sleeping in small spaces."

"Your room!" Felix put his shot glass on the bar.

"Hadley insisted I stay at the villa. I did read that the Hotel Le Toiny has heated towels and an outdoor Jacuzzi, but I'm sure I'll be perfectly comfortable." He paused. "Though I am starving. I make an excellent turkey sandwich." He looked at Felix. "Would you mind showing me around the kitchen?"

"Do you really think you can just show up after twenty years and ask to use our kitchen?" Felix spluttered. "And if you think the Hotel Le Toiny has better accommodations you can stay there." He turned to Hadley. "Someone needs to tell me what's going on."

"Olivia asked Sebastian to stay," Hadley said quietly. "She was delighted that her father arrived for her birthday."

"I see." Felix nodded. "Olivia, of course. She must be thrilled."

"My god, is that a signed Kandinsky?" Sebastian gazed at a painting in a silver frame. "That's more valuable than gold bouillon. And what a marvelous piece, I've never seen such bold use of color."

"I'd like to talk to Sebastian alone." Felix propelled Sebastian toward the study. He turned to Hadley and his jaw was tight. "We'll only be a minute."

Felix's and Sebastian's voices drifted up the staircase and Hadley sank onto the bed. She shouldn't have left Sebastian and Felix alone together. Felix would do anything to protect her and Olivia if he thought their happiness was threatened. And Sebastian! She tried to imagine what he was saying to Felix and shuddered.

How could she have let Sebastian stay at the villa? Finn was almost certain to propose to Olivia; what if Sebastian messed up Finn's plans? And she had had enough to worry about: she had to plan Olivia's birthday and she was anxious to talk to Felix about what was going on between them. It couldn't continue much longer. She tried so many times in New York but the phone rang or she got called away to the gallery or Felix had to meet a client.

She pulled open her drawers and noticed a black lace camisole. She remembered when the customs officer had unzipped her suitcase and she'd glanced over to see if Felix was watching.

Now she stuffed the camisole to the back of the drawer and took a deep breath. She couldn't let Sebastian look too closely at her marriage. Or the whole birthday week would be ruined.

Chapter Three

OLIVIA SAT AT Bar de L'Oubli and nibbled melon and papaya. It was mid-afternoon and the cobblestone streets were filled with men and women in linen shorts and leather sandals. She sipped an iced coffee and felt like she had been in St. Barts forever.

After Sebastian left, she swam laps at Shell Beach. The clear water was filled with Jet Skis and white sailboats and silver yachts. The air smelled of exotic perfume and the sky was a sheet of Tiffany blue wrapping paper.

Now she watched the bright parasails and thought how she loved sitting at an outdoor table on the harbor. Couples strolled along Quai de la Republique and bought chocolate croissants at Boulangerie Choisy. Olivia tipped her face up to the sun and was glad she wasn't in New York.

She had been disappointed when Sebastian injured his foot and had to go back to the villa. She couldn't wait for him to meet Finn; her father and fiancé would finally be together!

But now she ate a slice of coconut and remembered when she took an English midterm in college. She'd studied for days but had worried that the professor wouldn't like her essay. She never really knew what grade she would receive until he handed back the paper.

Finn was the most loyal person she'd ever met. Whenever he visited his family in New Jersey he spent hours walking their fourteen-year-old golden retriever, Molly. Finn said Molly gave him so much joy when he was a boy; she deserved to have someone take care of her.

She knew he didn't approve of Sebastian missing her entire childhood. But it was impossible to not like Sebastian in person; he was like chocolate ice cream dipped in sprinkles. You couldn't resist the brightly colored coating, and when you bit inside, the chocolate ice cream was even more delicious.

Sebastian had swum at Gouverneur Beach and his stroke was as confident as that of an Olympic athlete. And he was so charming. He offered to take the pretty young lifeguard to lunch for bandaging his foot. When she declined he scribbled down her name so he could recommend her to her supervisor.

And his French was perfect! He'd insisted on buying Olivia a cover-up and they sifted through the caftans at Lolita Jaca. He engaged the salesgirl in a conversation on silkworms in Tibet and the garment trade in India. They were about to exchange phone numbers when Sebastian noticed the price tag on a Hermès wrap and steered Olivia out of the store.

They entered Bijoux de la Mer and Sebastian had a long discussion with the owner about deep-sea diving in Tahiti. Then Sebastian fastened a black pearl necklace around Olivia's neck and told her to look in the mirror. She gazed at her and Sebastian's reflection and her heart lifted. Did she ever imagine seeing their heads so close together?

Of course Finn would be thrilled Sebastian was here. After all, he was her father. If she welcomed him back after twenty years, how could Finn possibly argue?

"There you are." A young man approached her. He had short blond hair and wore a polo shirt and tan shorts. "I'm sorry I took so long. A poultry truck overturned on the road back from Lorient and I helped collect the escaped chickens. And then I had to stop at the club and see your father."

"My father!"

"I waited until he finished his tennis match." Finn smiled. "Luckily he won or he would have kicked me off the court."

"Oh, you mean Felix," Olivia said and felt relieved.

"Who else would I mean?" he asked.

Olivia debated waiting to tell Finn until he met Sebastian at the barbecue. But she'd spend the whole afternoon with a lump in her throat and an ache in the pit of her stomach.

She took a deep breath and slipped off her sunglasses. "Sebastian is in St. Barts."

"Sebastian, your father!" Finn gasped. "Why didn't you tell me?"

"He showed up at the front door wearing a straw hat," she continued. "I didn't recognize him at first. But once he told me, I saw the resemblance immediately. I have his eyes and I get my freckles from his grandmother."

"Nobody has green eyes like you," Finn murmured. "And everyone has freckles when they spend the morning swimming in the bay."

"He couldn't wait to meet you." Olivia fiddled with her napkin. "We drove down to the beach, but he hurt his foot and had to take care of it."

"Why is he in St. Barts now?" Finn asked. "He hasn't seen you for twenty years."

"To celebrate my twenty-fifth birthday, of course. My mother invited him to join us at Maya's."

"I suppose he can come to your birthday dinner." Finn nodded. "What else will he do while he's here?"

"He wants to spend all his time with us." Olivia's eyes sparkled. "We can see the turtles at Lorient and windsurf at Grand Cul de Sac. And he's a great chef; he learned to cook in Marseilles. He's going to make us goat cheese omelets and café au lait for breakfast."

"I don't think Felix and Hadley will let him take over their coffeemaker." Finn drummed his fingers on the table. "But we can join him at his hotel for orange juice and scrambled eggs with bacon."

"He's not staying at a hotel," Olivia corrected. "He's staying at the villa."

"Sebastian is staying at Sundial?" Finn choked.

"I don't think he has much money," Olivia explained. "His paintings still sell; everyone wants a Sebastian Miller. But he has a lot of expenses: airfare and taxis and buying the correct wardrobe."

"He never paid a dime in child support and he let Felix finance your education."

"He gave my mother *The Miller Girls*. Not that she would ever sell it." She paused. "It's like Felix's summer cottage in Nantucket. The roof always needs to be repaired and heating costs a fortune. But Felix wouldn't dream of giving it up, it's been in his family for decades."

"How does Felix feel about having his wife's ex-husband sleep in the guest bedroom?"

"I don't know." Olivia studied him. "She hadn't told him about inviting Sebastian."

"Hadley invited Sebastian without asking her husband?"

"This is the twenty-first century and it's Hadley's villa too." Olivia straightened her shoulders. "I don't know why you're so upset. He's my father, I'm the only one who has to forgive him."

"Of course, you're right, you're just so smart and beautiful. You juggle temperamental artists and demanding clients like a symphony conductor. And when you enter a room, everything seems brighter." He touched her hand. "I can't bear the thought of anyone hurting you."

"I wasn't any of those things when Sebastian left," Olivia said and bit her lip. "I was a five-year-old who planted daisies in Sebastian's paint jar and made everyone eat plain spaghetti with butter for dinner."

"All five-year-olds get into their parents' things and I'm sure your mother grilled chicken and vegetables after you went to bed," Finn replied. "Raising children isn't easy. You don't board a plane and send a birthday card once a year."

"Artists have always been terrible husbands and fathers," Olivia insisted. "Gauguin left his wife and children and lived in a treehouse in Tahiti. Sebastian did say he was sorry, he thought of me every night before he went to sleep."

"Sebastian convinced Hadley and Felix to let him stay in their private villa with a swimming pool and one-hundred-eighty-degree views of the island," Finn said. "I doubt he spent the last twenty years living in a thatched hut and eating bread rusks."

"He does appreciate a fine bourbon." Olivia smiled. "And he mentioned the week he stayed as the guest of a prince in Mumbai."

Finn leaned across the table and kissed her. His lips were warm and Olivia felt a shiver of excitement.

"What was that for?" she asked.

"I'm sitting at an outdoor café on a Caribbean island with the most beautiful girl in the world." He took her hand. "I don't want to spend the afternoon arguing about your father."

Olivia laughed. "What did you have in mind?"

A chill ran down her spine and she wondered if he was going to propose. But Finn wasn't the kind of guy who would ask her to marry him while she was wearing a swimsuit and halter top.

Finn was right. When they returned to New York, Sebastian would be a fond memory, like the shells they collected at the beach. They shouldn't spend their holiday arguing about whether he behaved selfishly or couldn't have done any better.

"We could drive to Flamands Beach." Finn kissed her again. "It's practically deserted and the sea is as warm as a bath."

Finn went inside to pay and Olivia saw a familiar figure leaning against the railing. Sebastian wore a patterned shirt and his dark hair was covered with a straw hat.

"I was hoping you'd still be in Gustavia." He approached her. "You look even more beautiful than this morning, your skin is a shade darker."

"I thought you had to rest your foot," Olivia replied.

"Some ice and a shot of bourbon and it was good as new." He shrugged. "Felix and your mother were home, and I know when three is a crowd. It's hard to find time for romance at our age, I thought they might appreciate being alone."

Finn walked toward them and Sebastian's face lit up in a smile.

"This must be the young man everyone is talking about." He held out his hand. "You've received more glowing endorsements than a presidential candidate. I'm Sebastian Miller, Olivia's father."

"Olivia told me you went up to the villa to rest," Finn said, shaking Sebastian's hand.

"That makes me sound like a grandfather," Sebastian laughed. "I could say I had a sudden urge to watch the hang gliders but the truth is I couldn't wait to meet you." He looked at Finn. "From the time Olivia learned to blow her first kiss, I wondered when she would fall in love. I'd stare at her when she was asleep and want to guard her from any guy who might trample on her heart.

"Then Hadley told me about you and I knew I didn't have to worry. It seems Olivia bypassed callous thugs and discovered a prince on the first try."

"I wouldn't say that." Finn's cheeks flushed.

"Princeton graduate, associate in a Manhattan law firm." He paused. "And she mentioned you are a wine connoisseur."

"I spent a summer in Burgundy." Finn nodded. "I learned about varietal grapes and the correct temperature to store wine."

"Young people today are more interested in microbreweries and Peruvian coffees that cost forty dollars a pound. But does anyone celebrate a silver anniversary with a bottle of pale ale or sip espresso while they recite Shakespeare's sonnets?" He paused. "Wine has been the elixir of the gods since Homer wrote about Dionysius in the *Odyssey*. It's a pleasure to meet a young man with my sensibilities."

"Are you interested in wine?" Finn asked.

"When I was in Beijing, I stayed at the home of the French consul. I'd been living for weeks on bean pods and some kind of meat I couldn't put my finger on." He paused. "Jean-Luc poured a glass of Château Margaux and I suddenly had the wisdom of Confucius. I'm buying a bottle of wine as a housewarming gift for Felix and hoped you could help me."

"The local wine shops are terribly overpriced," Finn said. "Are you sure you want to spend the money?"

"I'm not a heathen, I know the value of a king-size bed and marble bath." Sebastian took a cigarette out of his cigarette case and lit it with a pearl-tipped lighter. "Kindness is the most precious commodity of all, and everyone likes receiving a gift."

"I suppose we could visit Ceillier de Gouverneur," Finn suggested. "The owners, Thierry and Frederic, know everything about wine and they have the best selection on the island."

They walked along the waterfront and entered a blue building with white shutters. Sebastian stubbed out his cigarette and took off his straw hat. He studied the wooden racks as if he were discovering the Magna Carta.

"What a magnificent selection. I'm so tired of supermarkets that arrange the bottles by price." He selected a Château d'Anglès. "People don't understand that a great wine is like a piece of art. It's difficult to describe and even harder to replicate, but when you find it you can't buy anything else."

"I know what you mean," Finn agreed. "Last year I discovered a bottle of Villa Antinori and it was the best thing I ever tasted."

"The Italians do spoil us," Sebastian sighed. "They have the greatest sculptures and most delicious pasta and wine like liquid honey. I spent a week on the Amalfi coast and lived on seafood linguini and glasses of Chianti. But if we're having lobster tonight, we might try a dry champagne or chardonnay."

"How did you know we are having lobster?" Finn asked.

"Olivia told me but if there's not enough I completely understand." Sebastian waved his hand. "I can make do with salad and summer vegetables." He patted his stomach. "I probably shouldn't have tender lobster meat in drawn butter, at my age you have to watch every ounce."

"I can never finish a lobster and Esther is making tomato gazpacho with avocado and lemon tarts for dessert." Olivia put her arm through Sebastian's. "There will be enough for a small army."

"In that case I'd love some lobster." He beamed and turned to Finn. "What would you suggest?"

"We could try a Sonoma chardonnay." Finn handed a bottle to Sebastian. "The Hanzell is excellent."

"A California wine is a safe choice but we want something more exotic," Sebastian mused. "I had the good fortune to paint the fjords in New Zealand. They really are spectacular, better than anything you see in Sweden. I stayed in a fishing village and we had cracked lobster in a cream sauce with a New Zealand sauvignon blanc." He gazed at the shelf. "How do you feel about pairing it with an imported wine?"

The salesgirl poured three thimblefuls of wine and Finn inhaled the aroma. He sipped it slowly and looked at Sebastian.

"It's subtle and smooth but has a hint of aged wood," he said eagerly. "I've never heard of the label, we'll have to buy some."

"Sadly, it's out of my price range," Sebastian said, glancing at the price tag. "I'm sure we can find something more affordable, a pinot noir from the Hudson Valley."

"This is a special occasion." Finn reached into his pocket and drew out his wallet. "I'll pay for it."

Sebastian hesitated. "Are you sure?"

"Quite sure." Finn nodded. "I can't imagine a better pairing with lobster."

"Hadley said you had a great nose." Sebastian handed the bottle to the salesgirl. "It's exhilarating to meet someone who understands the nuances so thoroughly."

"I thought you wanted to buy Felix a housewarming present," Olivia said to Sebastian.

"Of course I do. But if Finn insists on paying for the wine, I'll choose something else. Your mother loved salted nuts." Sebastian picked up a small bag of nuts. "I'll get them a packet of macadamia nuts."

They walked into the sunshine and Olivia slipped on her sunglasses. She was thrilled Finn and Sebastian were getting along, but shouldn't Sebastian have paid for the wine?

Sebastian and Finn talked animatedly and Olivia relaxed. Finn made an excellent salary; he could afford an imported wine. What was more important than her father and boyfriend forming a bond?

"That was more fun than I've had in weeks. The great thing about young people is they are willing to try things," Sebastian said. "You bring a bottle of wine to a dinner party and unless the label is as recognizable as a Ralph Lauren shirt, no one will taste it."

"We're going to buy the lobsters and take them up to the villa and then drive to Flamands Beach," Finn replied. "Would you like to come?"

"I don't want to outstay my welcome on the first afternoon." Sebastian laughed. "I'll stroll down to Shell Beach and get a glass of lemonade."

"Are you sure?" he asked. "You're welcome to join us."

"For years I wondered what Olivia would be like when she grew up. She would be beautiful, of course, with Hadley's genes she couldn't miss. I hoped she'd like art because there is no greater joy than sharing the thing you are passionate about with someone you love." Sebastian took out his wallet. "I still have the first drawing she ever made."

He handed Olivia a sketch of a vase of brightly colored flowers. "You kept this?" she gasped.

"I wanted to keep everything you touched," he explained. "Old books and dresses you outgrew and discarded teddy bears. But overweight luggage is more expensive than an extra seat. This piece of paper has seen more airport lounges than Taylor Swift's entourage. I would as easily part with it as rip out my heart."

"I wasn't very good but I do appreciate art." Olivia clutched the paper and suddenly felt like she was five years old. She looked at Finn and her voice was wobbly. "We should go, Felix is expecting the lobsters."

"The one thing I didn't know is whether you would be happy," Sebastian continued. "After all, what kind of role model did you have? A father who abandoned the most important person because he didn't know what he'd do with himself if he stayed." He paused. "But look at you! Glossy blond hair and a smile as wide as the beach." He turned to Finn. "I'm sure you have something to do with that, I can't thank you enough."

"It's nothing." Finn shrugged, taking Olivia's hand.

"You are wrong," Sebastian said and looked at Olivia. "It's absolutely everything."

Olivia stood on the balcony and inhaled the scent of fresh-cut grass and bougainvillea. It was late afternoon and a soft breeze rustled the gauze drapes. She loved the view at this time of day. Sailboats bobbed in the harbor and Jet Skiers jumped over the waves and the horizon was milky white.

Felix and Finn made a last-minute trip to the market for Esther, and Olivia decided to relax at the villa. She remembered sampling wines with Finn and Sebastian and a warmth spread through her chest. It had been wonderful to see her father and boyfriend together. And they had so much in common! She had no idea Sebastian knew so much about wine.

"I'd like one of those, but preferably with vodka," Hadley said, pointing to Olivia's glass of orange juice. She wore a print dress and white sandals.

"You never drink before six p.m.," Olivia laughed, walking back into the living room.

"Sebastian never occupied a guest bedroom." Hadley sat on the silk sofa. "Thank god he's taking a nap. He can't cause too much trouble when he's asleep."

"He met us in Gustavia," Olivia began. "At first I was worried about how he and Finn would get along, but they started talking about wines. Finn is so knowledgeable and Sebastian is quite the connoisseur, they had a wonderful time."

Hadley bit her lip. "How surprising that Sebastian and Finn have something in common."

"We went into a wine shop and Sebastian told stories about the fjords in New Zealand. He really has lived in the most interesting places." Olivia's green eyes sparkled. "Then Sebastian wanted to buy Felix a housewarming gift but the wine he found was too expensive." She paused. "So Finn insisted on paying for it."

Hadley raised her eyebrow. "How thoughtful of Sebastian."

"It was Finn's idea and he can certainly afford it," Olivia protested. "It must be difficult for Sebastian. An artist's life is so precarious. One painting sells for a fortune and the next by the same artist hangs in the gallery for months."

"Sebastian is the president and chief executive officer of the Sebastian Miller Preservation Society." Hadley fiddled with her earrings. "I doubt he'll ever run out of expensive cologne or silk suits."

"He has led the most fascinating life," Olivia sighed. "He told us about the time he lived in New Guinea; a tribal chief offered him his daughter's hand in marriage in exchange for a painting. Sebastian had to leave by rowboat in the middle of the night so as not to hurt the chief's feelings."

"It sounds thrilling." Hadley smiled. "I can't wait to hear all about it."

"I know I should be angry that he missed my whole childhood, but artists are wired differently," Olivia continued. "Can you imagine Cezanne getting a job at a factory, or Matisse working in Le Bon Marché? They have to roam the world or where would they get the inspiration to paint?"

"I haven't seen Sebastian's art on the walls of the Metropolitan or the Guggenheim. But I'm sure some Fifth Avenue penthouses would be darker without his paintings of tropical birds in Bali."

"He did come all the way to St. Barts for my birthday and he brought you those lovely red slippers," Olivia insisted. "Maybe we've been thinking of him all wrong."

"He's your father and you deserve the chance to get to know him." Hadley squeezed her hand. "I'm going to help Esther with the tossed salad."

Hadley disappeared into the kitchen and Olivia thought she would go upstairs and take a bath. She noticed a figure on the veranda and walked back outside. Sprinklers played on the lawn and a hummingbird hovered over the rosebushes.

"What are you doing out here?" she asked Sebastian. "I thought you were upstairs taking a nap."

Sebastian turned around and fiddled with his cigarette case. His forehead was creased and there were lines around his mouth.

"I couldn't pass this up, it's better than evenings in the outback." He waved at the milky horizon. "You'll have to join me in Australia sometime. The sun is a copper ball and Ayer's Rock is so majestic."

"I do love the view at this time of day." Olivia gazed at the infinity pool. "But I really should go upstairs and get ready. Felix gets irritable if we're not all drinking rhum vanilles at six o'clock."

"Olivia, wait," Sebastian said. "I want to talk to you."

"We spent the whole morning together." Olivia smiled. "And Finn and I had a wonderful time this afternoon. He couldn't stop talking about the wines we sampled at the wine store."

"I mean really talk to you," Sebastian urged. "Not comment on how lovely you look in a cotton caftan or how we both love James Bond movies."

"I'm listening," Olivia gulped. Was Sebastian going to say he couldn't stay for her birthday after all? He had to leave right away and didn't know when he would see her again . . .

"When I said that I left you and your mother because you deserved more than I could give, it was the truth. I didn't know how to be an artist and a husband and father at the same time, and I made everyone miserable. But I know now that's a pretty flimsy excuse and I want to apologize."

"Apologize?" Olivia repeated.

"Children don't need fancy schools or expensive clothes," he continued. "Those things are wonderful and one shouldn't turn them down. But the only thing a child really needs is to know she is loved. How could you know that when I disappeared and never returned?"

"You had your reasons," Olivia answered. "And you sent wonderful letters. I keep them all in a box."

"Don't make excuses for me, I've done enough of that myself." He shook his head. "There is only one thing I can do. Tell you I'm sorry and hope you will forgive me."

Sebastian kissed her on the cheek. She touched her skin and a smile spread across her face.

"Of course I forgive you," she murmured.

"Then I'm the luckiest guy on earth." He slipped his cigarette case into his pocket. His eyes were wet and he turned away.

"I really should go upstairs," she said quickly. "I don't want to be late for cocktails."

She raced up the staircase and closed the door of her bedroom. She sank onto the bed and tried to stop trembling. Sebastian had apologized to her; he really loved her! She slipped off her sandals and had never been so happy.

Chapter Four

HADLEY ARRANGED PURPLE ORCHIDS IN a crystal vase and glanced around the dining room. It was her favorite room in the villa with its geometric rug and glass table and high-backed velvet chairs. Abstract paintings lined the walls and French doors opened onto the garden.

When Hadley first arrived at Sundial almost twenty years ago, the furniture was all faded chintz and dark wood and Oriental rugs. She had loved everything about the villa: the beige ceiling fans and striped wallpaper in the hallway and the kitchen with its tile floor and beamed ceiling.

But she'd entered the dining room and longed for bright colors and clear surfaces and the wonderful feeling that the ocean was just outside. And she had achieved it! The velvet chairs were sea green and the crystal chandelier reflected on the glass table and the paintings were the colors of the beach at sunset.

Felix and Finn were putting scallops on the grill and Esther was preparing meringue in the kitchen. Hadley inhaled the scent of chrysanthemums and thought how much she missed fresh flowers when she was in New York. The duplex was always filled with cut flowers and here they reminded her of taxicabs and the window at Bloomingdale's. In St. Barts foliage was everywhere: banana plants and calla lilies and palm trees as tall as a house.

Of course, she loved living in Manhattan. She and Felix had season tickets to the ballet and symphony. If last year they didn't do more than attend the occasional gallery opening, that was to be expected. Felix took so long to recover from injuring his back playing tennis, and Hadley got used to coming home early and heating up a roasted chicken.

Sometimes the duplex seemed too quiet, with Felix reading his economics journals in the study and the coffeemaker blinking in the kitchen. But she could always curl up with a classic movie or paperback book she had put off reading.

Then why did she feel like her marriage was perched on the edge of a cliff, and a strong gust of wind could tip it over? She was being too sensitive. Just last month Felix had bought her an emerald bracelet to celebrate the sale of a painting. She thought about the black camisole stuffed into the drawer and was determined to talk to him.

She heard footsteps overhead and shuddered. She had run into Sebastian in the upstairs hallway, draped in a towel and holding a can of shaving cream. How could she talk to Felix when Sebastian occupied the room down the hall? And why was Sebastian really here? He had missed twenty birthdays and there had to be a reason he was in St. Barts other than to blow out the candles on Olivia's cake.

And Olivia was behaving like a starstruck teenager. Hadley couldn't blame her. Every girl wanted a father; it was as normal as having a crush on your third-grade teacher. And what a father! He was like a movie star and game hunter rolled into one. If he told one more story about outrunning a leopard in Kenya, she couldn't stand it.

She was worrying too much; Sebastian always needed people to admire him. He was like a hothouse flower. He only blossomed when he was bathed in others' adoration.

She remembered when they sold his first painting. It was late August in Cape Town and the wildflowers were in bloom. Every morning she woke up and wished she could stay there forever.

Hadley put the last cup in the sink and took off her apron. She looked out the kitchen window and saw a hummingbird poised above a bed of yellow roses.

After the first week it stopped raining and Hadley understood why people traveled from everywhere to see the South African light. It was like a photo spread in a glossy magazine. You were sure the pictures were touched up because you'd never seen such vibrant greens and liquid turquoises.

The owners of the guesthouse offered her free room and board in exchange for serving breakfast and Hadley decided to stay in Cape Town. After all, there was so much to do: tour Robben Island, where Nelson Mandela was imprisoned for twenty years, visit the wine farms in Constantia, and see the spider crabs at Two Oceans Aquarium.

But Hadley knew it wasn't the views from Signal Hill or the delicious curries the guesthouse served at night that kept her from catching the bus to Johannesburg. Ever since the third day, she and Sebastian had become inseparable.

He lounged around the kitchen, reading out loud from magazines he found in the library. They laughed over how the owners needed to subscribe to something other than *Ladies' Home Journal* but he could make an article on how to bake a sweet potato entertaining.

When they explored Cape Town it was as if her nerve endings were on fire. He pointed out things she wouldn't have noticed: the mosaic floor at City Hall, a pastel-colored sailboat entering the harbor. And everywhere they went he talked to other tourists, so they ended up sharing a plate of vetkoeks with a couple from Sweden.

Sometimes he tried to kiss her but she pulled away. It would be too easy to fall in love with his green eyes and wide smile. What would happen when she went on to the art course in Florence she had signed up for and he started law school in Chicago? It was better to stay friends.

"It's a beautiful day, I thought we could visit the Botanical Gardens." Sebastian had entered the kitchen. "You can wear your yellow dress and new floppy hat. I'll paint you in a bed of wildflowers."

"You've painted me surrounded by pansies and daffodils," Hadley laughed. "I feel like I'm living in a flower shop."

"I can't stop thinking about the colors. I lie awake at night and dream of ochre and magenta." He ran his hands through his hair. "If I shared my bed with someone it would be easier to sleep."

"Use a thick blanket and drink a glass of warm milk and honey." Hadley walked to the fridge. "It's the perfect cure for insomnia."

"I'm not ten years old and I don't sleep with a teddy bear," he groaned, taking a banana from the fruit bowl.

"I've already cooked two pots of mealie with powdered sugar and you haven't even shaved." Hadley gazed at the stubble on his chin. "You're getting plenty of rest."

"Tossing and turning in a single bed isn't the same as sleeping,"

Sebastian grumbled. "Let's take the cable car to Table Rock, the clear air always invigorates me."

Hadley fiddled with the dish towel. "Actually I'm going to the airline office. I have to book my flight to Italy."

"Your course doesn't start until September." Sebastian ate a red cherry. "You have plenty of time."

"I'm supposed to arrive in Florence a week early to see the museums and get settled," she replied. "I'm leaving on Monday."

Sebastian poured a cup of coffee and added cream and sugar. He took a small sip and looked at Hadley. "You can't go to Florence now."

"I did want to travel around Italy first, but I've run out of time and I probably couldn't afford it anyway. The guidebook says an espresso and pastry in Milan cost more than a platter of boerewors." She hesitated. "I suppose I could stay a few extra days. When is your flight to Chicago?"

Sebastian placed his coffee cup on the counter. "I canceled my flight, I'm staying in South Africa."

"But law school orientation is in three weeks."

"Do you think I could sit in a lecture hall with fluorescent lights and linoleum floors after I've seen this?" Sebastian pointed to the window. "Or inhale the smell of copy paper and vending machine coffee when I've breathed the scent of marigolds and juniper? I'm not going to law school, I'm going to be an artist."

"Of course you're going to be an attorney. You'll drive a sleek foreign sports car and own six pairs of Italian loafers. On Friday evenings you'll go to an upscale bar and tell stories about the summer you spent in Cape Town." She paused. "And then you'll go home to your penthouse with the framed Jackson Pollock and be glad you didn't change your reservation." She wiped her hands. "But if it will make you happy, we can have a picnic in the Botanical Gardens. I'll visit the airline office this afternoon."

"I don't want a sports car and I can wear the same jeans every day but I can't breathe if I'm not holding a paintbrush," he said urgently. "I didn't choose this. I'd give anything to want to be like my father with his two-martini lunches followed by a vigorous game of squash so he doesn't die young from a heart attack. But I have to paint, it's the only thing that makes sense." He looked at Hadley. "And I have to do it with you."

"But I'm going to Florence."

"Why would you sit in a stuffy classroom and discuss dead artists when you could be exploring Africa?" He touched her hand. "You must come with me, I have to paint you. You are Aphrodite and a swimsuit model rolled into one."

"Aphrodite was brunette," Hadley laughed.

"To me she's a blond with blue eyes and slender cheekbones and a mysterious smile like Mata Hari's."

Hadley fiddled with a ceramic bowl and wavered. She could take the course anytime and she was in no hurry to return to America. She still didn't know if she wanted to teach art history or work at a museum. And Sebastian was right; South Africa in the springtime was like a child's fairy tale come to life.

But if she left the guesthouse she'd have to pay for food and lodging. Her money would disappear in a couple of weeks and she wouldn't be able to go to Florence at all. And was she really that interested in the penguins at Foxy Beach or couldn't she bear the thought of leaving Sebastian?

"What did your parents say?" she wondered.

"I haven't told them." He shrugged. "I'm twenty-two years old, I can do whatever I like."

"What will you do for money?" she asked. "Even staying in guesthouses gets expensive, and you'll need bus fare and meals."

Sebastian was terrible with money. He behaved as if the world were a giant Monopoly board, and the rand in his wallet could be replaced by a trip to the American Express office. But his parents wouldn't send packets of traveler's checks if he turned down his acceptance to law school.

"Many great artists survive without chaining themselves to a desk," Sebastian retorted. "I can wait tables or become a tour guide."

"You'd be a terrible waiter, you'd sit down and have a conversation with every diner," Hadley laughed. "Anyway, you said all you want to do is paint."

Sebastian paced around the kitchen. He looked at Hadley and his eyes were bright. "We'll sell my paintings."

"How will you do that?"

"An artist can't sell his own paintings, it would be like a playwright reviewing himself on Broadway." He looked at Hadley. "You'll sell them for me."

"I've never sold anything in my life!" she exclaimed.

"I'm sure you had to write an essay convincing your college professor on the relevance of Renaissance paintings," he urged. "We all learn to sell from the moment we convince our mothers we must have an extra scoop of chocolate ice cream. And you'll be selling something you believe in."

Hadley did think his artwork was glorious. His colors belonged on the finest fabrics and his brushstrokes made something stir deep inside her.

She studied his long eyelashes and had to laugh. Was Sebastian special or was she falling in love despite herself? No matter what he told her, she believed it.

She was young and in one of the most exotic countries on the planet. Why shouldn't she take a chance? The worst that could happen is she ran out of money and flew home. She looked at Sebastian's firm jaw and had the sudden urge to kiss him.

"Will you do it?" he asked.

She turned to the sink so he wouldn't see her cheeks flush. "I'll do it."

Hadley wore her best floral dress and pair of pumps and took Sebastian's paintings to every gallery in Cape Town. She visited the modern galleries on the Victoria & Albert Waterfront with their chrome surfaces and slate floors. She lugged his portfolio to the elegant galleries in Old Town, where the air smelled of lemon polish and old wood.

But when anyone asked where Sebastian had shown his work or if he had studied at art school, she fumbled and bit her lip. Sebastian said everyone shaded the truth, but she was incapable of making up a degree from Pace, or an artist's cooperative in Chicago. The gallery owners handed her the sketches and said he had talent, but they couldn't take a chance.

"Everyone has to start somewhere." Sebastian opened a box of cigarettes and tapped a cigarette into his palm. It was the first time Hadley had seen him smoke and he looked older, like a troubled Marlon Brando.

The guesthouse was closing for its annual vacation in a few days and they would have to go their separate ways. Hadley felt a tightness in her chest and brushed it away.

"Why do you have to show your work in a gallery? You could

be an attorney and paint on the weekends," she suggested. "All you need is brushes and a canvas."

"You think this is a hobby? Something I discuss at a dinner party in between conversations about the World Cup and my boss's summer vacation in Madrid? 'How terribly interesting, an artist,'" he mimicked. "'I've dreamed of retiring to a South Sea island and drinking daiquiris and painting the sunset. We all have artistic aspirations but luckily we put them away so we can afford this bottle of sauvignon blanc and these Kobe steaks.'"

Hadley started to laugh and put her hand over her mouth. "I'm sorry, I told you I was terrible at selling things."

"It's not you, it's the damn dealers." He shrugged. "In New York and Chicago they are a bunch of lemmings but I thought in South Africa they'd be willing to take a risk. But they're like children eating their first bite of gelato, they need someone to tell them it tastes good."

Suddenly his eyes lit up and he ran up the staircase.

"Where are you going?" Hadley asked.

"To your room."

"Just because I failed doesn't mean I'm going to bed with you." Hadley followed him into her bedroom.

"I'm not going to seduce you." He walked to the closet. "I'm going to find you the perfect thing to wear."

Hadley gazed at the crystal chandelier and Oriental rugs and paneled walls. Waiters passed around samosas and rusks topped with caviar. The wood floor was scattered with leather ottomans and she felt as if she were in a private home instead of one of the oldest galleries in Cape Town.

Sebastian stood on the other side of the room in navy slacks and a white button-down shirt. He nibbled a canapé and she noticed how his cheeks were tan and his dark hair touched his collar. He hadn't told her why they were here, so she clutched a champagne flute and tried to look interested in the splotches of paint behind silver frames.

"Fascinating how the artist uses color to portray human emotions," an older man said as he approached her. He wore gold cuff links and tasseled shoes. "The swirl of green is envy, and the yellow represents hope."

"It's interesting but honestly I prefer portraits or landscapes," Hadley mused. "Bouguereau's *The Broken Pitcher* or Monet's *Garden at Giverny.*"

"We only get so many geniuses per century," he sighed. "Though most of us will cross the globe in the hopes of discovering one. I once traveled to an olive farm outside of Seville because a colleague told me he'd discovered the next Picasso. He turned out to be the man's nephew and barely knew his way around a set of watercolors."

"Great art is like a red light at an intersection," Hadley said.

She wore the only cocktail dress Sebastian had found in her closet. A black chiffon with a plunging back.

"You can't inch your car forward, it would be breaking the law. But by the time the light changes you're so transfixed, you don't want to move at all."

The man looked at her thoughtfully and moved closer. "Which artists do you admire?"

"I love the Renaissance, of course, no one understood the human body like Donatello and Botticelli. And the French Impressionists make you think of Belle Époque Paris and smoky nightclubs with showgirls dressed in lace stockings and satin bustiers." She paused. "But of the current artists, I'm a big fan of Sebastian Miller."

"Sebastian Miller?" he asked.

"He's somewhat reclusive," she continued. "You know how true artists are, letting go of a painting is like giving up a piece of their soul. But his use of color reminds me of Chagall and his portraits have a hint of the *Mona Lisa*."

"Perhaps you could send him my way." The man handed her his card. "I own the Lang Gallery on Church Street. I'd be interested in showing his work."

"I can't make any promises." Hadley smoothed her hair and smiled. "But I'll try to persuade him."

"Charles Lang." Hadley waved the card in front of Sebastian. It was almost 10:00 p.m. and the living room of the guesthouse was empty. The reception had seemed to drag on for hours and Hadley couldn't wait to tell him her news.

"He asked me which artists I admire and I told him Sebastian Miller was a genius." Her blue eyes sparkled. "I don't know why he was interested in my opinion but he wants to see your portfolio. I'm sure he will show your work."

Sebastian walked to the bar and poured a glass of scotch. He sipped it slowly and ran his fingers over the rim. "I may have mentioned to a few people that you were Hadley Stevens, the daughter of an important East Coast collector with a keen eye for new talent."

"You did what?" she spluttered. "I've never owned a painting in my life."

He put the glass on the side table and took her hand. He led her up the staircase and opened the door to her bedroom.

"You own all these."

Canvases were propped against the bed and desk and dresser. There was a sketch of Hadley standing on the edge of Table Rock, wearing a floral dress and sandals. The waves crashed below her and the sky was rinsed with color. There was a painting of Hadley in front of a colonial-style building in Old Town. She wore a floppy hat and clutched a bunch of daisies.

"I painted them all for you, now you can sell them to the gallery and we'll split the proceeds." His face broke into a smile. "I already wrote up an itinerary. We'll take the Garden Route all the way to the Eastern Cape. We'll cross mountain passes and swim in lakes as clear as diamonds and at night we'll stay in guesthouses and eat potjiekos and bread pudding."

Hadley knew she should be angry that he said she was a collector. But she felt suddenly brighter, like she was part of a team.

"I didn't say I would go with you." She paused and bit her lip. "But I have come all the way to South Africa, it would be wonderful to see ostriches and elephants."

"I'll paint landscapes and you'll sell my artwork. We'll be like Bonnie and Clyde but instead of running from the law we'll be creating our own adventure."

Hadley was almost dizzy, as if the room were too warm and she'd drunk too much champagne. Sebastian reached up and touched her hair. He pulled her close and kissed her.

She kissed him back and tasted caviar and scotch. She pressed against him and wondered why she'd waited so long. His lips were soft and he smelled of musk cologne.

"You know, it would be cheaper if we share a room," he offered. "We can take it slowly. I want your first time to be wonderful."

"My first time?" Hadley pulled away. "Do you think I'm a virgin?"

"Well, yes." He loosened his collar. "Why else wouldn't you want to sleep with me?"

Hadley gazed at his green eyes and furrowed brow and stifled a laugh. Sebastian had chiseled cheekbones and broad shoulders like a young Paul Newman. He wore polo shirts and leather loafers and his smile could light up a room. He had probably never been turned down by a girl.

She thought of all the ways she could get her heart broken: they would get tired of each other jammed together on rattling buses, Sebastian might meet an impossibly elegant European model. But if she didn't see the world now, when would she? And no one had talked about love; they were just two young people exploring South Africa.

"I didn't go to bed with you because I don't know how I feel about you." She looked up.

"I know how I feel about you," he whispered. "I'm falling in love with you."

Sebastian slipped one hand beneath her dress and caressed her breasts. Hadley felt his fingers on her nipples and gasped. She unbuttoned his shirt and ran her hands over his chest.

He slid his fingers under her panties and touched the wet spot between her legs. She felt a sudden thrill, like a shot of electricity. She put his hand on her zipper and her dress fell to the floor.

"Are you sure?" he asked. "We have plenty of time."

"I don't need time," she murmured. "I want you right now."

He took her hand and drew her onto the bed. They laughed at

the lumpy mattress and hard pillow and frayed sheets. Then he put his finger to her mouth and covered her breasts with his chest.

"Have I told you how beautiful you are?" he whispered.

"I can't remember. Tell me again," she gasped, wrapping her arms around him.

He paused and stroked her cheek. "You're the most beautiful girl I ever met and I've never wanted anything more."

Sebastian moved slowly, as if he was memorizing her smooth skin and the heart-shaped mark on her thigh. Then he pushed in deeper and she felt the infinite warmth and delicious tension. She urged him to go faster and he picked up speed and they came together in one dizzying thrust.

"I'll never forgive you," he said, when their breathing had slowed and they lay on their backs.

"For what?" Hadley gazed at the ceiling. Her breasts were slick with sweat and she felt wanton and dangerous.

"For making me wait so long," he groaned, draping his arm over her stomach.

Hadley watched the stars light up the sky and felt like Meryl Streep in *Out of Africa*. She was young and in love and in a foreign country. No matter what happened, it was going to be a great adventure.

Hadley placed the vase of orchids on the glass dining room table and thought how much she loved the colors in St. Barts. Africa had been all golds and browns and yellows, but St. Barts was blues and pinks and shimmering turquoise.

She opened the French doors to the garden and was so happy to be back at the villa. The air smelled like the most exotic perfume and she could live in cotton dresses and let her hair curl to her shoulders.

Footsteps sounded in the hallway and she turned around. Sebastian wore navy slacks and a white shirt and carried his straw hat.

"This place suits you," he said, entering the dining room. "Crystal chandeliers and priceless artwork and diamond earrings the size of birds' eggs."

"Not all the artwork is priceless and my diamond earrings are barely two carats." Hadley touched her ears. "Felix is very understated, nothing we own is ostentatious."

"But you can smell the wealth." He walked to the French doors. "The manicured gardens and silk sofas in the living room and ivory chess set in the library. I bet if I opened the sideboard there'd be stacks of sterling silverware and Wedgwood china."

"Most people collect things during a marriage," Hadley replied. "It doesn't take a family fortune to accumulate a few pieces of jewelry and fine china."

"I always imagined you surrounded by luxury." Sebastian tapped a cigarette into his palm and looked at Hadley. "Do you mind? Most Americans are appalled by a whiff of secondhand smoke. But in many societies sharing cigarettes is a sign of friendship."

"The surgeon general would disagree but you can do whatever you like." She shrugged. "Just don't smoke near Esther, she'll toss the cigarette pack in the garbage."

"Do you remember when we took the bus over the Garden Route in South Africa?" he asked. "It was September and the rain was supposed to have stopped and we left our raincoats in Cape Town. It started pouring outside of Plettenberg Bay and we couldn't leave the bus. I finally convinced a couple from Amsterdam to part with an umbrella in exchange for a carton of Marlboros."

"It was a long time ago." Hadley's cheeks turned red. "All I remember is wanting a shower so badly, I dreamed of fresh towels and Dove soap."

"You were splendid, you were up for anything," Sebastian continued. "I wanted to go ziplining in Tsitsikamma but I came down with a fever. You took my place at the last minute and only told me later that you were terrified of heights."

"We'd already paid for it, it seemed silly for the money to go to waste." She smoothed her hair. "Felix and Finn are in the garden. If you want to be useful you can help with the lobster."

"I need to talk to you about something." Sebastian perched on a velvet chair.

"I don't have time." Hadley walked across the room. "Felix likes to eat the salad course at seven, and I have to help Esther with dessert."

"It's about Olivia."

"What about Olivia?" Hadley turned around.

"She's gorgeous, of course." Sebastian waved his hand. "Those cheekbones could grace the cover of a magazine. And she's received a first-class education. You and Felix knew exactly which schools to send her to and which social circles she should move in."

"You make that sound like a bad thing," Hadley said warily. She studied Sebastian's tan cheeks and wondered what he was up to. Olivia was everything one could hope for in a daughter, intelligent and kind and beautiful.

"It's fine if you want her to move straight from a Central Park duplex to a Fifth Avenue penthouse," he cut into her thoughts. "But I get the impression she's never been anywhere she wouldn't feel comfortable wearing Prada pumps and a Tiffany bracelet."

"You should talk." Hadley glanced at his leather loafers. "You dress like the father in a Patek Philippe ad."

"I have to keep up appearances or collectors won't buy my paintings." Sebastian fiddled with his collar.

"Olivia is doing wonderfully," Hadley said, folding napkins. "She has her own apartment and a thriving career and a caring boyfriend."

"That's the thing," Sebastian insisted. "She manages an art gallery in Chelsea, and dates a Princeton graduate who is being groomed to take over his family's law firm. You may as well buy her a string of pearls and sign her up for the Junior League."

"I own the art gallery and Felix went to Yale and works in his family's business." Hadley's eyes flickered.

"But when you were Olivia's age you had slept in a tent in the Imfolozi National Park and taken a river cruise to see hippopotamuses. Olivia moves between the helicopter pad on top of the Time-Life Building and the private landing strip of a Caribbean island."

"Felix would never take a helicopter, he doesn't even fly private," Hadley bristled. "We lead a quiet life. I work ten hours a day and come home to a bowl of butternut squash soup and an episode of *Homeland*. Felix plays tennis most weekends and we spend a week in Nantucket and three weeks in the Caribbean. That hardly qualifies us for guest appearances on *Desperate Housewives of New York*."

"Do you ever wonder what would have happened if we hadn't gone to Thailand?" Sebastian asked. "We would have gotten Olivia a tutor, of course, she had to learn how to read and write. But we could have traveled to Morocco or Croatia. The portraits I could have painted of you wearing an emerald green bikini and swimming in the Baltic."

"I thought you wanted to talk about Olivia," Hadley said sharply.

"She hasn't been exposed to enough of the world," Sebastian explained. "She's only twenty-five and she's like a character in Edith Wharton's *House of Mirth*."

"Not everyone needs to be Humphrey Bogart in *The African Queen* to be happy," Hadley said angrily. "She spent a semester in Florence and takes the train regularly to Boston to visit museums. She even came out at the International Cotillion at the Pierre." She looked at Sebastian. "I sent you an invitation."

"I'm sure she looked stunning but she's going to think the whole world consists of hotel ballrooms with waiters passing around smoked salmon and bottles of Dom Pérignon." Sebastian ground his cigarette into a glass ashtray.

"You are quite happy drinking Felix's bourbon and sleeping on our Frette sheets."

"But I've also spent nights on the floor of a hut made of banana fronds. There's nothing wrong with Russian caviar and Cuban cigars and Swiss watches." He moved closer. "But don't you want her to watch the sunrise from the top of a cliff where all you see is lush forests and a sparkling ocean? Or experience the moon like an astronaut, with just a black sky and silver stars?"

"We're in St. Barts." Hadley suddenly felt uncomfortable. She moved away and smoothed her hair. "The whole island is full of amazing views and spectacular sunsets."

"But the harbor is dotted with yachts and the boutiques sell designer sunglasses and you probably run into a member of your New York book club at the butcher." He lit another cigarette. "She needs to meet grungy poets and struggling artists and young people who don't know what they want to do but are trying to figure it out."

Hadley heard voices in the hallway and rubbed her lips. She turned around and looked at Sebastian. Suddenly she was so angry she could hardly breathe.

"You were quite happy to walk out that door twenty years ago and leave us to our own devices. How dare you show up now and question our whole lives? The only reason I'm being the least bit civil is because our daughter deserves to spend four days with her father and I'm not going to spoil it." Her eyes flashed. "And Olivia didn't rebel because her father was busy doing it for her. Finn is thoughtful and dependable and they are going to have a wonderful future." She waved her finger. "If you do anything to ruin it, I will toss you on the barbecue with the scallops and sweet potatoes."

"You are your best when you are like this," Sebastian said and smiled. "A fierce lioness protecting her cub from anyone who hurts her."

"I'll see you in the garden." Hadley glowered and entered the hallway. "If you say one wrong thing at dinner, I'll slice you with a butter knife."

Hadley sipped rum and pineapple juice and fiddled with her sunglasses. They decided to have drinks near the pool and she thought the garden never looked so vibrant. The rosebushes were pink and yellow and the frangipani was purple and white and the pond was filled with neon-colored fish.

Felix and Finn sipped ti punch with a squeeze of lime and Hadley remembered why she loved cocktail hour on St. Barts. Felix recounted his winning serve and Finn described the sea turtles at

Colombier Beach and even Esther came onto the patio and tried her own deviled eggs. And Olivia! She wore a print dress and silver sandals and her arms were as brown as a native's.

Olivia kept glancing at the French doors to see when Sebastian would appear, and Hadley wondered if she had been too hard on him. After all, he only wanted what was best for his daughter.

Then she remembered all the years Olivia had helped mail him her birthday invitations and wanted to stab him with a pineapple wedge. If he had shown up ten years ago, Hadley would have let Olivia spend her summer exploring the Galápagos Islands or seeing the parrots in Senegal. Lots of couples got divorced, but they didn't leave a trail of forwarding addresses like bird seed in a Grimm's fairy tale.

Now was not the time to disrupt Olivia's life, when she was managing the art gallery and Finn was about to propose. Sebastian's timing was as poor as a kicker making a winning field goal after the clock runs out.

Hadley put her glass on the side table and thought she'd tell Sebastian there was a change of plans. A room had opened up at Hotel Eden Rock and they would pay for it.

Sebastian was used to being alone, he didn't want to be woken by Felix doing his morning exercises. He would be more comfortable in a hotel suite with a private balcony and complimentary newspaper and orange juice.

But there probably wasn't a room available on the whole island and when she looked at Olivia she couldn't do it. Since Sebastian had arrived, everything about Olivia seemed brighter. Her green eyes sparkled and her smile was wide and she skipped across the patio like a child at a birthday party.

The French doors opened and Sebastian appeared carrying a

paper sack. He wore a striped blazer and had a silk handkerchief in his pocket.

"This looks like a scene from *Tender Is the Night*," he said, glancing at the crystal pitcher of daiquiris and silver tray of grilled codfish. "I read Fitzgerald in college, but I always preferred Hemingway. How many people can relate to a couple lolling around a villa on the French Riviera and drinking absinthe? I'd rather read about big-game hunting in Africa or running with the bulls in Pamplona."

"I'm glad you decided to join us." Hadley glanced at her watch. "Drinks started at six."

"I'm sorry I'm late. I spend so much time on airplanes, sometimes I don't remember if it's a.m. or p.m." He placed his straw hat on a chair. "Though it can be terribly freeing to not know what day it is. I once spent a week on Norfolk Island without any connection to the outside world. When I returned to Melbourne, I discovered I'd missed a bombing in Phuket and an outbreak of Legionnaires' disease in Philadelphia.

"You'd be surprised how much time we spend soaking up other people's dramas. What good does it do, unless we are Tolstoy or Chekhov?" he finished. "I'd much rather eat a roasted pig and enjoy the sunset."

"It's called having empathy for the human race," Hadley bristled.

"Sebastian has a point." Felix joined the conversation. "The same disasters are replayed all day on social media. I enjoy watching Stone Phillips read the headlines with my evening martini, but it's unsettling when they pop up on my phone during a board meeting."

"Young people have to believe the world is a wonderful place or what would be the point?" Sebastian looked at Olivia. "One of the best months of my life was spent on a sheep farm in New

Zealand. There were no outside distractions so the bathwater seemed hotter and the bacon was saltier and when I fell into bed, I could sleep for days. And the sketches I made! I traded them to a former America's Cup winner for a week on his catamaran. You can't realize your full potential until life is stripped to its bare essentials."

"What an inspiring talk, I'm surprised you haven't been asked to speak at college commencements," Hadley murmured. "You should have attended Olivia's graduation, she was class president. She gave a wonderful speech about the importance of family."

Olivia put her arm through Sebastian's and smiled. "Everyone is here now, and I couldn't be happier. Finn mixed a pitcher of daiquiris, let me pour one."

"I am the luckiest guy in the world, and I have to thank Felix." Sebastian accepted the frosty glass and turned to Felix. "Not only did you do a tremendous job raising Olivia, Hadley has never been more radiant. When I spoke to her in private, she said she couldn't have a happier marriage."

"In private?" Felix said sharply.

"It was only for a few minutes and it was completely aboveboard. She was folding napkins in the dining room." Sebastian shrugged. "But she did make me appreciate all you've done for Hadley and Olivia: season tickets to the ballet and vacations on Cape Cod and the Caribbean." He handed the paper sack to Felix. "I can't give you anything to match my gratitude but I got you a housewarming present."

"I didn't do anything at all." Felix accepted the brown bag. "I was just lucky enough to meet the loveliest woman in New York. I remember when I first saw her at the gallery. She wore a black cashmere dress and I was too nervous to say hello."

"She can be reserved at first. But when you get to know her, you realize she'd do anything for the people she loves." He stopped and looked at Felix. "What am I saying, you know her better than anyone. Does she still pour cream into her coffee mug first?"

"I hadn't really noticed." Felix frowned and opened the sack. "My god, is this a Cloudy Bay sauvignon blanc? I read about it in *Wine Connoisseur Magazine*. I can't accept this; it must have cost a fortune."

"I can't take full credit, Finn discovered it and insisted on buying it." Sebastian sipped his drink. "Olivia has chosen a fine young man: educated, ambitious, and with a good instinct about wines." He looked at Finn. "He's going to be a great addition to the family."

"Sebastian suggested we try it." Finn ran his hands through his hair. "New Zealand sauvignon blancs are renowned for pairing with lobster."

"I still wasn't going to let Finn pay," Sebastian continued. "But I remembered a meal I shared with the Raj Mahi at his palace near Mumbai.

"You should have seen it," he whistled. "Mosaic ceilings and an indoor swimming pool and floors made of eighteen-karat gold. I just finished a trip down the Ganges and arrived with one change of clothes and a clean pair of socks." He leaned back in his chair. "We sat at the marble dining room table and ate pork jalfrezi and tandoori chicken and lamb masala.

"The Raj opened a bottle of 1978 Montrachet and I was about to refuse. How could I drink a wine he bought at auction for nine hundred thousand rupees? But after the first sip, I was glad I accepted.

"We talked for hours about the poverty levels in India and the need for better irrigation. He shared his dreams for building drinking wells and I told him about the villages I visited where whole families shared a bath.

"By the time we moved into the paneled library for snifters of Grand Marnier and Portuguese cigars, we were both flushed from the wine and curried samosas. I even told him to donate some of the rupees he owed me to the water project." He paused. "He insisted I take my whole fee but I knew we would stay close friends." He fiddled with his glass.

"Drinking the perfect wine with dinner is almost a mystical experience. You will never forget the way your taste buds respond as it slides down your throat, and it creates a special bond with your dinner companions that lasts for life."

"I'm suddenly starving." Felix shifted in his seat. "We'll have to tell Esther to hurry with the baked yams."

"But I couldn't arrive empty-handed," Sebastian mused. "It can't be easy having your wife's first husband staying down the hallway. Though don't worry about me, I sleep with earplugs." He drew a napkin out of his pocket. "I've been saving this for nine years, but I want you to have it."

"What is it?" Felix examined the linen napkin.

"I attended a state dinner at the White House in 2008 and was seated next to Jeff Koons. We discussed cynicism in modern art and where he finds inflatable toys for his work." Sebastian paused. "Did you know his latest piece, *Balloon Dog (Orange),* sold at auction for fifty-five million dollars?

"He encouraged me to try a new medium, but an artist can only paint what's inside him," he continued. "He signed this napkin for me, it has a drop of Béarnaise sauce on it. Whoever said you can't get a good meal in Washington has never eaten in the State Dining Room."

"Jeff Koons!" Felix gasped. "I remember when I saw his 'Banality' series at the Whitney. The critics dismissed it as 'Michael Jackson and Bubbles' but it became a touchstone in modern art." He nodded eagerly. "Pop star with his pet monkey. Koons is a visionary."

"You were invited to a state dinner in Washington?" Hadley sat forward. She suddenly felt queasy, as if the lime juice in the daiquiris were spoiled.

"They wanted Julian Schnabel but he was in Seville," Sebastian explained. "The chief of staff was very gracious. He paid for my airfare and hotel and gave me a complimentary tour of the West Wing."

"Nine years ago you were in Washington and didn't come to New York to see your daughter," Hadley repeated, trying to keep her voice steady.

"Well, yes." Sebastian's cheeks paled. "But it was a quick visit. You know how busy the president is, I didn't even shake his hand."

She turned to face Sebastian. "You were so allergic to living in Manhattan. You had to keep moving like a modern-day Columbus who decided to leave America to the Indians. But you were four hours away from New York by Amtrak and didn't visit Olivia."

Sebastian drew a cigarette out of his gold cigarette case and tapped it into his palm. He lit it and inhaled deeply.

"All I thought about was Olivia. She was sixteen and I imagined her with a blond ponytail and her first touch of lipstick," he sighed. "I couldn't wait to take her to Katz's Delicatessen for a pastrami sandwich or Carvel for a hot fudge sundae.

"But then I arrived in D.C. and realized I didn't know American teenagers at all. How could I relate to my own daughter if I didn't know what music she listened to or which authors she read or what flavor Life Savers she liked?" he continued. "I couldn't have my first interaction with Olivia be at a pivotal moment in her life. She'd think I was hopelessly out of touch and never want to see me again."

"That's the most self-centered thing I ever heard. It doesn't matter what Olivia thought of you, the important thing was to be there for her. Anyway, parents are supposed to be out of touch," Hadley said. "That's how teenagers form their own opinions."

"Yes, but you need some history to draw on. You nursed Olivia through the stomach flu and let her cry when her eighth-grade boyfriend broke up with her without telling her. But we had nothing! If I made some comment about her velvet jeans or ankle-length boots, she'd never forgive me."

"Hadley's right. I would have given anything for you to visit," Olivia said to Sebastian. "Why would it have mattered what you thought about my outfit?"

"You believe that now but it would have been different," Sebastian replied. "I would have made some terrible gaffe on the way back to the airport. You would be secretly glad I was leaving because I didn't understand you at all," he finished. "I stayed away for both of us, I didn't want to disappoint you."

"I'm sure that's the logic the Cowardly Lion used when he was afraid to meet the Wizard of Oz," Hadley murmured, refreshing her glass.

"If I thought Olivia needed me, I would have been on the first plane." Sebastian turned to Hadley. "The year I left, I checked the art catalogs and *The Miller Girls* never went on the market. I knew you were making ends meet and neither of you was going hungry.

"Then I came across the wedding photos in *Town & Country*. Olivia was the most charming flower girl with her pink satin slippers and wreath of baby's breath." He lit another cigarette. "I sat at Internet cafés in Beijing and searched Olivia's name. I knew she was made co-captain of the volleyball team at Brearley and was awarded the art history prize at graduation." He exhaled. "You and

Felix were doing a tremendous job, I thought it was best if I kept out of the way."

"Why did you come now?" Hadley asked, sitting back on the chaise longue.

Sebastian studied Olivia's blond hair and the light freckles on her nose.

"Look at her, I couldn't stay away any longer. I knew I'd probably be vilified from the moment I walked through the door but I had to take the chance." He stubbed out his cigarette. "Twenty years is a long time to consider my mistakes and I've come to make amends. I'll do whatever it takes to earn your and Olivia's forgiveness if it means I get to sing 'Happy Birthday' and help Olivia blow out the candles."

They moved to a long glass table on the patio and Esther brought out wooden bowls of green salad with Parmesan cheese and hardboiled egg. There was curried cauliflower and squid risotto. The lobster was tender and the drawn butter tasted of garlic and basil.

"God, what a feast. What kind of family business paid for this piece of paradise?" Sebastian swirled the pinot noir and turned to Felix. "The *Town & Country* article didn't mention what you actually do."

"Felix's family is in rubber," Hadley answered, sitting forward in her chair.

She had to stay on her guard. Sebastian was already settled in the guest bedroom and had invited himself to Olivia's birthday dinner. Why was he being so nice to Felix?

"Rubber!" Sebastian exclaimed. "How inspiring."

"Inspiring?" Felix asked, eating a forkful of Brussels sprouts.

"I can't think of anything more vital. We wouldn't be eating this succulent lobster if we couldn't get on a plane. And highways would be useless without rubber for the wheels of a car," Sebastian continued. "Without rubber we wouldn't even be able to bicycle to the harbor for a carton of milk."

"I never thought about it like that," Felix demurred.

"I once painted a sketch for a guy in Hawaii whose grandfather invented the plastic part of a shoelace. He used his inheritance to buy an estate and filled it with artifacts from ancient Crete. His collection rivaled anything at the Louvre but he was ashamed to say how he financed it," Sebastian mused. "The men who provide the most mundane essentials are the real heroes. The rest of us just try to leave this world putting in a little more than we take out."

"Sebastian should have appeared in our lives earlier." Felix turned to Hadley and laughed. "Maybe I wouldn't feel guilty when I leave the office early to watch the Wimbledon finals at the club."

"Yes, what would we do without our own personal Plato." Hadley stabbed an asparagus spear. "I can't wait to hear his views on global warming and the European economy."

Olivia and Hadley cleared away plates and Esther brought out silver bowls of coconut sorbet. There was a tray of lemon and kiwi tarts and meringue topped with strawberries.

They talked about Olivia's duties at the gallery and the charities Hadley and Felix supported. Sebastian pulled his chair close to Olivia and she rested her head on his shoulder.

"I want to propose a toast," Sebastian said, raising his brandy snifter. "When I walked out of that Morningside Heights apartment twenty years ago, I was wracked with misery. I wanted so much for Hadley and Olivia, but I was incapable of giving it to them." He paused. "But look at them now, they have everything I could have imagined. I want to thank Felix and Finn for taking such good care of the Miller girls."

"Excuse me." Hadley stood up and smoothed her skirt. "Esther needs me in the kitchen."

"I didn't hear anything," Olivia said.

"You have to listen carefully." Hadley glowered at Sebastian. "Or you might miss something."

Hadley entered the kitchen and turned on the faucet. Finn and Olivia had driven down to the harbor and Sebastian joined them to buy a pack of cigarettes.

Olivia had offered to help with the dishes but Hadley wanted to do them herself. Running her hands under hot water was as soothing as doing the ironing. She filled the sink with plates and felt a prickle at the back of her neck.

How dare Sebastian call them the Miller girls, as if they still belonged together? And why had he given Felix a napkin signed by Jeff Koons! Sebastian could be generous, but usually when it served his best interests.

And he had been so flattering to Felix and Finn. Sebastian was like the curry in the squid risotto. A pinch of it gave the dish flavor, but too much made it hard to swallow.

Footsteps sounded in the hallway and she turned around. Felix stood at the door, carrying a brandy snifter in one hand and silverware in the other. His silvery hair glinted and his cheeks were slick with aftershave.

"We do pay Esther to clean up." He entered the kitchen. "You don't have to soak your hands in bubbles."

"I enjoy doing the dishes." Hadley flushed as if he could tell she had been thinking about Sebastian. "It's as calming as practicing yoga."

"Don't say that out loud. You'll put the dishwasher manufacturers out of business," Felix laughed and picked up a dish towel. "You know, I may have misjudged Sebastian."

"Misjudged him?" Hadley repeated.

"I can never forgive him for abandoning Olivia and staying out of her life for two decades," Felix continued. "But I can see that in his own way he truly does love her and thought he was doing what was best for her."

"Yes, he does." Hadley nodded and bit her lip.

Maybe Felix was right; the only thing Sebastian wanted was to be with Olivia. In four days he would be gone and their lives would return to normal. She mustn't spoil Olivia and Sebastian's time together with groundless suspicions.

"I was thinking, we should invite him to spend a few days with us in Manhattan this fall," Felix continued. "If Olivia and Finn hold the wedding this Christmas, Olivia won't have another chance to be alone with her father."

"You want Sebastian to stay at the duplex?" Hadley raised her eyebrow.

"He is an excellent guest, the sauvignon blanc was superb," Felix said. "And he is an interesting conversationalist. It's invigorating to get another view of the world."

"I thought you played tennis to be invigorated," Hadley murmured.

"We don't have to decide now." Felix placed the dish towel on the counter. "I just hate to think of Sebastian leaving on Friday and Olivia missing him. Isn't it worth making up the pull-out couch in the den, so Olivia can get to know her father?"

"The fall is so busy with Fashion Week and new exhibits at the gallery." Hadley turned the faucet all the way so the water was scalding. "Olivia might not get to spend time with him at all."

"Just think about it." Felix kissed Hadley on the cheek. "I'm going upstairs to bed. Esther's meringue was so rich, it always makes me sleepy."

Hadley walked down the hallway and entered the library. The French doors were open and she inhaled the scent of bougainvillea.

She couldn't blame Felix for wanting Sebastian to stay with them in New York. Everyone fell under Sebastian's spell. He appeared carrying a fine bottle of wine and a precious souvenir like a Boy Scout earning his merit badge.

But could she really stand to have him in her house again, and how dare he say Olivia had been too sheltered. It would be better for everyone if they didn't see him again until the wedding.

The portrait of the Miller girls hung on the wall and she looked up. Had she ever been so young? Her blond hair was glossy and her shoulders were brown and even the way she held her head seemed different.

Footsteps crossed the upstairs hallway and she heard Felix humming "Unforgettable" by Nat King Cole. She caught her breath and wondered if he was going to come downstairs. But the master bedroom door closed and soft jazz began to play on the bedroom's stereo.

She slipped off her sandals and lay down on the leather sofa.

Why did she feel like there was a growing distance between her and Felix? And when could they talk without Sebastian asking to refill his scotch or Esther needing help in the kitchen?

There was a sharp pain in her chest and she felt a sudden longing. She pulled the cashmere blanket over her shoulders and thought it had to be soon, or she didn't know what she would do.

Chapter Five

OLIVIA OPENED THE FRENCH DOORS of her bedroom and thought mornings in St. Barts were glorious: the red-tile roofs gleamed and the lawn was wet from the sprinklers and the swimming pool was a dazzling turquoise. She stepped onto the balcony and wondered why anyone would want to travel anywhere else. You could spend hours hiking in the lush hills and at night the air was filled with the sound of laughter and music.

New York in April was like the seesaw she played on as a child. One day she woke up to blue skies and puffy white clouds and slipped on a linen dress and strappy sandals. The next morning the weather report predicted light snow and she returned to her winter uniform of a wool coat and leather boots.

But in St. Barts she could slip on a cotton caftan without checking the temperature. Every day there was a warm breeze and the sun was as shiny as the copper pans in the kitchen. And the ocean! She watched speedboats leave a small wake like ripples of fresh cream and thought how much she loved scuba diving and snorkeling. There was a whole world under the sea: pink coral and neon fish and pastel sponges.

Last night's dinner was delicious with Esther's salade Niçoise and tender lobster and fruit tarts for dessert. The moon had been a glittering Fabergé egg and the stars were a sheet of diamonds.

She had been nervous about Sebastian and Felix and Finn sitting around the same dining room table. Sebastian was charming and worldly and his laugh was as smooth as warm brandy. But would Felix resent him eating his chilled prawns when he never even sent a note thanking him for raising Olivia?

But Sebastian and Felix got along like two old fraternity brothers. Felix said Sebastian must see the leaves change in the Hudson Valley and Sebastian recounted trekking through the jungle in Honduras. They agreed Andrew Wyeth was the greatest landscape artist of his generation and they both admired Jackson Pollock.

And Sebastian was so thoughtful! After they'd finished their dinner last night, Sebastian took Olivia and Finn to the Pipiri Palace for a nightcap. Olivia entered the leafy garden with its tall birds of paradise and thought Sebastian could have suggested one of the livelier clubs: Nikki Beach with its white canvas couches and parquet dance floor. But Finn didn't like loud music and the Pipiri Palace was so intimate.

Sebastian insisted they share an apple tatin and bought a round of rhum vanille. It was only when Finn reached into his pocket for the tip and a velvet jewelry box fell out that Olivia's heart turned over. Had Finn been planning on proposing and now the evening was ruined? But Finn mumbled something about a birthday present and stuffed the box in his pocket.

There was a knock at the door and Olivia answered it.

"I wanted to wait until you came downstairs, but I'd like to talk to you in private." Felix stood at the door. He wore white shorts and a knit shirt. "Do you mind if I come in?"

"Of course." Olivia ushered him inside. "I was just coming down to the kitchen."

"The villa is busier than a bed-and-breakfast." Felix walked onto the balcony. "It's hard to find a corner to be alone."

"I'm sorry I asked Sebastian to stay. I should have consulted you first," Olivia said quickly. "He had nowhere to go and I couldn't turn him away. But if you're not comfortable . . ."

Felix shook his head. "That's not why I'm here. I'm a grown man, I can handle a few days with Sebastian. I'm worried about you."

"I'm terribly happy! All the people I love are in the same place."

"I watched you at dinner last night and you were like an umpire observing a tennis match," he continued. "You were afraid someone was going to smash the ball over the net and everyone would get angry."

"I was worried about Sebastian and Finn getting along," Olivia conceded. "And I thought you might be angry that I asked Sebastian to stay."

"Do you remember when you were seven years old? Sebastian wrote you a letter and you wanted to send him a reply. Hadley had the flu, so you asked me to go with you to the post office.

"But there was a postal strike on the island, and no letters went out for days. I discovered you sitting in the garden and crying," Felix continued. "You were worried if you didn't reply to Sebastian, he'd never write again."

Olivia remembered clutching the tear-stained letter and Felix appearing on the porch.

"You said you knew exactly how to send him a letter, islanders had been doing it for years," she picked up the story. "We should put the letter in a bottle and send it over the ocean." She looked at

Felix and smiled. "But first we had to use up all the milk. We went into the kitchen and had milk and Esther's fresh-baked cookies. Then we stuffed the letter in the bottle and drove to Colombier Beach. I tossed the bottle into the waves and you said Sebastian would be sure to receive it.

"I was worried that you would be upset that I missed Sebastian, when you were always there for me," Olivia continued. "But you said sending the letter was the most fun you had in weeks and we should do it again. When else would we have an excuse to drink a whole bottle of milk and finish off Esther's desserts?"

"You were seven years old. You needed your father," Felix said. "We want to be loved by the people who made us, it's the most basic instinct. You don't have to wonder if Finn and Sebastian are getting along or if I'm bothered that Sebastian is wearing my swim trunks. Sebastian is here to see you and you should enjoy it."

Olivia reached up and kissed him on the cheek.

"I'd suggest we go down and have milk and cookies but that wouldn't be a healthy breakfast," Felix said and looked at his watch. "And I have to run an errand before I go to the club."

"Thank you," Olivia said as he walked to the door.

Felix turned and smiled. "I only want you to be happy."

Olivia ran down the circular staircase and entered the kitchen. The tile counter was set with a platter of sliced melon and pineapple wedges. There was a plate of croissants and pots of strawberry jam and honey.

She poured a cup of dark coffee and heard footsteps behind her. Finn wore a white shirt and shorts and carried a tennis racquet. His blond hair was freshly washed and his cheeks were tan.

"I'm surprised you are awake," Finn said and kissed her. "I thought after the rhum vanille, you'd lie in bed with the sun streaming through the French doors."

"You should have knocked on my door and found out," Olivia laughed, perching on a wicker stool.

"We agreed we wouldn't sneak around like teenagers in your parents' villa," he reminded her, buttering a slice of whole wheat toast. "Though three weeks is a long time to steal kisses in the pantry."

"I'm sure Felix and Hadley would understand. After all we're practically . . ." She bit her lip.

Finn was determined to surprise her. She couldn't admit she knew he was going to propose, that would ruin everything.

"I still wouldn't feel comfortable." He shrugged. "I'll just have to hit the tennis balls harder on the court."

"You can't play tennis today. Sebastian is taking us scuba diving."

"Felix and I are playing doubles." Finn glanced at his watch. "We're seeded number four and I couldn't disappoint him."

"But Sebastian asked us to go scuba diving last night and we accepted," Olivia replied.

"I don't remember Sebastian saying anything." He frowned. "I would have explained I had a prior commitment."

Olivia tried to remember when they started talking about scuba diving. Could it have been while Finn was figuring out the check with the maître d'? They were overcharged for the apple tatin and Finn insisted on fixing it.

"You have to come," Olivia insisted. "We are going to pack a picnic and stay on the boat all day."

"Ask Sebastian to reschedule," he suggested, dusting crumbs

from his shirt. "He can join us at the club and we'll have lunch after the match. You promised you'd watch our match. I play much better when you're around, and Felix and I are trying to win the tournament."

Olivia fiddled with her coffee cup and took a deep breath. Wasn't being with her father more important than clapping for Finn and Felix? Finn spent every free moment at the club, why shouldn't she do something for herself? And she loved scuba diving! Ever since she put on snorkeling fins as a girl, her mother laughed that she was a fish. The minute she jumped off the boat nothing existed except baby sharks and slow-moving turtles.

"I must have forgotten, but I have to go with Sebastian. Anyway, it will be good for us to be alone together. I think he feels like a prized bull under inspection." Olivia hesitated. "If it's just the two of us, he'll be more relaxed."

"He seemed quite at home," Finn insisted. "He had no problem offering me one of Felix's cigars."

"He's never really belonged to anything, it can't be easy walking into a family." Olivia jumped off the stool. "This will be perfect, we have so much to catch up on."

"You're hardly going to recount stories about how you loved finger painting when you have an oxygen tank strapped to your back," Finn said angrily.

"But we'll have shared something. You know what it's like under the ocean. There are long tunnels and mysterious caves and bright sponges. It's like discovering a magical kingdom." She stopped and looked at Finn. "You do want me to get to know my father?"

"Of course I do but we've spent quite a bit of time with him." Finn's jaw was tight. "He spent all afternoon with us yesterday and insisted on joining us for drinks last night."

"He was going to go upstairs to bed." She reminded him, "You said we were having a nightcap in Gustavia."

"I was being polite," he snapped. "I had to invite him."

"He is my father, of course he wanted to be together. But if you don't enjoy his company, it's better we go alone." She put her coffee cup in the sink and grabbed her hat. "I'll send your regrets. I'm sure we'll be back for dinner."

"Olivia, wait." Finn followed her to the foyer. His forehead was creased and she could see the tension in his neck. "I don't know Sebastian well enough to have an opinion about him, but you can't just change your plans. You promised you'd watch our match, we can't win without you."

"Of course you can. Anyway, you're not Roger Federer and this isn't Wimbledon." She turned away.

"It's the principle," Finn insisted. "You said you'd come and support us and now you're going back on your word."

"He's my father, and he's only here for three days," Olivia shot back. "I would have thought that meant something to you. Is all you care about winning another trophy?"

"Olivia, of course I care about you," Finn relented. He rubbed his chin and sighed. "Go with Sebastian if it's so important to you. I suppose Felix and I will manage. Why don't we have dinner alone tonight?"

Olivia gazed at his wide shoulders and the cleft on his chin and felt suddenly lighter. They could never argue with each other for long. And Finn had to play tennis if he already promised Felix. But Sebastian was only here for three more days; they might not get another chance.

"I'll make reservations at Le Toiny Beach Club," she suggested. "We'll eat freshly caught conch fritters on the sand."

"We could rent a private cabana." Finn pulled her close and kissed her. "I think they have quite good soundproofing."

Olivia inhaled his citrus aftershave and a tingle ran down her spine. Finn was warm and handsome and they were madly in love.

She kissed him back and whispered, "We'll have to find out."

Olivia watched Finn's car back down the driveway and wondered if she'd made a mistake. It was important she spend time with Sebastian, but she and Finn would be married soon and they should be part of a team.

When Olivia was growing up, Hadley never signed a new artist without showing Felix his work. Felix always asked Hadley's opinion before he bought tickets to a Broadway show or made reservations at a new restaurant. Olivia wanted the same closeness for her and Finn. And wouldn't she be disappointed if Finn went scuba diving without her?

A car stopped in front of the villa and Sebastian hopped out. He wore Felix's board shorts and a patterned shirt and carried a paper sack.

"I'm sorry I'm late," he said as he approached her. "I went to see Gerome first thing this morning. Apparently he was dancing at La Plage until two a.m. and forgot our appointment. I sat in the dive shop for two hours sipping day-old coffee," Sebastian took off his hat. "I can't blame him; when you're young and carefree you forget people count on you.

"But it's all set now. We have a forty-eight-foot catamaran and Gerome is going to escort us himself. He mentioned Pain du Sucre has the best scuba diving on the island."

"He has the biggest boat in St. Barts," Olivia protested. "You couldn't possibly afford it."

"I almost fainted at the prices. Every tourist in St. Barts must carry blocks of gold bouillon," he agreed. "But I believe in the barter system. Everyone has their price, you just have to figure out what it is."

"You bartered for use of his boat?" She raised her eyebrow.

"How do you think commerce works in most countries? If you live in a village in Japan you'll never wear suede loafers, but a pair of sturdy boots allows you to farm in adverse conditions. Next year you grow more rice than your neighbor and exchange them for a chicken coop." He paused. "Your wife sells the eggs at the market and the next thing you know you're opening your own grocery store."

"But what did Gerome want?" Olivia asked.

"I sat next to a couple of *Sports Illustrated* models on the plane." Sebastian took her arm. "They were here to do a photo session and one of them gave me her card. I told him I'd suggest they take scuba diving lessons."

How could she ask Sebastian to change his plans when he went to so much trouble? And it was a gorgeous day. The sky was pale blue and the clouds looked as if they had been painted with watercolors.

"Is there a problem?" he asked, noticing her expression.

"Finn didn't know you invited us," she said. "He's playing in a tennis tournament with Felix. I forgot that I promised to watch the match."

"I could have sworn he was at the table when I suggested it, but we can't go without him. I'll call Gerome and reschedule. I did stop in Gustavia for French bread and liver pâté and papaya." He glanced in the paper sack. "But the pâté will keep and the bread will be fresh tomorrow."

Olivia felt the hot sun on her cheeks and longed to be under the ocean. And really, Felix and Finn were perfectly capable of playing without her cheering them on. She couldn't plan her day around everyone's schedule.

"Of course we'll go today." She smiled. "Let me get my swimsuit."

"That's wonderful." Sebastian put on his hat. "Pâté never tastes the same when it's been in the fridge."

Gerome greeted them at the boat and Olivia knew she'd made the right decision. The deck had dark wood planks and creamy leather seats and jazz playing on the stereo. She stood next to Sebastian and her heart swelled. She was about to do the thing she loved most with her father!

"I haven't scuba dived since I was in Micronesia," Sebastian said when they reached Pain du Sucre. "The boat was nothing fancy and my tank was slightly rusted, but once you hit the bottom there's nothing like it. Shoals of neon fish and blue ribbon eels and baby sharks. I almost forgot to come up."

"I'm the same way." Olivia felt the familiar tingle of excitement before a dive. "It's so still and I've never seen such bright colors. I want to explore the coral reefs forever."

"You must get it from Hadley." Sebastian strapped on his fins. "When we were on Koh Tao island, I had to limit her to two dives a day, like a gambler you steer away from the roulette table." He shielded his eyes from the sun. "She must love it here, her own aquatic playground."

"My mother doesn't dive," Olivia said.

"That's impossible, it's the thing she loved most." Sebastian frowned. "In South Africa she swam in a cage surrounded by sharks. We were going to go together but I got food poisoning. At least I thought that's what it was," he laughed. "It was probably nerves. She jumped into the cage wearing a blue bikini. God, I was jealous of those sharks being so close to her small waist and long legs," he sighed. "It was the second most frightening fifteen minutes of my life. I made her promise to never do it again."

"She never told me." Olivia frowned.

"I suppose that's smart. It's like not telling your teenager you had a fake ID or rolled a joint in your parents' bedroom." He shrugged. "But these days they have all sorts of safety mechanisms, it's like riding a bicycle."

"Felix gets claustrophobic underwater," she explained. "She wouldn't want to dive without him."

"She gave up all this," he waved at the dappled sea and sun glinting on the boat, "because her husband doesn't want to strap on a pair of fins?"

Olivia suddenly felt uneasy, as if she was being disloyal. "I'm sure there are other reasons. She says swimming in the pool is the best exercise."

Sebastian was about to say something and changed his mind. He signaled to Gerome and stood up. "Well, I can't wait another minute."

Olivia jumped into the clear water and everything faded away: the heated discussion with Finn at the villa and wondering when he was going to propose and if she was being foolish letting Sebastian into her life. There were pink coral and manta rays and fish like fluorescent lamps.

A sea lion swam by and there were iridescent blue tangs and brightly colored parrotfish. Olivia saw a reef shark and a whole school of yellow silversides. The blue water enveloped her and she felt like she'd slipped inside a jewelry box.

"Being on the water is more invigorating than staring down a herd of water buffalo," Sebastian said when they put away their gear and lay on striped towels on the deck. "Every time I dive I feel like Neptune in his private kingdom."

"Do you dive often?" Olivia adjusted her sunglasses and thought she had never been so content. Sebastian was easy to be with and they shared the same passions.

"Not as often as I like." Sebastian ate a bite of star fruit. "But I traded a painting for a day's diving in the Gili Islands and I once spent a week in Tahiti. The wonderful thing about diving is you always discover something different: parrotfish in Malaysia and humpback turtles in Fiji and leopard sharks in Sipadan."

"I wouldn't know," Olivia said. "I've only dived in St. Barts."

Sebastian sat up and looked at Olivia. "But surely if you're passionate about diving, you've been to Grand Turk or the Great Barrier Reef."

"Felix and Hadley spend every Christmas and April in St. Barts." She shrugged. "There's no time to go anywhere else."

"Felix and Hadley have the money, they should use it to travel." Sebastian frowned. "It's like owning a sports car and driving it to buy milk at the supermarket."

"Felix doesn't like hotels." Olivia ate a cherry. "The mattress can be bad for his back and he's allergic to some kinds of laundry detergent."

"But you and Finn are young," he continued. "You should build orphanages in Belize or ride llamas in Tibet."

"St. Barts is perfect, why would we want to go anywhere else?"

"I have an idea," he exclaimed. "A friend keeps a boat in Costa Rica. He invited me for a week at Christmas, you and Finn can join me. We'll eat mahimahi and drive inland to see the jungle."

"We always spend Christmas in St. Barts." She hesitated. "Esther makes a feast of stuffed eggplant and grilled codfish and strawberry shortcake. After lunch we sail in the harbor. It's glorious to soak up the sun instead of shivering in New York."

"Now is the time to make your own traditions," Sebastian urged. "What could be better than starting the year somewhere new?"

What would Hadley and Felix say if she announced they were going to spend Christmas with Sebastian? But if she said no, when would she see him again, and it was a wonderful invitation!

"You know when I said that watching Hadley swim with the sharks was the second scariest fifteen minutes of my life?" Sebastian began. "The scariest fifteen minutes was the moment you were born. We had you at an American hospital in Johannesburg; I painted a portrait of the surgeon's wife in exchange for a private room." He smiled. "Everything went smoothly until the doctor realized the umbilical cord was wrapped around your neck.

"I saw the look of terror on the doctor's face and prayed if God granted me this one wish, I'd never ask for anything else. Suddenly I heard you cry and your skin was wrinkled like a lizard and I'd never seen anything so beautiful," he finished. "I may not be the best father but I couldn't love you more."

"I'm beginning to understand that being a parent is more complicated than I thought," Olivia said slowly.

"It's not complicated really." Sebastian looked at Olivia. "You're grateful for being given the greatest gift and you only want to be worthy. You make mistakes for years and then finally there is a possibility to set things right. You hope and pray you haven't missed your chance." He paused. "You and Finn should come to Costa Rica at Christmas."

"It's a fantastic offer and I do appreciate it," Olivia said and smiled. "I'll ask Finn what he thinks."

Olivia opened the fridge and took out a jug of iced tea. It was midafternoon and Sebastian had gone upstairs to take a shower. Felix and Finn were still at the club and she could hear Esther running the vacuum cleaner in the living room.

Scuba diving with Sebastian had been so exciting. She thought about his invitation to Costa Rica and pictured underwater caves filled with exotic fish. But would Finn want to spend a week on a boat with her father?

"There you are." Hadley entered the kitchen. She wore a patterned dress and leather sandals. "I had lunch at the club. Finn said you went scuba diving with Sebastian."

"He invited us last night after dinner," Olivia sighed. "The ocean was like a sheet of glass and the fish were all the colors of the rainbow. We had a marvelous time."

"I'm glad you had fun." Hadley looked at Olivia. "Finn was concerned you went without him."

"Sebastian did invite him, Finn just didn't hear him." Olivia flushed. "And I had to go, Sebastian is only here for three more days. I couldn't miss out."

"You promised Finn you would watch the match, and he was very disappointed. Men can be so superstitious, he didn't think he could win without you. Just don't forget Finn is the man you're in love with." Hadley filled a glass with ice. "Sebastian is like a sailboat on the horizon. You're busy admiring its billowing sails and sleek wood and the next minute it's gone."

"Actually, Sebastian wants to be around more." Olivia took a deep breath. "He invited me and Finn to go scuba diving in Costa Rica at Christmas."

"He did what?" Hadley exclaimed.

"It would only be for a week," Olivia explained. "We could still come to St. Barts for New Year's."

"What an intriguing invitation." Hadley's eyes flashed. "Did he say why Christmas specifically?"

"His friend owns a boat and we would be his guests," she explained. "It would be nice for Finn and Sebastian to spend time together."

"Oh yes, it was very thoughtful of Sebastian." Hadley pursed her lips. "I'm surprised he didn't mention it to me."

"I think he just thought of it," Olivia said excitedly. "We were having so much fun, we didn't want it to end. We really are very similar, we like the same foods and books and movies."

"Sebastian makes a chameleon look like a simple lizard." Hadley fiddled with her earrings. "He wears more coats than Joseph in *The Amazing Technicolor Dreamcoat.*"

"I know we always celebrate Christmas in St. Barts but he's trying so hard." Olivia put her glass in the sink. "He's making up for all the years he missed."

"I'm sure that's exactly what he's doing," Hadley said and walked to the stairs. "I'm going to have a quick word with him."

"You might want to wait," Olivia called after her. "He was going to take a shower."

"In that case I'll fix him an iced tea with a splash of gin." She took a bottle out of the cabinet. "He's going to need it."

Olivia closed the door of her bedroom and untied her caftan. She thought about the conversation with her mother and wondered why she seemed upset. Didn't Hadley want Olivia to spend time with Sebastian?

The holiday in St. Barts was supposed to be about celebrating her birthday and Finn proposing and lying on a white sand beach. But now Finn was unhappy and even her mother seemed unsettled. Maybe she should tell Sebastian going to Costa Rica wasn't a good idea.

She opened her bedside drawer and took out the wooden box. She sifted through the letters and removed a red envelope.

> *Dearest Olivia,*
>
> *I've never written at Christmas before because I was afraid I'd say the wrong thing and spoil your vision of Santa Claus. What if I asked whether Santa Claus ate all the oatmeal cookies when you actually left him brownies? Or if I wondered if the reindeer enjoyed the carrots and you and Hadley fed them celery?*
>
> *But since you are now a teenager, it is safe to assume you know that Santa Claus means something different to everyone. I am in Tokyo and the Japanese have the strangest Christmas tradition. They all eat Kentucky Fried Chicken! You've never seen so many red and white tubs of drumsticks.*
>
> *I hope you have a wonderful day filled with fruitcake and presents. There is something magical about the holidays. All over the world people sing carols and drink eggnog with the people they love.*

Enjoy my gift. Your mother might be angry with me if you don't have your ears pierced, but I hope she lets you keep them.

Merry Christmas, my dearest Olivia. One day we will exchange presents in person.

Your loving father,

Sebastian

Olivia remembered the jade earrings nestled in the envelope and her heart turned over. How wonderful to finally celebrate the holidays with Sebastian! And it was only one Christmas; it wouldn't hurt to do something different. She slid the letter back in the envelope and stuffed it in the box. She'd just discovered her father; how could she give him up now?

Chapter Six

HADLEY POLISHED THE WALNUT CABINET in the living room of the villa and twisted the cloth in her hand. She had always loved polishing furniture; it was so satisfying to make the coffee table gleam and the crystal vases sparkle and the glass chess set glint in the sun.

Often she arrived home from a long day dealing with temperamental artists and demanding clients at the gallery and picked up a bottle of Lemon Pledge. She polished the grand piano in the conservatory and the bookshelves in Felix's study and silver picture frames in the den. Felix would see the fiery look in her eyes and laugh that they didn't need a housekeeper, no one could make a Regency desk shine like Hadley.

Now she heard Sebastian singing in the upstairs shower and grimaced. He was lucky she didn't shut off the hot water. How dare he invite Olivia and Finn to go scuba diving in Costa Rica at Christmas?

She tried to remember when Felix had come into the living room and told her Finn was going to propose. Sebastian hadn't been there; could it be a coincidence he suggested they go scuba diving the same week Finn wanted to get married?

But she remembered Felix and Sebastian spending time together admiring Felix's art collection and drinking aged cognac. Felix could easily have confided in Sebastian.

What would Finn say when Olivia mentioned Sebastian's invitation? Finn couldn't tell Olivia why he didn't want to go without ruining the surprise engagement, and they would get into another argument. If this were a boxing match, Sebastian would perform a knockout in the opening round.

She would tell Sebastian he had to take back the invitation before Olivia mentioned it to Finn. He'd already caused a small rift; he couldn't create a bigger tear.

The shower turned off and she thought no one could make her blood boil like Sebastian. She clutched the dust cloth and suddenly remembered the first year they were together, when his determination was intoxicating.

They had been traveling in Africa for ten months and Sebastian painted sunsets that were pink and yellow and orange. At night they ate bobotie and malva pudding and mapped out where to go next. And when they lay in each other's arms with the moon as big as a platter, Hadley couldn't imagine being anywhere else.

Hadley stood in front of the closet and admired the black chiffon dress. She glanced at the quilted evening bag and silver wrap. It had been so long since she'd worn anything but windbreakers and khakis, she wondered if she remembered how to apply lipstick and mascara.

It was late July and the African winter had been mild. Occasionally she and Sebastian waited out rainstorms in a farmhouse on the Laikipia Plateau or in the foothills of Mount Kenya, but mostly they rode buses and painted and fell more deeply in love.

Hadley kept telling herself they were just travel companions and eventually she would do a course in Italy or return to Connecticut. But every day was crammed with new adventures and when Hadley watched Sebastian hunched over his canvas, his dark hair streaked with paint, something hard pressed against her chest.

And the food! They ate Swahili cakes in Malindi and fried plantains in Ghana and lamb stew with spices in Tunisia. Hadley loved the food in South Africa best: breakfasts of milk tarts and dark coffee and dinners of boerewors and sweet potatoes. She loved everything about the country: the fragrant hibiscus and green valleys and sharp cliffs with views of the ocean.

Charles Lang called and said one of South Africa's wealthiest diamond merchants wanted to host Sebastian and Hadley at a house party. At first Sebastian hesitated: he didn't want to rent a tuxedo and sit around drinking dry sherry. But Charles reminded him that one good sale could finance months of traveling on the Ivory Coast. And how difficult was it to spend the weekend at an estate in the most exclusive suburb in Johannesburg?

The bedroom door opened and Sebastian entered, carrying a stack of boxes. He wore a wool sweater and loafers and his wavy hair touched his collar.

"Did you see the grounds on this place?" he whistled, setting the boxes on the four-poster bed. "It's big enough to house an elephant. And the swimming pool has gold-inlaid tiles. It would be like diving into Tiffany's."

"I thought you didn't like wealth and luxury." Hadley pulled her robe around her waist. She was getting over a winter cold and spent the afternoon reading magazines and taking a hot bath.

"Certainly not as a steady diet." Sebastian sunk onto a satin love seat. "But forty-eight hours of heated bathroom floors and a sideboard set with fresh oysters and bottles of Absolut isn't as bad as I thought."

"And a host predicting you're going to be one of the greatest artists of your generation." Hadley smiled.

"That's all about you." Sebastian was suddenly serious. "You walk into a gallery and tell people they should buy my paintings and they believe you." He kissed her. "You're elegant and sophisticated and I wouldn't be anything without you."

They rarely talked about their relationship. The future was like the African plains during a downpour. You knew there was a road somewhere but for the moment all you saw was mud and sheets of rain. When the rain finally stopped the sun was so bright and the hills were so green, you couldn't see anything else.

But sometimes Hadley wondered if she should be applying to graduate school or starting a career or doing something other than posing for Sebastian. But then she would see his sketch of her sitting under a jacaranda tree and her heart stretched.

"Maybe in the beginning," she smiled, "but now everyone wants a Sebastian Miller."

"In a small circle but not in New York or Paris." He shrugged. "But together we will conquer the art world. One day we'll visit the Guggenheim and see the portrait of you on top of Table Mountain."

"Right now we have to dress for dinner." Hadley held up the dress. "I only have the black chiffon, do you think it will do?"

"Derek's driver took me into Johannesburg." Sebastian handed her a box. "These are for you."

"We can't afford this," Hadley gasped, taking out a gold lamé dress. There was a pair of sheer stockings and black stilettos.

"If we want people to pay a lot for my paintings we have to dress the part," Sebastian explained. "We can't let Derek's guests think we're two American kids bumming around Africa."

"We'll have to go home if we don't save money," she protested. "This must cost more than the sale of your last landscape."

"You said everyone wants a Sebastian Miller, why shouldn't we enjoy it." He stopped and looked at Hadley. "And how could I resist, when the fabric makes your eyes look like cornflowers."

Hadley felt a heady rush, like she was standing on top of a waterfall. "Thank you, it's lovely. I can't wait to put it on."

"I brought you something else." He reached into his pocket and drew out a black velvet box. She snapped it open and discovered diamond teardrop earrings.

"These must cost a fortune, they're like the earrings the girls wore at Mount Holyoke. They received them for their twenty-first birthday or from boyfriends who attended Harvard and drove convertibles." She handed the box to Sebastian. "Take them back and I'll book our trip to Stellenbosch. A gallery there is interested in your work and we can stop at the Tsitsikamma National Forest and see the rhinoceros."

"I didn't buy them." He fiddled with the box.

"Then how did they end up in your pocket?" she asked.

"Derek gave them to me in exchange for sketching his trout farm in Magoebaskloof," he explained. "We'll stay in his guesthouse and eat grilled trout and sleep under a goose down comforter."

"You can't trade a piece you haven't painted for a pair of diamond earrings," Hadley spluttered. "What will we use for bus fare and fresh fruit and vegetables?"

"We'll hitchhike if we have to and I'll eat mealie for days to see your eyes sparkle," he grabbed her hands. "I may not be able to give you a penthouse apartment and steady paycheck and three weeks' vacation in Hawaii. But we'll never go hungry and we'll see the most amazing places. I love you and I couldn't do this without you."

It was impossible to resist Sebastian. He was like a boy looking through a telescope, explaining how he was going to reach the stars.

"Let me see them on you," he whispered. He led her to the mirror and fastened the earrings in her ears.

Sebastian kissed her hair and her neck. He ran his hands over her breasts and circled her nipples. She leaned against him and felt the exquisite tension.

"They're gorgeous," she breathed, a wetness forming between her thighs.

Sebastian stroked her cheek and whispered, "They'll look even better when you're not wearing anything else."

He untied the silk sash and let her robe fall to the floor. The diamonds glittered in the mirror and she felt wanton and sensuous.

She unbuttoned his shirt and ran her hands over his chest. He brushed her thighs and she wanted him so badly, her whole body trembled.

"Not yet," she murmured, guiding him to the bedroom.

"I thought we had to dress for dinner," he whispered, unzipping his slacks.

"There's plenty of time." She lay on the bed and drew him on top of her. "First we have to work up an appetite."

Hadley wrapped her arms around him and opened her legs. He moved faster and she felt the warm center forming inside her. He came first and fell against her, his chest slick with sweat. She waited and the center fell away and in its place were endless waves and the sensation of being completely happy.

"You see," Sebastian moaned, when they lay on their backs. "Diamonds are the way to a girl's heart."

Hadley took a deep breath and gazed at the velvet jewelry box. Sebastian was wrong; the heady feeling had nothing to do with diamond teardrop earrings. It was the certainty of being in love.

Hadley fiddled with her earrings and glanced around the dining room. The parquet floors were covered with geometric rugs and the cherry sideboard was set with crystal wineglasses and sterling silverware. Twelve-foot glass doors opened onto a lush garden and the walls were lined with abstract paintings.

Dinner was served at the long glass table filled with platters of lamb skewers and bunny chow and stuffed zucchini. There were plates of boerewors with chakalaka and meatballs smothered in chutney; long rolls filled with steak and stews made of every kind of vegetable. But all these South African foods Hadley loved suddenly made her stomach turn.

She watched Sebastian chat with a polo player and felt uneasy. They didn't belong with men wearing Armani tuxes and women in couture gowns. And she shouldn't be wearing the diamond earrings when they didn't know if Sebastian would sell another painting.

But it wouldn't do any good to give them back to Sebastian. She would talk to him tonight: they would keep a chart of their expenses and make a plan for the future.

After dinner the men moved to the library and Hadley sank onto a paisley sofa in the living room. She wondered why she was so tired. Maybe it was the rich food or central heating or that she was still slightly ill.

"You don't look like you're enjoying yourself," a woman said as she approached her. She was in her mid-thirties and wore a red dress and gold pumps. "You must try the banana cream pie. It's delicious, you can't help but feel better."

"I'm fine," Hadley said and smiled. "I'm just getting over a cold."

The woman nodded. "That's the problem with traveling to a different continent. When we left Texas it was one hundred degrees and the humidity was so bad, going outside was like taking a bath. I forgot it's winter in South Africa. We had to stop at a department store in Johannesburg and buy sweaters and boots."

"We've actually been in Africa for almost a year," Hadley replied. "But the weather can be unpredictable and it's easy to get chilled."

"A year, how fabulous!" she exclaimed. "My husband and I went on safari on our honeymoon. But it rained the first three weeks and I came down with stomach flu. Of course it wasn't the flu at all, I was pregnant!" she laughed. "Ten years and three children later and we're finally finishing our vacation. I love being a parent but I miss grabbing a passport and getting on a plane," she sighed. "You don't know how many years we've sipped French champagne on New Year's Eve and tried to imagine we were in Paris."

"Sebastian is an artist," Hadley explained. "We started in Cape Town and took the Garden Route through South Africa. We visited waterfalls and game preserves and ostrich farms."

"You're married to Sebastian Miller!" She beamed. "When we were first married we pictured ourselves as a modern-day F. Scott Fitzgerald and Zelda, without the alcohol and insanity, of course," she laughed. "A young couple should see as much of the world as possible. Though there is nothing more delicious than a baby; wait until you inhale their skin after a bath."

"We're not married," Hadley corrected. "We're just travel companions."

"I'm terribly sorry, sometimes I say the wrong thing." She glanced at Hadley's gold lamé dress and blushed. "I just thought . . ."

"Thought what?" Hadley asked, suddenly feeling queasy. She thought about the last few weeks when she didn't eat anything except rusks. Her blouses were too tight and she couldn't stand the smell of coffee.

"Texans have a reputation for being nosy but I noticed you didn't eat a bite of potjiekos at dinner. You haven't touched the desserts and you look like you'd give anything to climb into bed." She paused. "And I've never seen anyone with such glossy hair."

"My hair?" Hadley touched her blond hair.

"It's the best thing about being pregnant," she said as if she were sharing a secret. "For the next eight months you'll have lustrous hair like a supermodel."

Hadley sat at the dressing table and tried to stop her hands from shaking. She remembered the antibiotics she took in Pretoria and the last few weeks of feeling miserable and knew, of course, she was pregnant; how could she have not seen it sooner?

The diamond teardrop earrings glittered in her ears and she felt an unbearable sadness. All the adventures of the last year— falling asleep on Sebastian's shoulder and waking up to the smell of sweet pastries, looking out the bus window and seeing a herd of elephants—would be swept away as if by the winter rain.

She dabbed her mascara and thought it wouldn't help to cry. She'd go back to Connecticut and teach art at Miss Porter's School. Her parents would help with the baby and eventually she would move to New York and get a proper job.

She couldn't tell Sebastian, he was the least likely person to have a child. He slept until noon and thought a bowl of vanilla ice cream was an acceptable dinner. He hated making plans and got restless if they stayed in the same place.

She would say she was tired of traveling and needed to do something for herself. He could know the truth later, when his paintings were in the Sotheby's catalog and his name was a household word.

Her heart pounded and she put the earrings in the black velvet case. The door opened and Sebastian entered, holding a crystal brandy snifter.

"There you are," he said. "I was drinking Hennessy with a collector from London and he asked who I thought would win Wimbledon. You know I'm terrible at that stuff, I needed you whispering names in my ear."

"I had a headache," Hadley explained, slipping off her stilettos.

"I can make you feel better," he whispered and put his hands on her dress.

"Not now." Hadley jumped up. She turned to Sebastian and her voice softened. "I'm not feeling well, I'm going to take a bath."

"In that case, I'll warm up the bed." He untied his bow tie. "You'll never guess who I met, Hans Feinman! He loves my landscapes and wants to show my work at his gallery in Munich. Can you imagine, our first show in Europe at one of the most respected galleries in Germany? I'll have to work hard," his face broke into a smile, "but I know where to get my inspiration."

Hadley nodded. "That's a fantastic opportunity. I'm so pleased for you."

"From there we can introduce my work to galleries in Milan and Paris." He paused. "We'll buy you a whole new wardrobe, chic black dresses and designer pumps and some significant jewelry.

We'll be the darlings of the art world and you'll charm everyone with your perfect French."

Hadley looked at Sebastian and took a deep breath. "I'm not coming."

"What do you mean you're not coming?" he demanded.

"I can't follow you around forever, like the sidecar on a motorcycle," she continued. "I've had a wonderful time but I have to do something for myself. Where will I be in five years if all I do is sip champagne at gallery openings and pose in fields of flowers?"

"You'll be next to me, making sure I don't fall on my face," he spluttered. "Every artist needs a muse. Degas and Picasso had women who inspired them."

"Is that what I am?" Hadley was suddenly angry. "An insurance policy that guarantees you can paint? I'm sure there are dozens of models who would be happy to sit for you, and you don't need me to butter up gallery owners, you're doing a fine job."

"With one German who shared a taste for gewürztraminer!" Sebastian exclaimed. "But we wouldn't be sitting in this suite if it wasn't for you. Why would you want to leave, when we're having so much fun?"

It would be so easy to tell him the truth: she was pregnant and she had to have the baby, that's just the way she was. But he couldn't stop what he was doing. He'd be an empty shell if he didn't paint.

But it wouldn't change anything, so what would be the point?

"I'm going to live at home for a while and then dip my feet in the New York art world," she said slowly. "Work at the Frick or get a job at one of the impossibly sleek galleries in Chelsea."

"We're not going to traipse around the world forever." Sebastian ran his hands through his hair. "But right now there's so much to paint. I can't do it surrounded by honking taxis and half-empty garbage cans and vendors selling warm pretzels."

Hadley walked to the dresser and picked up the jewelry case.

"Sell these and you'll have enough to finance your next painting." She handed him the box. "If you'll excuse me, I'm going to take a bath."

"Hadley, wait." Sebastian touched her arm. "I love you, I thought we were going to do this together."

She turned away and thought her heart would break. "I love you too, but I can't."

Hadley dried her hair with a towel and wrapped a robe around her body. Sebastian had stormed out and she'd taken a long bath. She remembered his look of betrayal and wished she could tell him the truth.

Then she pictured everything ahead of her: booking her flight to New York, telling her parents, finding a doctor, and thought she had things to worry about other than Sebastian's feelings.

The bedroom door opened and Sebastian strode inside. His cheeks were pale and he still wore his white dinner jacket.

"I was just going to bed," she said. "I can sleep on the sofa if you like."

"I went downstairs to have a brandy and met a couple from Texas," he began. "The husband is an oilman and his wife is one of those chatty women who pulls out pictures of her children."

Hadley gasped and a chill ran down her spine.

"She met you after dinner and asked if you were feeling well," he said and looked at Hadley. "She said in her first trimester she couldn't get out of bed and all she wanted to eat was salted nuts." He paused. "Then she said you had the loveliest blue eyes and we were going to have a beautiful baby."

"She said all that," Hadley whispered.

"I'm sure she would have gone on but her husband pulled her away." He took a cigarette case out of his pocket. "Why didn't you tell me you were pregnant?"

"It only occurred to me this evening. I haven't had my period in weeks, I thought it was the bumpy bus rides and changing temperatures." Her lips trembled. "But I'm certain it's true."

"And you were just going to pack your passport and go back to New York?" he fumed.

"I'm sorry, I was going to tell you later." She hesitated. "I didn't want you to change your plans."

"But what will you do?"

Hadley looked at Sebastian and something shifted inside her. For a moment she thought he would say he loved her and they had to be together. But he just wanted to know what she was going to do about the baby.

"My parents won't be shocked. Their relationship started quite scandalously." She tried to smile. "And I do have a college degree, I can find a job."

"You can't just take my baby and move to a different continent." Sebastian lit the cigarette.

"You're hardly ready to be a father. You hate loud noise and don't know how to keep a budget." Her cheeks flushed. "Do you think a baby is something you keep in your backpack and show off to vendors you meet at an outdoor market?"

Sebastian stubbed out the cigarette and looked at Hadley. "I would have liked to have the choice."

"But that's the thing about a baby, it's not about you anymore."
She felt like a train picking up steam. "You said yourself you have
to paint. Could you really give it up for a house in the suburbs and
a weekly pass on Amtrak?"

"There are hospitals in South Africa," he argued. "Why couldn't
we have a baby and keep traveling?"

"We're not even married," Hadley said and bit her lip.

"We can change that." He reached into his pocket and drew
out a velvet case. He snapped it open and dropped to his knee.

"I knew the moment I met you at the guesthouse in Cape Town
you were beautiful and smart," he began. "And your smile is brighter
than all the stars in the African sky. I can't promise you the most
conventional life and you're right, I haven't a clue what to do with
a baby." He took her hand. "But I love you both more than anything in the world. Hadley Stevens, will you marry me?"

Hadley wondered if they really could do anything as foolish as
get married. It was easy when all they shared were cups of coffee
and wonderful nights in bed. But what happened when they had
to set up a 401(k) and visit two sets of parents at Christmas?

Sebastian was charming and talented but he was the worst idea
of a husband. He didn't know how to cook and could be terribly
impatient. And she could as easily imagine him wearing a suit and
going to an office as she could Peter Pan growing up.

But you didn't have to live in a gabled house to make it work.
When she was with him, she felt part of something bigger. Wasn't
the most important thing being in love?

"Where did you get that?" She pointed to the emerald-cut diamond on a platinum band.

"I gave Derek the diamond teardrop earrings and he let me
have this ring instead." He looked at Hadley. "I may have to paint

a couple more pieces but you're going to wear it for sixty years. It had to be perfect."

"It's beautiful," Hadley gasped.

"Will you put it on?"

She glanced at his green eyes and bright smile and all her reasons to say no disappeared. Of course she had to say yes, she couldn't imagine life without him.

"Yes." She nodded.

He slipped the ring on her finger and a warmth spread through her chest. They were going to get married and have a baby, what could be a greater adventure? She kissed him and never wanted the moment to end.

Hadley ran the cloth over the glass coffee table and thought she had been so young and foolish. Sebastian loved her and Olivia but he loved himself more. When he had to choose between the thing that made him what he was and his family, he packed his paintbrushes and favorite slippers and left.

She shouldn't be too hard on him; he had suffered. But it didn't excuse what he did. And he wasn't going to arrive now and stir up their lives like a chef on a television cooking show.

Was Sebastian right, were Olivia and Finn too young to get married? Finn was grounded and loyal and would do anything for Olivia. And Olivia didn't have to save turtles in Costa Rica or ride elephants in Thailand to know she was in love. They had been together for four years; getting married was the natural step.

She would tell Sebastian he couldn't extend any invitations to Olivia without asking her. And if he caused any more waves between

Olivia and Finn she'd put him on a rowboat and push him into the harbor.

Footsteps crossed the hallway and Sebastian entered the living room. He wore linen slacks and a pastel-colored shirt.

"Nothing like a cold shower to make you feel twenty years younger," he said, walking to the bar. "I spent a few days with a tribal chief in Ghana who only bathed in ice-cold water. He was sixty-nine and just fathered his sixteenth child."

"All you need is more children; you haven't done a good job with the one you have," she retorted. "Did you see your daughter this afternoon? She ran up to her room and she was quite upset."

"I don't understand, we had a fabulous morning scuba diving." He poured a glass of scotch. "Olivia is like a fish in the water, she must have inherited it from you," he sighed. "That and her long legs, she really is a beautiful girl. We did well."

"We didn't do anything. Her looks are a stroke of nature and her intelligence is a combination of hard work and good schooling." She looked at Sebastian. "You wouldn't know. You left before she finished her first *Fun with Dick and Jane* book."

Sebastian raised his eyebrow. "You are irritable this afternoon. Felix should hire a maid instead of making you do the housework."

"We have a housekeeper and I like to polish the furniture." She tossed the cloth on the side table and sat on the sofa. "A little honest labor is rewarding, you should try it."

"Drink this, it's your favorite scotch." He handed her the glass. "And tell me what's wrong."

"Don't treat me like a shopgirl you charm into giving you free cigarettes." She took the glass. "You asked Olivia and Finn to go scuba diving in Costa Rica at Christmas."

"I knew there was something bothering you. You always were as transparent as a sheer negligee," he mused. "But isn't it a little late to be discussing custody? Olivia is almost twenty-five. She can spend Christmas with her father if she wants to."

"You forgot the small fact that Finn is going to ask her to marry him," she replied and downed the scotch.

"I did invite them both. Though Finn played tennis this morning instead of going scuba diving." He shrugged. "If he doesn't want to come to Costa Rica, Olivia and I will have fun without him."

Hadley wondered if Sebastian really hadn't known that Finn wanted to hold the wedding at Christmas. Maybe his invitation was perfectly innocent and she was getting upset about nothing.

"You're absent for twenty years and suddenly appear like a cross between Santa Claus and the most dazzling movie star," she said finally. "Olivia and Finn never fight, and now she's defending you."

"I can't think of anything more boring. The best part of being with you was when we had a difference of opinion." He glanced at Hadley. "Making up was more electrifying than a swarm of fireflies."

"A relationship where you agree on things is called a lasting marriage." Her cheeks flushed. "Finn asked Felix to hold the wedding at St. Barts at Christmas but it's supposed to be a surprise. If Finn says he doesn't want to go to Costa Rica, Olivia will be furious."

Sebastian nodded. "That could be a problem."

"You didn't know?" Hadley looked up.

"How would I know? I hardly qualify as Finn's best man." He shrugged. "I'll tell Olivia we'll go next spring for her birthday."

"You would do that?" she asked hopefully.

She had been worried that Olivia and Finn would get into another fight, but now everything would be all right.

"Of course." He poured another glass of scotch. "You really don't see; there's nothing I care about more than Olivia's happiness. Though, frankly, I believe she's making a mistake. She's like a turtle content in its shell. Eventually it dives in the ocean and discovers neon-colored fish and glittering coral and realizes there's more to life than miles of white sand. But I would never sabotage her relationship on purpose," he finished. "That would be like destroying the *Mona Lisa*."

"I'm glad." Hadley's eyes filled with unexpected tears.

"There is something else bothering you." Sebastian sat next to her. "You're a beautiful woman with piles of wealth. You should be swathed in diamonds and rubies. You should own a collection of Louis Vuitton luggage and jet between Gstaad and Monte Carlo."

"I thought we should all be living in the jungle and eating coconuts," Hadley retorted.

"You wear nondescript dresses and flat sandals you find at Macy's."

"I come to St. Barts to relax, I can wear whatever I like."

"It's not just the clothes, though, you're wasting a fine pair of legs," he continued. "Olivia said you don't scuba dive anymore."

"Felix had a bad experience years ago." She fiddled with her glass. "He doesn't like to dive."

"He plays tennis every day and you don't own a racquet," Sebastian protested. "Why should you stop diving because he doesn't want to?"

"Sometimes you do things because your spouse asks you to. It's called putting the other person first," she replied. "That might sound as foreign as saving for your retirement but it's part of the marriage vows."

"Well, it doesn't seem to be working. You'll be forty-nine in a few days but you behave like you're seventy." He frowned. "You should be practicing yoga and eating exotic foods and planning trips to Portugal and Tenerife. Instead you're driving to the tennis club and mixing rum punch."

"We own a villa in St. Barts. It's one of the most glorious islands in the Caribbean." Hadley's cheeks flushed once more. "I have everything I could have dreamed of."

"But you're not even enjoying St. Barts. You could be scuba diving and snorkeling and sipping peach daiquiris at nightclubs. Look at you." He waved his hand. "You're wearing a housedress and wiping down furniture."

"I like to polish furniture and this dress is vintage Diane von Furstenberg. If I need fashion advice I'll read a copy of *Vogue*." She stood and smoothed her skirt. "Now if you'll excuse me, I'm going to take a bath."

"Hadley, wait." Sebastian touched her arm. "I can't help noticing the changes. Your beauty is still there, it's more spectacular than ever. But you're so busy with Felix and Olivia and Finn, you've forgotten about yourself.

"Where's the girl who climbed onto a rock to get close to the penguins or stood fifty feet from a rhinoceros? I don't expect her back altogether, we all age. But you can't extinguish her completely; what will be there instead?"

Hadley felt his hand on her arm and a chill ran down her spine.

"I'll tell you what's there, a mother who spent two decades making sure her daughter was loved and nurtured," she began. "And a wife who enjoys fixing her husband a dry martini because he always says thank you. We can't all lead big lives filled with African chiefs and spiritual awakenings, but some of us are happy." Her blue eyes flashed. "And I think you're feeling sorry for yourself or you wouldn't be here trying to charm your daughter."

"You're wrong, I—"

The front door opened and Felix stood in the foyer. His tennis bag was slung over his shoulder and his white shirt was damp with sweat.

"There you are! Finn and I made the final round." He kissed Hadley and nodded at Sebastian. "I'm glad I found you two together. I ran into an old friend from Yale. Eric is a big art collector and I told him Sebastian is staying with us." He paused. "He and his wife are staying at the Hotel Eden Rock and asked us to dinner. He invited the whole family but I think he's most interested in meeting Sebastian. He thinks your piece *Poppy Fields in Cambodia* is better than Monet's *Garden of Giverny*."

"I'm flattered but comparing me to Monet is like comparing a Toyota to a Bentley," Sebastian said, sipping his scotch.

"I told Finn to be ready at six," Felix said. "I'm going to go upstairs and shower."

"I have an idea, why don't we leave Finn and Olivia at the villa and go ourselves?" Sebastian suggested.

"Eric did invite the whole family," Felix wavered.

"Olivia and Finn are young, they don't want to listen to middle-aged men singing Yale fight songs or reminiscing about their first time in a German beer garden." Sebastian looked at Hadley. "It might be good for them to have the place to themselves. They can eat a romantic dinner and go for a late-night swim."

"That's an excellent plan," Hadley agreed. "I'll tell Esther to make baked chicken for two."

"Sure, why not." Felix nodded and walked to the staircase. "I can't wait to catch up with Eric. He was the only one at university who appreciated Rothko's early work."

Hadley waited until the master bedroom door closed and turned to Sebastian.

"Thank you," she said. "It will be good for Finn and Olivia to have time alone."

"I know you think I'm trying to shake up everyone's life but you're mistaken." He put his glass on the sideboard. "I'm like Jimmy Stewart in *It's a Wonderful Life*. I just want to know the Miller girls are okay."

Hadley walked to the foyer and turned around. "I appreciate the sentiment but that doesn't stop you from getting things wrong. I'm turning forty-eight, not forty-nine."

Chapter Seven

OLIVIA BUTTONED A FLORAL DRESS and slipped on white leather sandals. She smoothed her hair behind her ears and glanced at her watch. It was almost 6:00 p.m. and if she didn't hurry she'd be late for cocktails.

She rubbed red lipstick on her lips and thought it had been a glorious day. Scuba diving with Sebastian was exhilarating and their picnic of French bread and duck pâté was delicious. If only she and Finn hadn't gotten into a fight this morning, everything would be perfect.

She remembered suggesting they eat dinner at Le Toiny and bit her lip. How could she have forgotten to make a reservation? She had stayed in the bath too long soaking in lavender bubbles and reading a paperback book. But Finn was counting on it and she couldn't disappoint him again. He had been so angry with her, she didn't want to have another disagreement.

Suddenly she pictured eating apple tatin at the Pipiri Palace with Finn and Sebastian and gasped. Finn didn't have to figure out the check with the maître d', he was telling him not to bring out the champagne. Finn had been going to propose! If only

Sebastian hadn't joined them, she might be wearing a sapphire-and-diamond ring on her finger.

She would call Le Toiny and reserve a table. Then she'd put on Finn's favorite perfume and the diamond bracelet he gave her for Christmas.

There was a knock on the bedroom door and Olivia opened it. Finn stood in the hallway, wearing a navy polo shirt and beige slacks.

"I'm sorry I'm running late," she said. "Felix likes us to be punctual. Let me grab my purse and I'll be ready."

"Didn't Felix tell you?" Finn entered the room. "He and Hadley and Sebastian went to Hotel Eden Rock for dinner. An old college friend of Felix's is an art collector and wanted to meet Sebastian."

"I must have been in the bath and didn't hear him knock. I was about to book a table at Le Toiny. I meant to do it earlier, I just . . ." She hesitated.

She couldn't apologize for scuba diving with Sebastian; she had every right to see her father. But she hated tension between them; it made her feel slightly dizzy.

"I'm sorry about everything I said earlier," he began. "I'm glad Sebastian is here and you're spending time with him."

"I shouldn't have changed my plans, but I've waited so long for this moment. Sebastian really is quite sensitive and he does like you," she replied. "He wanted to cancel scuba diving because you couldn't join us."

"I think we can all get along perfectly for the next few days." He kissed her. "I have an idea. We have the whole villa to ourselves and Esther made coq au vin and polenta and coconut mousse for dessert. Why don't we stay home and eat in the garden?"

Olivia kissed him back and her shoulders relaxed. That was the wonderful thing about Finn, they hardly ever argued. She glanced out the French doors at the pink hibiscus and yellow frangipani and felt warm and happy.

Her green eyes sparkled and her face broke into a smile. "I can't think of anything I'd like better."

They sat at the glass table on the patio and ate shrimp salad and grilled tomato bread. Finn poured two glasses of zinfandel and they talked about the tennis match and a new client at the gallery. Olivia gazed at the lush palm trees and glittering ocean and thought she really was happy. All the people she loved were in one place, what more could she want?

She remembered when she met Finn the summer before her senior year at Vassar. The weather was unbearably humid and she thought she was the only young person in Manhattan. All her friends had escaped to their parents' Long Island estates or cottages in Maine. But Olivia wanted to get work experience and Hadley was happy to have her work at the gallery.

"Can I help you?" Olivia asked a young man standing near the door. He wore a dark suit and white shirt and his forehead was covered in sweat.

It was almost 5:00 p.m. and she was desperate to change into a cotton dress and sandals. But Hadley treated everyone who walked in as if they were old friends. She would never point out it was two minutes to closing time and she longed for a plate of tapas and chilled sangria.

"They're all fascinating." He studied a canvas painted in endless shades of blue. "I'm just not . . ."

"Interested in abstract art?" Olivia finished, smoothing her blond hair behind her ears. "To be honest it's not my favorite style of painting. At least when I study a Rueben or Rembrandt, I know what I'm looking at."

The man glanced at Olivia and laughed. "Shouldn't you not say that out loud? If the owner hears you, you might get fired."

"Art appreciation is individual." Olivia shrugged. "If everyone liked the same thing, all the art in the world could be housed at the Metropolitan and the Louvre. I can respect an artist without enjoying his paintings." She paused. "Besides, I'm Olivia Miller. The gallery belongs to my mother."

"If we're being completely honest, I came inside for the air-conditioning," he replied. "My boss sent me to deliver a letter to a client in Chelsea. I walked in circles and still can't find the address."

"Let me see." Olivia took the envelope from his hand. "It's around the corner. If you wait a minute, I'll show you."

"I really appreciate it, I was wearing out the soles of my loafers," he said when they delivered the letter. "Can I buy you an iced coffee or gelato?"

"I never go out with strangers." She hesitated. "How do I know you're not an international spy?"

"My name is Finn and I'm clerking at my family's law firm," he began. "I was crew co-captain at Princeton and vice president of the honor society. Besides," he looked at Olivia, "we just walked through a dark alley, you have to be able to trust me."

"I guess I'll take my chances," she said and noticed his eyes were the color of cornflowers. "Right now I'd give anything for a plate of spinach ravioli and frozen Negroni."

They sat at an outdoor table at Alta Linea and ate crispy artichoke with salsa. There was a basket of French bread and pots of sundried tomato butter.

"This is my first summer in Manhattan," he admitted, sipping his drink. "Everyone looks cool and relaxed and I feel like I spend all day in a sauna. Then I go back to my sublet and strip down to my board shorts. It's my fault; the landlord said it was air-conditioned. I didn't think he meant you had to stand in front of the freezer."

"New York City landlords aren't known for their integrity," she laughed. "But you're wrong, everyone in Manhattan in August is uncomfortable. But if they admitted they'd rather be sailing on the Long Island Sound or eating crab in Nantucket, other people will know they're miserable. They have to make everyone believe they stayed in New York because the restaurants are empty and you can get a ticket to the best show on Broadway."

"Then I'm afraid I'm not going to fit in. My parents taught me to be honest," he explained. "If you meet a woman with glossy blond hair and green eyes, you tell her she's beautiful. And if you want to see her again, you don't wait a few days and pretend you lost her phone number."

"Oh." Olivia blushed and looked at her plate.

"Would you go out with me this weekend?" He looked at Olivia. "I hear it's easy to get tickets to a Broadway play."

She studied his tan cheeks and the cleft in his chin and nodded.

"Yes, I'd like that very much."

"I want to ask you something," Finn interrupted her thoughts. "It's about this summer."

"This summer?" Olivia put down her wineglass and gulped.

Surely Finn wasn't going to suggest getting married in a few months? She wasn't going to be one of those brides who kept a daily notebook and spent nine months picking out centerpieces. But the best locations in New York booked months in advance and the perfect dress could take several fittings. She didn't want to rush into buying something off the rack and reserving a poorly air-conditioned restaurant because the ballroom at the Plaza was taken.

"I know we always spend a week in Nantucket with Felix and Hadley but an associate at the firm booked a cottage in Maine," he continued. "It's on the coast and there's whale watching and hiking. He asked if we'd like to stay there in July."

"Maine!" Olivia replied and wondered why she suddenly felt like a deflated balloon.

She'd been going to Nantucket since she was a child and loved everything about Felix's clapboard house and the village with its elegant boutiques and quaint shops. And Maine would be just as lovely; the scenery was breathtaking and the lobster delicious.

But she remembered Sebastian's descriptions of Kenya and felt somehow guilty, like when you read a whole book at a bookstore without paying for it. She and Finn didn't have to ride a camel in the Gobi Desert to be happy. And being alone together in Maine would be so romantic; they could visit lighthouses and watch the sunset.

"I know we love Nantucket but it would be nice to do something different," Finn urged. "We could go fishing and catch our own dinner."

Olivia looked at Finn and remembered why she loved him. He was always thinking about her and more than anything, he wanted to be together.

"That's a wonderful plan. I actually had an idea for Christmas."
She took a deep breath. "Sebastian has a friend with a boat in Costa
Rica. He invited us to go scuba diving."

"This Christmas?" Finn dropped his fork. "But that's impossible, we always spend Christmas in St. Barts."

"It's a wonderful invitation," Olivia insisted. "The underwater
caves in Punta Gorda are supposed to be magnificent."

"People come from all over the world to scuba dive in St. Barts,"
he protested. "Why would we leave a spacious villa with Esther's
home cooking and our own swimming pool for a week on a cramped
boat?"

"You don't know anything about the boat, it might be a luxury
cruiser," she fumed. "Sebastian has friends who are hedge fund
managers and CEOs of corporations. You don't want to go because
Sebastian asked us. If one of the law partners invited us on their
yacht, it would be different."

"That's not true." Finn put his hand on hers. "We always spend
Christmas in St. Barts. My parents travel during the holidays, and
you love it here. We don't have to worry about the lines at Zabar's
or being snowed in by a freak snowstorm on Christmas Eve. You
always say Christmas in St. Barts is your favorite time of year."

Olivia's eyes watered and she blinked. She adored opening
presents in the villa's living room, with the breeze drifting through
the French doors. And the island was so festive, as if everyone belonged to a special club. But she remembered Sebastian saying it
was time to make their own traditions. She was a grown woman;
could she spend every Christmas in the guest bedroom of her
parents' villa?

"Maybe that's the problem." Olivia looked up. "We always do
the same thing."

"I didn't know it was a problem," Finn said stiffly. "Do you remember the summer we met in Manhattan? It was so hot, we spent every evening at Amorino, drinking vanilla frappes and naming the coldest places we could think of: Iceland and Greenland and Antarctica."

Olivia pictured sharing lemon gelato and never wanting to be anywhere else. But nothing had changed; she still loved being together.

Finn was twisting everything. She wasn't planning on going with Sebastian alone; he'd invited both of them. And maybe Sebastian was right: they should broaden their horizons.

"Why shouldn't we try somewhere new?" she demanded. "Lots of our friends go to Club Med or Couples Resorts or even hiking in Patagonia. Your parents spend every December on a cruise of the Mediterranean."

"They're retired and my mother adores going on vacation," Finn said. "But when I was a child we spent every Christmas at home in New Jersey. And Hadley and Felix go to so much effort. Hadley ships the presents ahead of time and Felix spends hours making eggnog with real cream and nutmeg."

"What about Sebastian? Doesn't he deserve to be with his family?" she asked. "How can we let him be alone at Christmas when he wants to be together?"

"Sebastian walked away from his family," Finn said quietly. "Everything he wanted was available to him and he turned it down. Maybe he deserves to be alone."

"Because he made a mistake twenty years ago, he can never fix it?" Olivia asked. "Ever since Sebastian arrived he's done nothing but apologize. He brought my mother satin slippers and gave Felix a housewarming present and said how happy he was we are together." Her voice shook. "And all you do is say these terrible things about him."

Finn walked around the table and stuffed his hands in his pockets.

"Somebody needs to say terrible things about him if they're true," Finn began. "He thinks he can just barge in here as if he went out for coffee and the newspaper. He deserted you and Hadley. How can you forget that?"

"It isn't that simple and he's trying to make amends. You're just making it worse."

"I'm only trying to protect you, I don't want you to get hurt again. What if we agree to join him at Christmas and he gets a better offer?" He touched her hand. "How can you trust him when he only thinks about himself?"

"That's a horrible thing to say. He wouldn't have asked us if he didn't mean it," she gasped. "You're jealous of Sebastian because I'd rather go scuba diving with him than watch your tennis match. I'm sure you wish he never came." She pulled away. "I'm sorry you feel that way but he is my father."

She raced up the stone steps into the hallway. She grabbed her mother's keys from the end table and ran into the driveway.

"Olivia, where are you going?" Finn called, running after her.

She was about to answer but she couldn't think of anything to say. She backed the car out of the garage and put her foot on the accelerator.

Olivia parked next to the harbor in Gustavia and adjusted her sunglasses. It was early evening and the bay was filled with sleek yachts and wooden fishing boats.

Was it only two days ago that she and Finn sat at Bar de L'Oubli, nibbling melon and talking about the things they were going to do in St. Barts? They had the whole week ahead of them and she was excited about snorkeling and sailing and her birthday dinner in three days at Maya's.

But now she and Finn were barely speaking. He had said some terrible things and she regretted her own response. She pictured the black velvet jewelry box and her stomach clenched. What if they didn't make up and Finn decided not to propose?

She thought about Hadley and Felix and suddenly felt uneasy. Hadley wouldn't mind if they missed Christmas, she wanted Olivia and Sebastian to be together. But would Olivia offend Felix?

When she was a girl, Felix was the one who made sure the tooth fairy knew she lost a tooth and helped her mail a letter to Santa Claus. She remembered being afraid Santa Claus wouldn't come to St. Barts because it was so hot. Felix put out a platter of sliced watermelon and a bowl of water for the reindeer.

Was she caught up in Sebastian's spell and ignoring the people who were close to her? That was silly; Sebastian didn't want anything except to be part of the family.

She entered the double glass doors of Côté Port and sat at a table by the window. The waiter handed her a menu and she realized she was starving.

"Is this seat taken?" a male voice asked.

Olivia looked up and gasped. Finn's collar was crooked and his forehead was covered in sweat.

"What are you doing here and how did you find me?" she demanded.

"I checked all the cafés in Gustavia," he admitted. "I guessed you might be here, it's always been our favorite. You barely ate anything at dinner, I thought you might be hungry."

"If you came to tell me I'm being impossible, it can wait until tomorrow." She smoothed her napkin. "We've argued enough for one night. I'd like to enjoy a plate of seafood gnocchi and crisp vegetables."

"I came to tell you I'm sorry," he said and touched her arm.

"You did?" Olivia let out her breath.

"I was afraid that coming to St. Barts and spending a week in Nantucket isn't enough," he explained. "We'll be able to travel anywhere we want later. But you know how law firms work, the associates put in all the hours."

"I shouldn't have suggested we go away at Christmas." Olivia shook her head. "Felix might be offended and I never want to hurt him. It's just I understand how Sebastian feels. His life might sound impossibly exciting, riding elephants and big-game hunting, but I recognize the look in his eyes and all he wants to do is belong.

"I'm the luckiest girl in the world to have Felix, but I couldn't help wanting to meet the person who shared the same genes." She looked at Finn. "The funny thing is the minute Sebastian said he was my father, I felt the connection. We both like the same flavors of ice cream and get freckles on our nose from the sun. And sometimes even if I don't say anything, he knows what I'm thinking. It sounds silly, but I discovered part of me that was missing."

"We can go to Costa Rica if you want." Finn put his hand on hers. "I don't care if we're floating on a rust bucket in the Pacific Ocean as long as we're together."

"I doubt it's a rust bucket, Sebastian does like nice things." Olivia felt lighter, as if she'd stripped off a winter coat. "We should talk to Hadley and Felix first, maybe they'd like to join us."

"That would be a lot of people," Finn laughed. "It might capsize the boat."

He leaned across the table and kissed her. Olivia felt his lips on hers and a warmth spread through her chest. Finn was kind and understanding and everything was going to be all right.

"I'm starving," he said. "I'll order a cheeseburger and sweet potato fries."

"Do you think Esther will mind?" Olivia suddenly remembered the glass table set with shrimp salad and sweetbreads.

"We'll bring her a slice of raspberry charlotte," Finn said and smiled. "It's the best on the island."

Olivia slipped off her sandals and stood on the balcony. It was almost 11:00 p.m. and the villa was quiet. Sebastian and Hadley and Felix were still out to dinner and Finn had gone to his room. She felt the cool breeze on her shoulders and listened to the sound of sprinklers and longed to climb into bed.

After she and Finn ate cottage cheese mousse and drank Cointreau they drove back to the villa in Olivia's car. Olivia remembered Finn's mouth on hers and his hands on her breasts and shivered. They were like two teenagers hoping their parents wouldn't discover them kissing in the driveway.

But now she walked back inside and felt unsettled. She and Finn never had such heated arguments. Now they'd made up but was it going to be that easy? Finn had placed first in the long jump at Princeton; competition was in his nature. And Sebastian always got what he wanted; he never had to answer to anyone.

Surely they could get along for three more days. Sebastian wouldn't dream of causing a fuss on her birthday and Finn would be on his best behavior. She remembered when she was a child and competed in the three-legged race. It seemed like the easiest event: all you had to do was cross the field. But when you tied the rope around you and your partner, it was impossible not to stumble.

She unzipped her dress and climbed into the four-poster bed. She had to make Finn and Sebastian get along; she couldn't bear the thought of losing either of them.

Chapter Eight

HADLEY LEANED OVER THE BALCONY of the Hotel Eden Rock and wished she had a cigarette. But she inhaled the scent of frangipani and expensive perfume and remembered she didn't smoke. She listened to the band playing soft jazz and watched couples sharing warm chocolate cake and longed to be in her kitchen, drinking a large snifter of brandy.

Dinner with Eric and his wife, Priscille, was delicious. Eric had insisted on ordering and selected lobster medallions and beef tenderloin with shallot chutney. Even Sebastian was impressed by the bottles of Châteaux Margaux and platters of French imperial caviar and smoked salmon.

And Sebastian was being so charming, admiring the hotel with its white villas and red roof and breathtaking view of the harbor. The blackened cod was better than he'd had in a fishing village in Tenerife and the chanterelles were so tender they could have been picked in Provence. Hadley rolled her eyes and even Felix fiddled with his sorbet spoon.

Finally Hadley needed some air and told Felix she had to call Olivia. Now she knotted her pink pashmina around her shoulders and thought sitting between Felix and Sebastian was like being stranded on a lifeboat: you didn't know which was worse, the blazing sun or sharks circling in the water.

Even when Sebastian was being perfectly nice, she didn't trust him. He'd caused a rift between Olivia and Finn; she didn't want to put her marriage in the line of fire.

How dare Sebastian insist she'd changed. Of course people were different after twenty years. He could hardly expect her to be a girl with glowing cheeks and bouncy hair and a wardrobe of miniskirts and platform shoes.

But that didn't mean she wasn't generally happy. Her life was like a feature in a glossy women's magazine: her own successful gallery in Chelsea, a glamorous Central Park duplex, and a villa on the most gorgeous island in the Caribbean.

Maybe she and Felix hadn't gone dancing since he hurt his back and never got around to booking a romantic weekend in Paris. But how could you want anything more than being with the people you love and always having enough food and clothing?

She thought again of the sudden feeling of loneliness when she was near Felix and an ache formed in the pit of her stomach. She was blowing things out of proportion. Once they really talked, everything would be set right. But if talking could solve things, wouldn't they have already had a conversation?

She smoothed the folds of her silver cocktail dress and could almost hear Sebastian scoffing. Being content with having enough food and clothing was fine advice from Dear Abby, but did it make life worth living? You had to expect more, or how would you get more?

The moon glinted on the black ocean and she suddenly remembered the last spring they'd spent in Cape Town. Olivia was three with blond ringlets and creamy skin. Hadley had gazed at her round cheeks and pink mouth and thought she had everything she wanted: a charismatic husband and a vibrant daughter and a future as bold and brilliant as the African sun.

Hadley stood on the wooden deck and was glad to be back in Cape Town. Charles Lang was staging the biggest show of Sebastian's career and had invited them to stay at his beach house. The ocean was a shimmering turquoise and the mountains were emerald green and she remembered everything she loved about Cape Town's tropical climate.

The months of being pregnant had been glorious and Hadley was so happy to be at Derek's trout farm. Sebastian spent every minute painting and she pottered around Derek's garden like a character in an E. M. Forster novel.

And they were so in love! Sebastian couldn't get enough of her rounded stomach and heavy breasts. At night they shared platters of boerewors and bowls of malva pudding. Then they retired to their bedroom and made love in the white-canopied bed.

Now Hadley glanced at Olivia playing with her doll and thought the last three years were magical. What other little girl perched on top of an elephant and rubbed noses with a lion cub? They were like the Three Musketeers with sun-streaked hair and tan shoulders.

The sliding glass door opened and Sebastian appeared on the deck. His cheeks were smudged with paint and he wore a blue shirt and khakis.

"There are my two girls." He kissed Hadley. "I thought you'd be down on the beach with Olivia's new pail and shovel."

"You didn't have to buy her anything." Hadley smiled. "She's perfectly happy collecting shells."

"And have her be jealous of the other little girls wearing designer swimsuits?" Sebastian asked. "At least she can have a new bucket."

"She's three years old, she doesn't care if she runs down the beach naked," she laughed. "You should join us, we're going to pack a picnic and walk to Camps Bay."

"I don't have time to swim, the opening is tonight." Sebastian ran his hands through his hair. "Charles sent invitations to collectors in Dubai and Paris. He thinks this show will change my career."

"You work too hard," Hadley said and took a deep breath. "I thought we could take a vacation."

"Every day is a vacation." Sebastian leaned over the railing. "Do you see any office buildings or men eating soggy sandwiches and carrying rolled-up newspapers?"

"You said you don't have time to lie on the sand," she urged. "What about if we take the money you earn from the show and have a proper holiday?"

"Why would we do that?" he wondered. "You and Olivia love exploring new places and I do what I do best."

"I'd like to go home for a while," she continued. "Olivia only met her grandparents once when they came to Johannesburg and we haven't been to Connecticut at all. Olivia would have a snowy Christmas with turkey and gravy and stockings. I'm sure Monet stopped painting to be with his family and Turner put aside his brushes to enjoy the English countryside."

"I am with my family and I hate the snow. You're trapped inside with Monopoly and instant macaroni and cheese." He waved at the pink sand and tall palm trees. "Why would we trade this for winter coats and rubber boots?"

"Olivia has never known people who aren't carrying maps and binoculars," Hadley said. "And it's impossible to get your attention when you're painting. It's like traveling with a general preparing for battle."

"I thought you were happy." Sebastian's green eyes flickered.

"I am happy, I just want what's best for Olivia," she explained. "Children can be terribly selfish. They want to think they come first."

"Everything I do is for you and Olivia," he pleaded. "But stopping painting wouldn't be a holiday, it would be like a death."

"Never mind." Hadley glanced at her watch. "I better get Olivia showered and dressed."

"Hadley, wait." Sebastian touched her arm. "If this opening is a success, next year we could do a show in New York. We'll stay at the St. Regis and Olivia can drink Shirley Temples and eat room-service spaghetti."

Hoping Sebastian would take a break from painting was like imagining a tiger could be a pet. But it wouldn't help to discuss it now; Sebastian could be as stubborn as the donkeys they rode in Senegal. It had to be his idea, or it wouldn't happen at all.

"That sounds wonderful." She kissed him. "I need to get Olivia ready, and then I'm going to take a quick bath before the opening."

"We have time." He pulled her close. "Maybe we should get sweaty before you waste all that hot water."

She inhaled his scent of citrus aftershave and a tingle ran down her spine.

"It is early and Olivia needs a nap," she whispered. "She's been playing on the deck all morning."

Hadley glanced around the art gallery and rubbed her lips. No matter how many shows Sebastian did, she was as nervous as a director on opening night. Waiters in white dinner jackets carried silver trays and elegant men and women nibbled duck pâté and jumbo prawns.

"There you are." Charles Lang approached her. He wore a pin-striped suit and tasseled shoes. "You look stunning and Olivia is so grown-up, I almost didn't recognize her."

"Sebastian bought her a new dress," Hadley explained. "I told him she'll fall asleep before the end of the cocktail hour but he insisted she look like a princess. I can't imagine how he's going to spoil her when she's older. He keeps buying her hair ribbons and glass bracelets."

"Fathers can't help it. They want to make sure their daughters never look at another man." He smiled. "He does worship you and Olivia, you can see it in his latest painting."

"What painting?" Hadley asked.

"*The Miller Girls,* it's the best thing he's ever done," he continued. "We built the whole show around it. Surely you've seen it?"

"I must have and I've forgotten." Hadley blushed and took Olivia's hand. "Excuse me, I need to talk to Sebastian."

"Charles said you have a new painting called *The Miller Girls,*" she said when she joined Sebastian. "Why haven't I seen it?"

"Charles can't keep his mouth shut after two glasses of Dom

Pérignon," he laughed. "It was supposed to be a surprise. Come with me, and I'll show you."

They entered a small room with pinpoint lighting and wood floors. The painting almost took up the whole wall and was of her and Olivia at the foot of Mount Eglon. The sun touched their blond hair and the brushstrokes were so clear, she could see the freckles on Olivia's nose.

"When did you do this?" she gasped.

"I started it our last week in Kenya but it was too ambitious so I put it away," he answered. "I've been working on it for the last two weeks in Charles's studio." He looked at Hadley. "Do you like it?"

"I love it." She kissed him and the champagne floated to her toes. "We better mingle, everyone is going to want to meet the great Sebastian Miller."

Hadley wiggled her toes and clutched a plate of fruit tarts. It was almost 11:00 p.m. and she longed to go back to the beach house and slip on a cotton robe and slippers.

"Did you see the red dots on the paintings, we sold every one." Sebastian put his arm around her. "We'll take Olivia home and drink pineapple mojitos and go dancing at Rick's."

"I don't think I could stay vertical," she sighed. "I'm not used to wearing stilettos, my feet are killing me."

"We can stay in bed tomorrow and eat Olivia's pretend pancakes." He kissed her. "It's our first sold-out show, we have to celebrate."

"You can't leave yet," Charles said, interrupting their conversation. "I have some news, come into my office."

They followed him into a paneled room and Charles took out a crystal decanter. Olivia was asleep in a leather armchair. She wore a red pinafore and clutched a stuffed giraffe.

"It's Martell cognac, I only take it out for my most important sales." He handed them each a shot glass. "Yens Bergin owns luxury hotels in Norway and Sweden. He thought the work was spectacular, he bought the whole collection."

"One buyer bought everything in the show?" Sebastian gulped.

"He said *The Miller Girls* reminded him of Bouguereau's *The Broken Pitcher*." He picked up a piece of paper. "He wrote a check for a hundred thousand dollars."

"What did you say?" Hadley gasped.

"He loved the other pieces too. He's going to display them in his hotel lobbies." Charles beamed. "Can you imagine entering from a snowy street to find a painting of the African sun glaring down on a beautiful blonde and her daughter?"

"No, I can't." Sebastian jumped up. "*The Miller Girls* isn't for sale."

"What do you mean?" Charles spluttered. "It's the center of the whole show."

"You asked me to paint an important piece to get people in the door." Sebastian paced around the room. "You never said I had to sell it."

"Think what you can do with a hundred thousand dollars," Charles urged. "You won't be living from commission to commission like a nineteenth-century portrait artist."

"The money sounds lovely but the painting is not for sale," Sebastian insisted. "I'll paint something else and he can have the others."

"He doesn't want something else, he wants *The Miller Girls*."

Charles looked at Sebastian. "And I don't want to tell him he can't have it."

"You're going to have to." He scooped Olivia into his arms. "I need to put my daughter to bed. We'll discuss it in the morning."

"I can't explain it to Charles, he would never understand." Sebastian lit a cigarette and paced around the all-white living room.

They had driven back to the beach house in silence. Hadley pictured the check on Charles's desk and thought of everything it could buy: plane tickets to America, never needing to count every dollar in their pockets.

"*The Miller Girls* is the best thing I've ever done, it poured out of me like volcanic ash." He blew thick smoke rings. "What if I can never create anything as good? The art critics will say I peaked at twenty-six. 'Sebastian Miller never lived up to the early promise of *The Miller Girls.*'"

"That doesn't make sense." Hadley gazed out the sliding glass doors. The moon was a saucer and she could see the outline of Table Mountain. "Why shouldn't you paint anything like it again?"

"Vermeer only had one *Girl with a Pearl Earring* and Pissarro never replicated *A Sunday on La Grand Jatte*." He stubbed the cigarette into a ceramic ashtray. "The whole point of art is striving to be your best. If I've already produced it, I'm finished before I began."

"You're worrying about nothing," she replied. "Look at Chagall and Picasso. Whole museum wings are devoted to their work."

"What if I can't?" he replied. "Sometimes a painting just comes together. Olivia's green eyes and your colored shawl and the African light forming a halo on your hair."

"It's one hundred thousand dollars." Hadley tried a new direction. "We could put a down payment on a flat and never have to worry about money for clothes and paints."

"Art isn't about providing a stable future, it's about taking everything inside you and throwing it on the canvas." He lit another cigarette. "If I wanted to set up a 401(k), I'd have joined the law firm."

"You happened to be married with a child." She felt an odd stirring inside her, like a coffeepot coming to a boil. "In two years Olivia will start kindergarten. Do you expect her to learn to read and write in a tent on the Niger River?"

"We're hardly in a tent." He waved his cigarette at the polished wood floor and crystal vase filled with African violets. "I'll always get another commission and our lives are the greatest adventure. Isn't that what we wanted?"

She looked at Sebastian and remembered the young man she met at the guesthouse in Cape Town. He had the same blond hair and emerald eyes and narrow cheekbones. But they were older now. They couldn't exist with just enough money to pay for the next hostel.

"When we brought Olivia home from the hospital in Johannesburg we promised to always put her first." She stood and smoothed her skirt. "If someone offers you one hundred thousand dollars for a painting, you take it. I'm tired, I'm going to bed."

"Hadley, wait," he called after her.

"What is it?" She turned and tears swam in her eyes.

Sebastian was going to say he was wrong, of course they'd accept the money. Now they could go on holiday or buy a house in the country.

"I would walk on hot coals for you and Olivia." He flicked ashes into the ashtray. "But if I don't think my next painting will be •

better than my last, I won't be able to paint. I have to stay hungry, or I'll have nothing at all."

Hadley entered the bedroom and slipped off her stilettos. How dare Sebastian turn down $100,000? He should be popping a bottle of champagne instead of worrying about his next piece.

But maybe she was being too hard on him. How did she know what made Sebastian pick up a brush? And he was right: they had everything they needed.

There was a knock on the door and she answered it.

"I was going to come and see you." She fiddled with her earrings.

"The minute you walked upstairs I realized I was a fool." Sebastian entered the bedroom. "You think I forget about you and Olivia but you're wrong. It's as if you're beside me when I'm painting, connecting the brush with the canvas. The only thing worse than selling *The Miller Girls* is letting anything come between us."

"We'll keep *The Miller Girls*," she said and walked to the balcony.

"Are you sure?" he gasped.

"Do you remember when we met and thought we'd have to return to America because we ran out of money?" she asked. "Selling your paintings seemed as likely as the possibility that it would ever stop raining.

"I don't understand what motivates you to paint, just as I don't know why Botticelli's *Venus* is heartbreakingly beautiful. But if keeping *The Miller Girls* allows you to work, then we can't sell it." She looked at Sebastian. "I believe in you and me and Olivia and we're going to have a wonderful future."

He tucked her blond hair behind her ears and drew her close. She kissed him and all the tension drifted away like shells on the beach.

She unbuttoned his shirt and ran her hands over his chest. Desire shot through her and she felt almost wanton. They were staying in a glamorous beach house in Cape Town and were about to make love.

She unzipped his slacks and rubbed his hardness. Sebastian groaned and every nerve in her came alive. She wrapped her arms around him and they toppled onto the bed.

"Olivia is in the next room," he whispered, untying her robe. "Are you sure she is asleep?"

"She was so exhausted she'd sleep through a monsoon," she whispered back.

Sebastian balanced on his elbow and stroked her cheek. He ran his fingers over her lips and between her breasts.

"Then let me show you how much I love you," he murmured and buried his head between her thighs.

Hadley clutched him against her and felt the waves build inside her. Her whole body shuddered and she gasped. The sweet wetness subsided and all that was left was exquisite nothingness.

"Come here." She opened her legs and pulled him on top of her. Her fingers gripped his back and she coaxed him to go faster. He collapsed against her breasts and the heat and sweat were replaced by unbearable spasms.

"Oh," she whispered, when her breathing slowed.

"I love you," he lay on his back. "You and Olivia are the best things that ever happened to me."

Hadley gazed out the window at the moon glinting on the ocean. Her blond hair was tousled on the pillow and she felt almost giddy. They were young and in love and Sebastian was immensely talented. She couldn't worry about the future; she had everything she ever wanted.

Hadley drew the pink pashmina around her shoulders and saw Felix motion to her from the restaurant. She wasn't ready to return to the table; the night air was intoxicating.

Over the years she wondered whether Sebastian told the truth. Did he refuse to sell *The Miller Girls* because he was afraid he couldn't replicate it? Or was it because he didn't want to accept $100,000?

At first she thought that was ridiculous: no one loved money more than Sebastian. He couldn't buy Olivia enough hair ribbons and he loved surprising Hadley with silver jewelry. But he was allergic to the kind of money that paid a mortgage and created a college fund. Sebastian was at his best when all he had to worry about was finding a pressed shirt to wear to meet a new collector.

Of course, how could she have forgotten he was so restless! Sebastian was no more interested in becoming part of their lives then he was in working at the Chrysler Building. He was simply between commissions and decided to spend a few days in St. Barts.

In three days he would pack his leather overnight bag and move on to his next destination. He would leave relationships a little strained and the vodka bottle half empty, but there would be no lasting damage.

The glass door opened and Felix walked onto the balcony. He looked handsome in a polo shirt and pleated slacks.

"What are you doing out here?" he asked. "Sebastian was describing the week he spent on Tin Can Island in the South Pacific.

It doesn't have a natural harbor so natives have to paddle canoes to obtain supplies from passing cruise ships."

"I needed some air," Hadley explained. "Sebastian sucks up oxygen like a vacuum cleaner."

"He loves to talk," Felix said and smiled. "Eric was so enthralled he almost set his sleeve on fire with his banana flambé."

"Sebastian must be in heaven," she laughed. "There's nothing he loves more than an audience."

"When he arrived in St. Barts I was disturbed by the idea of him sleeping in the guest bedroom," he began. "But I never thought how it might affect you. It can't be easy greeting your ex-husband over scrambled eggs and grapefruit juice."

"Whatever Sebastian says bounces off me." Hadley shrugged. "I was worried about him interfering with Olivia and Finn. He seemed determined to star in his own remake of *Father Knows Best*.

"But I realized if he wanted a relationship with Olivia he would have appeared years ago. Of course he loves her, like he loves a new shirt. He holds it up to the mirror and suddenly he looks younger and more handsome."

"Aren't you being a little harsh?" Felix wondered. "He is her father and Olivia is his only daughter."

"That's just the way he is, he has to move forward." Her eyes dimmed. "That's why Olivia and I were lucky to find you. You're capable of staying still and enjoying yourself."

"I was looking at you through the window. You are as beautiful as when I first saw you at the art gallery." He paused. "I'm the lucky one."

Hadley heard the band play "Fly Me to the Moon" and remembered it was their song. She turned to Felix and was about to say something. But she couldn't talk to him now, with everyone waiting at the table.

"What is it?" he asked.

"We should go inside," she sighed and took his arm. "Priscille would never forgive us if we let her husband catch on fire."

Hadley moved the ivory chess piece around the chessboard and sighed. The silver clock chimed midnight and she wished she could fall asleep. But the minute she laid her head on the pillow, her eyes flew open and her heart raced.

In the last year she had tried drinking warm milk and honey and watching classic movies and sipping heated brandy. But the milk turned her stomach and watching movies made her temples throb and brandy gave her a headache.

After dinner at Hotel Eden Rock they dropped Sebastian in Gustavia to buy cigarettes and returned to the villa. Olivia and Finn were already asleep and Esther had left banana bread in the kitchen. Felix kissed her and said he was going to bed and Hadley busied herself preparing the morning coffee, before moving to the library to turn off the lamps.

She heard footsteps and a figure stood in the doorway. Sebastian's blazer was slung over his shoulder and he clutched a packet of cigarettes.

"Can I join you?" he asked, entering the library. He lit a cigarette and walked to the bookshelf.

"I'm busy," she looked up. "You shouldn't smoke in the library, Felix would be furious. Some of his books are first editions."

"I've always thought the smell of cigarettes is sensuous." He inhaled. "It reminds me of Parisian nightclubs and kissing in dark alleys."

"I think it's vile. Thank god Olivia never smoked." She shuddered. "She had a good role model, Felix never touched a cigarette."

"Ah yes." He poured a glass of cognac. "He only indulges in aged cognac and Cuban cigars."

"He might smoke a cigar on special occasions," she countered. "But he doesn't make his clothes smell like a taxicab and leave cigarette butts around the house."

"You're right, it is a terrible habit." He stubbed the cigarette in an ashtray and sat across from Hadley. "That's the thing about being divorced. No one tells you to exercise or watch your cholesterol."

"You seem to take care of yourself." Hadley pursed her lips. "Your stomach is flat as a board."

"I didn't think you noticed," Sebastian said. "I must say you look stunning in that dress. You haven't changed as much as I thought. In the right outfit you're still the most beautiful woman in the room."

"Save your greeting card prose for a new conquest." She smoothed her hair. "I'm a happily married woman."

"Then why are you playing chess at midnight when your husband is asleep in a four-poster bed?"

"I came in here to get a paperback book." She hesitated. "The chessboard looked inviting."

"You hate chess. Do you remember when I tried to teach you on the Orient Express because there was nothing else to do from Venice to Istanbul?" he asked. "You didn't see the point of moving a white knight across a wooden chessboard."

"That was years ago," she mused. "Felix taught me and I quite enjoy it."

"I've been watching you the last couple of days." He rubbed his fingers over the rim of the glass. "Olivia thinks you get up early to swim but you never go to bed at all. Last night you slept in here and the first night you curled up on a sofa in the living room. If you're happily married why aren't you sharing a bed with Felix?"

"How dare you poke around the villa!" she exclaimed. "It's none of your business where I sleep. For your information, the sofa is very comfortable."

"When Olivia was born we made a list of things we wanted to teach her: to work hard and not be afraid of new adventures and be kind to others." He paused. "You re-did the list a dozen times but the most important lesson stayed the same: to always tell the truth. You've always been easy for me to read, I can tell when something's wrong." He looked at Hadley. "If you tell me what it is, maybe I can help."

Hadley listened to the hum of the sprinklers and bit her lip. It would be nice to tell someone her problems. She couldn't confide in Olivia and her friends in New York were always running from a gallery opening to a new restaurant.

Wasn't it easier to talk to someone who wasn't part of your life? Like a therapist who knows your most intimate secrets but never sees you carrying your dry cleaning down Fifth Avenue. And Sebastian could be a good listener when he wanted to; he had a knack for seeing right through you.

Sebastian leaned forward and she jumped. She must have had too much wine at dinner. She'd rather swim in shark-infested waters than confide in Sebastian.

"A lot of people get insomnia at my age." She turned back to the chessboard. "It's perfectly normal and nothing to worry about."

"You're not even forty-eight and you've always slept like a baby," he answered. "You could sleep through a sixteen-hour bus ride surrounded by chickens.

"All these years I hoped that you and Olivia were happy, that was the point of leaving. But I can't help worrying about the Miller girls," he finished. "Even if I'm absent, you're still the two most important people."

Hadley stood up and glowered at Sebastian.

"You might like to imagine the Miller girls as some mythical creature, like Pegasus. But the only place you'll find them is behind that picture frame." She waved at the gold frame. "Olivia is all grown up and I've been Hadley London for nearly twenty years. We all move on, maybe it's time you do the same."

"I'm going to bed." Sebastian picked up his blazer and walked to the door. "Good night, pleasant dreams."

"Sebastian, wait," she urged. He turned around and the lines around his mouth were deeper. "I'm sorry, I didn't mean it."

"Yes, you did." He nodded. "And you were right."

Hadley wiped the sideboard and her shoulders tightened. How dare Sebastian make her feel sorry for him? And what did he know about her marriage? She had a lovely evening, she felt closer to Felix than she had in weeks. Just tonight at dinner, Felix told her she was still beautiful.

All she had to do was get through the next three days. Then Sebastian would be gone and she could enjoy the cool breezes and warm ocean of St. Barts. She curled up on the leather sofa and pulled the cashmere blanket over her shoulders.

Chapter Nine

Olivia stood on the patio and inhaled the scent of tiger lilies. It was mid-morning and the ocean was a sheet of glass. Wooden fishing boats bobbed in the harbor and the roofs of Gustavia shimmered like bright red lipstick.

She and Finn had gone for an early-morning stroll on Flamands Beach. It had been wonderful to drive across the island with the sky turning pink and orange and yellow and to kick off her sandals and feel the white sand under her feet.

The best part was being with Finn. They splashed in the water like children and when they stopped to kiss, Olivia never wanted to be anywhere else.

Now Finn was at the tennis club and Olivia had the day to herself. In two days it was her birthday and she was so excited! She clutched her coffee cup and wondered whether she should sunbathe at Shell Beach or browse in the boutiques in Gustavia.

"You remind me of a Japanese geisha I met in Tokyo." Sebastian appeared on the patio. He wore a linen shirt and his straw hat. "She always had a secret smile, like someone told her a fabulous joke." He paused. "Of course, I never mastered Japanese. For all I know I was the punch line."

"It's such a beautiful morning." Olivia turned to Sebastian. "There's a slight breeze and the water is eighty degrees."

"I know that smile." Sebastian studied her sparkling green eyes and pink mouth. "It's the look of someone young and in love. It seems your night alone with Finn went well. I'm glad."

"It was a lovely evening." She nodded. "And we had a romantic walk this morning. Sometimes when we're together, I'm so happy I think my heart will explode."

"If only you could bottle that feeling for when you can't agree on who takes out the garbage." He reached for his cigarette case. "Young people think love is all you need. It's imprinted in their minds like the myth that you should spend two months' salary on an engagement ring. But if marriage was that easy, divorce attorneys would be out of work."

"I don't want to talk about divorce," Olivia said. "Finn and I are in love and we are going to have a wonderful life."

"Of course you are," Sebastian agreed. "You're a Miller, I wouldn't expect anything less. Where is everyone? I woke up late and all I found were fresh towels in the bathroom and fried bacon in the kitchen."

"Felix and Finn are playing tennis and Hadley and Esther went to the fish market in Gustavia," Olivia said. "It's a gorgeous day, I just want to lift my face to the sun."

"Lucky sun." Sebastian lit a cigarette. "I'm surprised Finn isn't with you. If I was in my twenties and my girlfriend had your warmth and intelligence, I wouldn't waste my time whacking a ball over a net."

"Tonight we're going to have a romantic dinner at La Plage," Olivia replied. "It overlooks the bay in St. Jean and the tables are right on the sand. I have a feeling Finn is going to propose."

"Oh, I see," Sebastian said. "Then never mind."

"Never mind what?" Olivia asked.

"I thought we could browse in the shops in Gustavia and I could buy you an early birthday present," he began. "But you probably want to work on your tan or get your hair done. We can do it another time."

Olivia had been looking forward to lying on a chaise longue with a book and perhaps going for a swim. But she couldn't let Sebastian spend the day alone.

"I have an idea!" she exclaimed. "We'll go to the beach at St. Jean and have lunch at Sand Bar. It has the best people watching on St. Barts."

"That's a marvelous suggestion." Sebastian took her arm. "I don't know why I didn't think of it myself."

They sat at an outdoor table at Sand Bar and drank piña coladas and ate grilled fish sandwiches with chipotle mustard. There was sautéed green beans and seafood risotto. The sun warmed Olivia's brown shoulders and she felt light and happy.

Canvas sofas littered the sand and there were white beach umbrellas and vases of yellow tulips. Men wore linen shirts and Italian loafers and women were dressed in silk sarongs and had chunky gold bracelets on their arms.

"I thought they would check my passport to see if my last name was Vanderbilt or Windsor." Sebastian ate an asparagus tip. "It seems you can't get a table unless you're an American steel magnate or European royalty."

Olivia laughed. "Felix and Hadley used to bring me here when I was a child. The women were all swathed in diamonds and rubies. I thought they were princesses come to life from my storybooks."

"It reminds me of the Emerald Coast in Sardinia," Sebastian said. "Your mother and I were invited on a yacht when you were two. The minute we docked I went to a boutique and bought a yellow linen dress for Hadley. She was the most beautiful woman on board; she couldn't play shuffleboard in a cotton blouse.

"You look just like her," he finished. "Hadley is still lovely. I told her last night when we were playing chess that she's one of the most beautiful women I've ever seen."

"You and Hadley played chess?" Olivia looked up.

"We played in the library underneath the portrait of *The Miller Girls*." Sebastian nodded. "It made me quite nostalgic. You were too young to remember, but the three of us had a good time. You even rode on the back of a tiger. The game hunter was holding you, of course," he laughed. "The look of anger on your mother's face would have scared any big cat. You loved it but I promised never to do it again."

"Did Felix play chess with you?" Olivia felt slightly off, like a french fry had stuck in her throat.

"He was already in bed. I envy a man my age who can lie down and fall asleep. Sometimes I prowl around at night like a lion with a splinter in his paw." He paused. "I gather Hadley is the same. She was wide awake."

"She was probably preparing the coffeemaker," Olivia explained. "She brews it fresh every morning with nutmeg and cinnamon."

"I am happy for her." Sebastian looked out at the bay. Jet Skiers jumped over the waves and a striped sailboat billowed in the breeze. "I always thought she deserved a life filled with beautiful clothes and elegant dinner parties."

"Hadley didn't marry Felix for his money," Olivia retorted. "They have a wonderful marriage. She isn't interested in cocktail parties or galas, she loves being at home."

"Do you think so? She seems a little on edge." He paused. "I hate to ask, but I do worry about her."

"What do you mean?"

"She looks a little skittish," he continued. "I thought she might have said something to you. You are close and we all need someone to confide in."

"If there was anything bothering her she would tell Felix," she answered.

"A spouse is the perfect person to tell your problems to," he agreed. "Your mother and I spent many nights lying under the stars worrying about when your first tooth would come in or if the rash on your cheek was normal." He looked at Olivia. "But it's difficult if the person you are married to is part of the problem."

"I don't know what you're talking about," she said. Suddenly the sun was too bright and she longed to go inside. "They're the best couple I know."

"Then I'm sure I'm imagining it." Sebastian squeezed Olivia's hand. "Let's talk about something else. I called my friend Rufus. He can't wait to have us on his boat in Costa Rica."

"I talked to Finn." Olivia nibbled a green bean. "I don't think we can go this Christmas."

"It's always good to compromise in a relationship. But you can't let your partner walk all over you. Just because Finn doesn't want to come, you shouldn't miss out."

"Finn was quite happy to go to Costa Rica."

"Then why aren't you coming?" he asked.

Olivia put down her fork and took a deep breath. "Hadley and Felix do so much to prepare for Christmas and the holidays are very important to Felix. I wouldn't want to offend him."

"Felix?" Sebastian exclaimed. "What does he have to do with it?"

"I remember the first Christmas we spent in St. Barts. I was only six but I thought Christmas had to include sledding and hot chocolate with marshmallows. Felix took me to the harbor and we watched the boat parade. Dozens of boats lit up with colored lights like an illustration in a storybook. It was the prettiest thing I'd ever seen.

"Christmas is important to Felix, we have to be here," she finished. "You could join us. Felix makes homemade eggnog and we watch *It's a Wonderful Life.*"

Sebastian sipped his piña colada and a smile lit up his face.

"I have a better idea. I just got a commission to paint the gardens of a villa in Capri in July. You should join me. We can explore the grottos and take a day trip to Amalfi."

"I've never been to Capri!" Olivia's eyes were wide. "It sounds lovely but I can't."

"Hadley would give you time off from the gallery," he insisted. "If Finn is too busy, you can come alone."

"Finn suggested we spend a week in Maine," she explained. "A friend booked a cabin and we could bicycle and shuck oysters."

"Maine! That's as exciting as a barn door," he spluttered. "You have to hear foreign languages and sample other cuisines."

"Most people in St. Barts speak French and I did spend a semester in Florence in college."

"Capri might not be the Serengeti but at least it's somewhere new," he tried again. "You don't know how much I've regretted not having you join me on at least some of my adventures. We could have climbed Mount Kilimanjaro or rode elephants in Thailand. This is our last chance to be together before you and Finn get married."

"Why didn't you?" she asked.

"Why didn't I what?" Sebastian ate a pineapple wedge.

"You sent me Japanese kimonos and Russian dolls; why didn't you ask me to join you?" she answered. "Hadley would have let me when I was older."

Sebastian rubbed his forehead. He sat forward and his voice was soft.

"It was hard enough walking away from you and Hadley, for what I thought were the right reasons. I could never give your mother the life she deserved and I was as easy to live with as a black bear.

"I thought about inviting you to visit, but I was too afraid I couldn't part with you again. I knew once we were together, I'd never want to let you go."

"That's ridiculous." Olivia's eyes flashed. "Lots of families are divorced. We could have had wonderful summers."

"I got used to being away from you. The pain was always there but it was manageable, like a chronic illness that needs the right mixture of medicines." He paused. "But if I had to give you up again, I don't think I would recover."

"I see." Tears swam in Olivia's eyes.

The waiter replaced their plates with silver bowls of rum raisin sorbet. There was Caribbean chocolate pie with caramel sauce.

"It is a wonderful invitation." She picked up a dessert spoon. "I'll have to think about it."

After lunch Sebastian bought a silk handkerchief at a boutique in St. Jean. He offered to take Olivia dress shopping but she wanted to go back to the villa.

"I'm going to walk off that chocolate pie," Sebastian said when they pulled into the driveway. "At my age if you lie down after lunch, the butter goes straight to your waist."

"Thank you, I had a lovely time." She stepped out of the car.

"I couldn't ask for a better lunch partner." He smiled. "Perhaps don't mention to your mother that I am worried about her. She thinks she's the strongest person there is."

"Of course I won't mention it." Olivia adjusted her sunglasses. "She's perfectly happy and there's nothing to worry about."

Olivia entered the living room and saw her mother arranging a vase of yellow tulips. She wore a linen dress and her blond hair loose.

"Darling, there you are." Hadley looked up. "Esther and I returned from the fish market and the villa was empty."

"Sebastian and I ate lunch at Sand Bar." Olivia put her purse on the glass side table. "He went for a walk and I'm going to take a nap."

"A nap!" Hadley raised her eyebrow. "Are you feeling all right? You look a little pale."

"I'm fine," Olivia said and smiled. "It's so thrilling catching up with Sebastian. I feel like I'm living my life all over again."

"Did he mention Costa Rica?" Hadley asked.

"I told him we couldn't go," Olivia replied. "He's staying at a villa in Capri this summer and asked me to join him. It sounds heavenly but Finn couldn't get time off. I don't know whether I should go alone."

"What a fascinating invitation. I hadn't thought he was so clever." Hadley pursed her lips. "Sebastian is like a cat. He always lands on his feet and then he's right back to creating mischief."

"I've wanted to join him for years but somehow it seems wrong to go now." Olivia hesitated. "Like I'm picking Sebastian over Finn."

"That's how Sebastian wants you to feel. Though Capri is gorgeous." Hadley paused. "I didn't think it was Sebastian's style. He favors islands in the South Pacific."

"Perhaps he thought I'd be more interested in Italian handbags than thatched huts," Olivia laughed. "It does sound wonderful. I'll talk to Finn about it at dinner. We have reservations at La Plage."

"Oh dear. Esther is making grilled snapper and pumpkin foam soup." Hadley frowned. "Eric and Felix are having a boys' night out so it was going to be the four of us."

"I can ask Finn to cancel the reservation," Olivia suggested.

"You mustn't change your plans." Hadley shook her head. "I'll have Esther just make enough for two."

"You and Sebastian are going to eat alone?" Olivia gasped.

"Don't look so frightened, I can handle Sebastian," Hadley smiled. "Though being his only audience can be exhausting. I'll ask Esther to join us."

"Sebastian said something at lunch," Olivia began. "I always thought Sebastian left because he had to paint. But he said you should have beautiful clothes and attend glamorous parties and he couldn't give you the life you deserved."

"Did he really?" Hadley's blue eyes flickered. "And did he also say Judas never had any intention of turning Jesus over to Pontius

Pilate or that Columbus knew all along the Earth was round? Sebastian should be a writer as well as an artist; he has a knack for rewriting history.

"I had everything I wanted: a husband and beautiful daughter and part-time job at the gallery. When he walked out the door it was for the benefit of Sebastian Miller."

"That's what I thought." Olivia let out her breath.

Suddenly she remembered Sebastian wondering if Hadley was unhappy and bit her lip.

"But you aren't sorry he left?" she began. "I mean, you're glad you married Felix."

"What a silly question." Hadley smiled. "You don't know what a relief it was not to have to tiptoe around Sebastian's moods like a flight attendant in the first-class cabin of an airplane."

"And Felix?" Olivia asked.

"Felix is intelligent and kind and we like the same books and movies. He never forgets an anniversary and he knows exactly which flowers I like." Hadley paused. "There's only one thing I regretted."

"What?" Olivia asked.

She waited for Hadley to reply and felt a prickle on her neck.

"That you didn't grow up in the same house as your father," Hadley said.

"That's all?" Olivia breathed.

"Of course that's all." Hadley smoothed her skirt. "What else could there be?"

Olivia leaned over her balcony and inhaled the scent of frangipani. The sun glinted on the ocean and white clouds were as fat as cotton balls.

She wanted to ask Hadley if she and Sebastian had played chess but she didn't know how to bring it up. And what if they had? Just because two old friends played a board game didn't mean they were doing anything illicit.

Sebastian hadn't seen Hadley in twenty years; how could he know if she looked happy? And how could Hadley not be content in St. Barts! The bay was shimmering turquoise and the hills were lush green and the air smelled like the most expensive perfume.

She didn't have time to think about it, she had to shower and get dressed for dinner. Royal palm trees wafted in the breeze and she wondered when everything got so complicated.

Chapter Ten

HADLEY FILLED A SILVER TRAY with a bowl of pumpkin soup and a basket of baguettes. She added a glass of pinot noir and changed her mind. Sebastian had drunk enough of Felix's wine and bourbon; tonight he could have soda water.

Esther had to go home and Hadley decided the last thing she wanted was to trade barbs with Sebastian over grilled snapper and stuffed artichoke. She would prepare him a tray and he could eat in the study.

She sliced green shallots and thought how dare he question her sleeping arrangements. He knew nothing about marriage. When they divorced they were practically children and as far as she knew he never had another long-term relationship.

Maybe she never experienced that same heady excitement when Felix entered a room or spent all afternoon choosing a dress for a romantic dinner. But that didn't mean their lives weren't filled with warmth and laughter.

She drizzled olive oil on spinach leaves and remembered their honeymoon in St. Barts. It was the first time Hadley stayed at Felix's villa and she loved everything about the island: the friendly people and shimmering ocean and white houses cascading down to the bay.

Every morning they swam in the pool and ate papaya and kumquat and passion fruit the color of rubies. In the afternoons they climbed into the four-poster bed and peeled off each other's robes. Felix was a surprisingly good lover: he kissed her in all the right places and never finished until her body twisted in delight.

It was only after they returned to New York that there was a strain in the relationship. She and Felix both wanted more children and Olivia was anxious for a brother or sister. Hadley was certain she was pregnant; she drifted through Bloomingdale's admiring pink booties and soft yellow blankets.

But each month her stomach remained flat and she had an uneasy feeling. She knew why she couldn't get pregnant and should have thought of it sooner.

And they were so lucky to have Olivia! Olivia and Felix spent countless hours exploring Manhattan. They went ice skating in Rockefeller Center and attended children's hour at the New York Public Library.

Perhaps their sex life had ebbed but they enjoyed long walks in Central Park and intimate dinners at Per Se. Felix gave her a dozen red roses every anniversary and never forgot her birthday.

She added cottage cheese to the pumpkin soup and thought about the last year. It had been so natural for Felix to sleep alone after he injured his back. But now he was well enough to play tennis but they still didn't share a bedroom. Was it because of his injury, or was there another reason? She hadn't asked him because she was afraid of his answer.

Anyway, you couldn't rely on sex to keep a marriage together. She remembered when she and Sebastian were in Thailand and couldn't keep their hands off each other. When the sex was taken away, everything that was wrong between them reared its head like a dragon in a street parade.

Hadley gazed at the room service tray of spicy prawn soup and green curry. There was soft egg tofu and wok-fried rice and hot basil. She ate a bite of khao soi noodles and had never tasted anything so delicious.

The hotel suite had dark wood floors and rattan sofas and red lacquered cabinets. Hadley had never seen so much red! The silk pillows on the window seat were red and the towels next to the claw-foot bathtub were red and the robes hanging in the walk-in closet were red silk.

Chiang Mai was the most fascinating city. The guidebook said it was built in the thirteenth century and surrounded by a moat to ward off invaders. Now it was a mix of ancient monuments and modern apartments. Hadley loved the red pickup trucks that served as taxis and Olivia could spend hours visiting the giant pandas and chimpanzees at the zoo.

Sebastian received a commission from a British collector who wanted to fill his estate with original art. He spent all day replicating the landscape: lush waterfalls and terraced rice paddies and temples made of gold.

At night he joined them for coconut curry on a floating restaurant or a massage at the market on Chang Klan Road. They climbed three hundred steps to the monastery in Doi Suthep and saw the giant boulders at Luang National Park.

The best part was for the first time in months they had their own bedroom. Olivia slept on a rollout in the suite's living room and Hadley and Sebastian shared a king-size bed with a quilted headboard.

When they shut the sliding doors and Sebastian stripped off his boxers, Hadley felt wild and wanton. All Sebastian had to do was caress her breast and she couldn't wait to get tangled in the embroidered sheets.

"There you are." She looked up. Sebastian wore a patterned shirt and leather sandals. "Room service left pork with crispy noodles and lychee sorbet. I still can't believe Walter put us up in a suite at the Four Seasons."

"He keeps it for out-of-town guests and wanted me to have peace and quiet." Sebastian tossed his hat on the bamboo coffee table. "Though he didn't realize how distracted I'd be by my wife wearing a red silk robe and gold slippers."

"I just took a shower." Hadley smoothed her hair. "The fixtures are solid brass and when you look out the window you see the mountains."

"We drove out to the Mae Rim Valley." Sebastian sat on a wicker love seat. "Wait until you see my sketch. It's the whole city from the top of the tea plantations."

Hadley gazed at his wide shoulders and thought ever since he turned down the offer for *The Miller Girls,* he had been so confident. His skin was golden and he looked like a male model.

"Olivia is getting dressed, the parade starts in an hour." Hadley poured a cup of Darjeeling tea. "She made me promise to tell her when the dragon appears so she can close her eyes. She said hiding from the dragon is the best part."

"I'm afraid I can't go. Walter is taking me to see the underwater caves at Doi Inthanon National Park." Sebastian ate a tangerine. "I'm going to cover canvases with magenta and indigo and turquoise."

"Olivia has to ride on your shoulders," Hadley insisted. "She can't see the parade from the ground."

"I can't say no. He gave us a two-room suite at the Four Seasons and an unlimited budget for art supplies." He paused. "And he has an exciting new project. When I've finished these paintings, we're going stay at his beach house in Phuket. It has glass walls and a tile floor imported from Istanbul."

"Olivia's fifth birthday is in April." Hadley looked up. "She has to start kindergarten."

"She's not learning physics, you can teach her to read." He shrugged.

"Kindergarten is one of the most important years of her life, she'll remember it forever."

"We can't stop now. Look how far we've come." Sebastian waved at the coffee table. "We're eating off Royal Doulton china and sleeping on one-thousand-count Egyptian cotton sheets."

"I thought you were happy staying in a cramped guesthouse," Hadley bristled.

"I don't give a fig about the money but I do care that someone loves my work," Sebastian replied. "Walter could afford any artist but wants to fill his walls with Sebastian Millers. One day he'll donate the whole collection to the British Museum."

"We can't cart Olivia around like a pet monkey." Hadley fiddled with her fork. "She needs friends and a bookshelf filled with *Anne of Green Gables*."

"She's getting a wonderful education. She can say thank you in three languages and knows the names of a dozen different flowers,"

Sebastian answered. "Can we discuss this tonight over mango and sticky rice? You can wear what you're wearing now and I'll come in boxers and socks."

Hadley gazed at the dimple on his cheek and hesitated. Sebastian could stop any argument with his smile. And Olivia was happy and wasn't the most important thing for a child to see her parents doing what they love?

"All right." She nodded. "But I'm not going to change my mind."

"We'll see about that." He kissed her. "I can be quite persuasive."

Hadley sat on a pink chaise longue and sipped a mai tai. Palm fronds flanked the infinity pool and there was a pagoda with stone lions. Olivia licked an orange Popsicle and waiters carried colored drinks with paper umbrellas.

The street parade had been filled with fire-eating dragons and floats made of pink and yellow flowers. Women in silk kimonos twirled parasols and vendors sold candies wrapped in rice paper. Hadley and Olivia had watched the lion dance and waved at children riding elephants.

"Your daughter is lovely," a woman said, reclining beside her. She was in her forties with dark hair and diamond earrings. She wore a red sarong and silver sandals. "It's wonderful when they still want to be with you. My daughter, Grace, is fourteen and only allows me in her room to deliver her *Seventeen* magazine."

"Olivia is almost five," Hadley said and smiled. "We visited the street parade and she's exhausted. I had to carry her to the taxi."

"You never think you're going to miss your children clinging to your skirt," the woman sighed. "But then you drive them to the mall and they don't want their friends to see you. It usually happens around the time your husband would rather play golf than massage your back with suntan lotion. All those years of wishing for time alone and suddenly you spend your day reading spy thrillers."

"My husband and I have been married five years and still have romantic dinners," Hadley mused.

"When you're young you think you're immune to migraines or bouts of indigestion. But eventually it's easier to sleep in the guest room." She paused. "But there are rewards. I can afford to spend all day at the spa and the Four Seasons offers heavenly chakra treatments."

Hadley nodded. "I'm excited to be here. My husband is an artist and we've traveled all over Asia and Africa."

"You're clever traveling while your daughter is so young," the woman agreed. "My husband is a stockbroker. We dreamed of spending a year in Paris and renting a flat on the Rue Saint-Honoré. But now Grace is in high school and would never leave her friends. We'll have to wait until she graduates and then we'll be too old to go to the nightclubs."

"I'm sure your daughter would adjust," Hadley replied.

"I understand Grace's position. She's addicted to American television and pop music." She sipped her drink. "If I could do it again, I'd be like you. See the world before life is about choir concerts and school dances."

"We do have fun and the Four Seasons is spectacular," Hadley said, suddenly feeling light and happy. "Olivia saw pink flamingos in the garden."

"What is your husband's name? Maybe I've heard of him."

"Sebastian Miller," Hadley replied.

"The artist with chiseled cheekbones who was featured in

British Vogue?" She raised her eyebrow. "Well, you are lucky. Who knows, maybe you'll defy the odds and still be romantic at our age."

Hadley wrapped her hair in a towel and slipped on a silk robe. Candles flickered on the walnut sideboard and a vase held floating hibiscus. There was a bottle of melon liqueur and a plate of goat cheese and macadamia nuts and honey.

She waited for Sebastian to arrive and thought maybe the woman at the pool was right. Olivia was seeing places she'd only read about and what better way to teach her about different cultures than to visit ancient temples? And wasn't beauty an education in itself?

"You can't walk around looking so gorgeous," Sebastian said, entering the suite. "I'll have to stop everything and sketch you."

"Olivia wanted to show you her face painting but I insisted she wipe it off before she went to bed." Hadley offered him a bowl of water chestnuts.

"I'm sorry I missed it." Sebastian loosened his collar. "The waterfalls at Mae Sa were so blue, I couldn't possibly replicate the color. And the view from the tea plantation was all gray mists and green fields and wooden temples."

"Thailand is beautiful," Hadley sighed. "I met a woman by the pool and she was quite jealous of our lifestyle."

"Artists have painted provincial scenes in France and Spain for centuries but no one has captured the magic of Asia and Africa." Sebastian sat on the rattan sofa. "I know you're worried about Olivia, but in a few years we'll buy a flat in Paris or London. She'll attend school and I'll paint abstracts or still lifes. But I only come alive when I hold a paintbrush, and right now I have to paint waterfalls and rain forests."

Hadley took a deep breath and looked at Sebastian. "I think you're right."

"You do?" he looked up.

"We're young and you're so talented," she continued. "Perhaps Olivia can get a tutor or go to an international school. She'll have experiences she'll remember forever."

Sebastian drew her close and kissed her. She kissed him back and he slid his fingers beneath her robe. God! She wanted him. Nothing existed except his smooth skin and warm mouth.

"We better go in the bedroom," he whispered, pulling her up. "Olivia might wake up and I want to do things to you that you can't imagine."

She followed him into the bedroom and closed the sliding doors.

"Lie down on the bed," he instructed, sliding her robe off her shoulders.

"What are you going to do?" she asked, lying on the silk bedspread.

"We are at the Four Seasons in Thailand," he said and smiled. "I'm going to give you a massage you'll never forget."

He disappeared into the bathroom and returned with oils and lotions. He dimmed the lights and lit a scented candle. The air smelled of ginger and cloves and Hadley shivered.

He kneaded lavender oil into her shoulders and massaged her thighs. He turned her on her stomach and rubbed her back with almond milk. Her skin throbbed and her heart raced and she wanted to pull him inside her.

"I love you," he whispered. "I will spend a lifetime making you happy."

"I love you too," she murmured, turning onto her back.

Sebastian lowered himself onto the bed and kissed her breasts. He stripped off his shirt and she pulled him on top of her. She wrapped her arms around his waist and urged him to go faster. His buttocks were slick and he came in one long thrust.

Sebastian waited until her breathing subsided and lay on his back.

"This is for you," he whispered. He pressed one hand on her stomach and inserted the other inside her. She caught her breath until the wetness became unbearable waves and her whole body shuddered.

"I could do this forever," he moaned, lying on his back.

"So could I," Hadley sighed, feeling wild and spent.

He traced a pink dot on her stomach and looked up. "What's that?"

"A mosquito bite." She shrugged. "Mosquitos were everywhere at the parade."

"I can't blame them for wanting you." He kissed her. "I've never tasted anything sweeter."

Hadley stood in front of the suite's walk-in closet and touched her forehead. She and Olivia had spent all day at the zoo, visiting the panda house and the aviary with its colored peacocks and silvery finches. She stood in line to buy coconut Popsicles and suddenly her head throbbed and her skin was like paper.

Now she slipped off her sandals and thought she was not used to the Thai climate. The mornings were misty and cool but by noon the sky was pale blue and the sun was bright white. All she needed was a cold shower and she'd be fine.

The door opened and Sebastian entered the bedroom.

"There you are." He tossed his straw hat on the bedside table. "I thought we'd go to the Loi Krathong festival. People launch paper boats filled with candles and flowers in the Ping River. The air is thick with incense and vendors sell sticky rice wrapped in banana leaves."

"It sounds lovely," Hadley said, fiddling with her zipper.

"I'll help you." Sebastian touched her dress. "You're quite hot, are you feeling all right?"

"We visited the zoo, Olivia can't get enough of the giant lizards," Hadley said and smiled. "I was in the sun too long. I'll hop in the shower and be fine."

Hadley entered the bathroom and gazed out the window. The sun was setting and the fields were mauve and gold. She reached for a towel and suddenly everything went black and she crumpled to the tile floor.

Hadley propped herself against the silk pillows and sipped a cup of green tea. A silver tray was filled with bowls of miso soup and pickled vegetables. She nibbled a lychee nut and wished she had an appetite.

The last month had been the most harrowing of her life. After she had collapsed, she woke up in the hospital surrounded by doctors and nurses. It was only later, when her cheeks were cool and her lips were no longer blue, that Sebastian told her she had dengue fever and almost died.

She'd never heard of the disease, carried by mosquitos in

Thailand. Her fever had spiked to 105 and she had pains all over her body. The doctor said it would take weeks to recover and she needed rest and a nutritious diet.

Now she picked at a piece of sweet fish and thought Sebastian had been wonderful. He patted her forehead with moist towels and kept the suite filled with orchids and violets. Olivia sat with her in the afternoons and they read stories and painted in coloring books.

"You look like a Brueghel painting." Sebastian opened the gauze curtains. "All alabaster skin and large blue eyes."

"I do feel better." Hadley put the cup on an enamel saucer. "Perhaps we can walk in the garden. I haven't left the suite in a month, I forgot what fresh air smells like."

"I'll bottle the air and bring it inside." Sebastian smiled. "The doctor said to take it slowly."

"A stroll around the grounds isn't going to exhaust me," Hadley said, tucking her blond hair behind her ears.

"Olivia and I are going to perform a puppet show and I ordered a feast: banana blossom salad and sea scallops and mango mousse cake for dessert."

"You haven't painted in weeks," Hadley reminded him. "Walter isn't going to pay for our suite if you don't complete the commission."

"I told Walter I couldn't finish the paintings." Sebastian stopped and looked at Hadley. "We're paying for the suite."

"We can't afford jasmine-scented bath salts and heated towels," she protested. "We barely have enough for clothes and bus fare."

"The doctor said I shouldn't move you. We didn't have a choice." He paused. "I pawned your engagement ring."

"You did what?" she gasped.

"You haven't worn the ring since you got sick. It's the only valuable thing we own besides *The Miller Girls*," he explained. "I'll get it back. When you're better we'll stay at Charles's beach house in Cape Town. I'll paint and you can recuperate."

"We're not going to stay in a beach house in Cape Town or guest cottage in Kenya or yacht in Sardinia." Hadley's cheeks flushed. "We're going home."

"What are you talking about?" Sebastian snapped.

"What if Olivia had gotten sick? Can you imagine our daughter fighting for her life in a Thai hospital?" she demanded. "Or if you were unable to paint and we didn't have enough money to eat. A friend is subletting her apartment in New York and I'll find a job in a gallery."

"I'm an artist. I need fresh air and open space." He ran his hands through his hair.

"It doesn't matter what you want." Hadley's blue eyes flashed. "Olivia needs to go to school and take dance lessons and have birthday parties."

Sebastian walked to the bed and kissed her.

"We'll talk about this later." He slipped his hand under her robe. "After a plate of steamed sea bass and warm chocolate cake."

Hadley studied his chiseled cheekbones and something tightened inside her. Usually Sebastian could convince her to do anything by kissing her. But they hadn't made love since she fell ill and she couldn't imagine being sweaty and spent.

Suddenly everything they had done—traveling over the Garden Route in South Africa and camping at the foot of Mount Elgon—seemed from another time. She was a mature woman and couldn't build her future around Sebastian's boyish dreams.

"I already had the concierge buy the plane tickets." She pulled the sheet around her shoulders. "My parents lent us the money. They can't wait to see Olivia."

Hadley tossed the spinach salad and wondered if she had been hard on Sebastian all those years ago. He had loved her and Olivia; it was as obvious as the paint strokes on his canvas. And going to America was like removing a wild animal from its natural habitat.

She had nothing to feel guilty about; Sebastian was the one who left. And Olivia had to have a normal life. She couldn't have done anything else.

She carried the tray down the tile hallway and entered the study. Sebastian nursed a shot glass and flipped through a magazine.

"You didn't have to go to so much trouble, I could have eaten in the kitchen." He jumped up. "Pumpkin soup is my favorite and the scalloped potatoes smell heavenly."

"Esther made the soup, I didn't do anything except fix a salad." Hadley placed the tray on the glass coffee table. "And you'll be more comfortable in here with the television."

"You must join me for a cocktail." He walked to the bar. "Scotch and soda, no ice? And have some of these Brazil nuts, they're delicious."

"No, thank you. My dinner is in the oven." Hadley smoothed her hair. "You can leave the tray here, Esther will get it in the morning."

"I was looking at Felix's *National Geographic*." Sebastian handed her the magazine. "Do you remember Chiang Mai? The Doi Suthep temple was eighty feet tall and made of solid gold. Olivia was certain if you rubbed the surface a genie would pop out."

"I hardly remember." Hadley bit her lip. "It was more than twenty years ago."

"It was the most beautiful place we'd seen. Valleys covered in dew and fields like velvet carpets. And the food! Crispy noodles and pork that tasted so good, we were sure it was steak."

"I don't know why we're talking about this." Hadley twisted her hands. "Your soup is getting cold."

"Because I always felt guilty." He paused. "And I never said I'm sorry."

"Guilty?" Hadley looked at him.

"If I had gone to the parade you wouldn't have been bitten by a mosquito." He traced the rim of his glass. "One insect bite changed three lives."

"It was time to go home. Olivia was starting kindergarten."

"Do you remember Olivia wearing a kimono and serving us tea and fortune cookies?" he asked. "I never wanted to leave. Everything I wished for was in that hotel suite."

"I have to go," Hadley said and walked to the door.

"I always wondered why you didn't have more children," Sebastian mused. "You were such a good mother. Even when you were ill, you only thought about Olivia."

"That's none of your business." Hadley turned the door handle.

"I admit I was glad." He sipped his scotch. "It was the one thing Felix never gave you."

Hadley sat at the kitchen counter and tore apart a baguette. How dare Sebastian talk about Felix while he was eating from his china? And why did she let Sebastian reminisce when she was generally happy? She didn't have time to think about Thai feasts; she had to get ready for Olivia's birthday.

And really, was sex so important when you were older? There was much more to marriage: being with someone who went out in a snowstorm to get aspirin when you had a migraine and knew exactly when you wanted to leave a party.

She was a grown woman; if she wanted to make love with her husband she would tell him. She put the bowl in the sink and smoothed her skirt. They would have to talk about it soon, or she didn't know what would happen.

Chapter Eleven

OLIVIA KNOTTED A SARONG AROUND her waist and slipped on her sandals. She glanced at the emerald-green sheath she'd worn last night to La Plage and thought it had been a lovely evening. The table was set with a sea-green tablecloth and flickering candles. Finn ordered a bottle of French champagne and it was so romantic.

Then why had she wished she was sitting at a café in Capri, sipping limoncello and eating pizza napoletana? Even when she and Finn had strolled along the sand, she pictured blue grottos and chipped fishing boats and men chatting in Italian.

St. Barts was full of fishing boats and she could eat pizza at Isoletta in Gustavia. But wasn't that the point? It would be wonderful to go somewhere new where she didn't know the names of every restaurant.

She smoothed her hair and felt slightly guilty. Finn was so furious about Sebastian's invitation to Costa Rica, she hadn't mentioned Capri. But why shouldn't she spend a week in the summer with her father?

She thought about going on holiday with Sebastian and felt a surge of joy. The pasta was the best in Italy and the gelato was to die for. They could visit Tiberius's villa in Ana Capri and take the ferry to Sorrento.

She opened her bedside drawer and pulled out the wooden box. She untied the red ribbon and read out loud:

> *My darling Olivia,*
>
> *Today is your tenth birthday and I am so sorry I can't be there. I am staying at a guesthouse in Guiyang, China. Have your mother show it to you on the map. It is a fascinating city with a lake and 400-year-old temple.*
>
> *Did you know that in China it is traditional to eat a plate of long noodles on your birthday? You have to slurp it as long as possible for good luck! And in Australia they have bread and butter sandwiches with colored sprinkles.*
>
> *And you should be glad you don't live in Vietnam. They don't acknowledge birthdays at all. Everyone celebrates together on New Year's Day.*
>
> *I may sound like a schoolteacher, but that's not the point of my letter. Everywhere I go; I store up information like shells in a sand bucket. Someday I hope you'll look through my letters and see that every day I was thinking of you.*
>
> *Happy birthday, my darling Olivia, and I hope you like the red purse. My love for you is bigger than the Chinese full moon and you are the most beautiful ten-year-old girl on two continents.*

Olivia folded the letter and opened a piece of yellow paper. She glanced at the date and read out loud:

My darling Olivia,

I'm staying on the edge of a copper mine in Western Australia and your mother's invitation just arrived. To be honest, I forgot the date. But even if I left today, it would be a thirty-six-hour flight and I'd miss your sixteenth birthday party.

I hope you like the gold nugget necklace; the owner of the mine gave it to me himself. There's so much more I want to give you now that you're almost grown up: jewelry and beautiful clothes, because you shouldn't wear anything else. But more than anything I want to show you the world: poppy fields in Tibet and windmills in Crete.

Eventually you will realize everyone has problems: the violinist in Vienna worries he won't strike the right chord and the Japanese rice farmer prays for rain and the baker in Toulouse is afraid he'll run out of flour for his daughter's wedding.

No matter how big your problems may seem there are only two things that are important: to go to bed with a clear conscience and get up the next morning.

I promise one day we will celebrate your birthday together. Then we'll make up for all the years we missed by having the greatest party on two hemispheres.

Olivia riffled through envelopes with postmarks from Venezuela and Brazil. There was a pink hair ribbon and a colored-glass bracelet. She placed the box in the drawer and walked to the balcony.

She had been dreaming of Sebastian's world since she was a child. How could she pass up the opportunity to go away with him now?

She slipped on her sunglasses and felt strangely unsettled. Suddenly she wanted to see bullfights in Pamplona and ride donkeys in Tunisia and explore the Greek Islands. She was not even twenty-five; maybe she and Finn were rushing into things.

She fiddled with her earrings and remembered when she knew Finn was the one. It was a few weeks after they started dating and they were invited to a Labor Day party in Bridgehampton.

Olivia smoothed her hair and glanced at her watch. It was almost 5:00 p.m. and any minute Finn would arrive at the gallery. They were going to walk along the High Line and eat oysters at John Dory Oyster Bar.

She thought about the last few weeks and smiled. Finn appeared every day after work and they looked for antiques at the Chelsea Market or flipped through the clothing racks at Artists & Fleas. Afterward they ate three-cheese pizza at Co. and lobster fettuccine at Del Posto.

He always brought a little gift: daisies from a flower stall, a box of Jacques Torres chocolate, a magazine he picked up at the newsstand. And they had so much to talk about: Finn's plans after law school and Olivia's passion for the gallery.

Sometimes she wondered if they were moving too fast. In a couple of weeks she'd return to college and Finn would work full-time at the law firm. What if the distance was too great and he broke her heart? But then she studied his blue eyes and broad shoulders and knew she could trust him.

"You look beautiful." He entered the double glass doors. He wore a tan blazer and clutched a bunch of lilacs. "I'd grab you and kiss you but the people walking by might disapprove."

"These are lovely." Olivia accepted the flowers. "I'm starving. I can't wait to slurp oysters and drink ice cold pale ale."

"I ran into a friend from Princeton and he invited us to his parents' house in Bridgehampton for the weekend," Finn continued. "There will be a clambake and fireworks over the Long Island Sound."

"It sounds wonderful but I told Hadley I'd stay for the opening. The florist delivers wilted tulips if I'm not here and the caterer never keeps the champagne as cold as Hadley likes."

"I'll tell him we can't make it." Finn's face fell.

"You must go. You can't miss the fireworks," she said and smiled. "I'll come out after the show."

"You don't mind?" Finn asked.

"As long as you don't eat all the clams without me." She kissed him. "It's perfectly fine."

Olivia glanced around the gallery and bit her lip. She had assured Hadley she could handle the opening herself. But the florist's truck broke down and the caterer called and said the waiter had a summer cold.

Now the space was filled with men in pastel suits and women wearing linen dresses and everyone looked hungry and thirsty. Olivia could grab a tray, but how would she sell any paintings.

She looked up and saw a man walking toward her. He wore a pressed shirt and his blond hair was brushed over his forehead.

"Finn, what are you doing here?" she asked. "You're supposed to be in the Hamptons."

"I decided I'd rather sip champagne and nibble duck foie gras with you than listen to hedge fund managers discuss their stock portfolios." He grinned. "We'll leave together in the morning."

"The waiter got sick so there's no one to serve the canapés," she gulped. "And the florist's truck broke down so the crystal vases are empty. It's a complete disaster and Hadley will never trust me."

"Wait here. I have an idea," Finn said.

She entered the office and decided she'd serve the hors d'oeuvres herself. If people didn't eat soon they'd get irritable and leave. She heard footsteps and saw Finn wearing a white dinner jacket and carrying a bunch of freesias.

"Where did you get those?" she gasped.

"I asked the owner of the café next door if I could buy all his flowers," he explained. "He said they were free for the beautiful young woman at the gallery, as long as we come in after the opening for coffee and dessert."

"They're perfect but why are you wearing a dinner jacket?" she asked.

"I borrowed it from a waiter." He picked up a tray and smiled. "Now where do I find the napkins?"

Olivia gazed at the royal palm trees and wondered whether she fell in love with Finn because he was always there when she needed him. But that was ridiculous. Even if Sebastian walked out when she was five, Felix had been a wonderful father.

She loved everything about Finn: his clear blue eyes and broad shoulders and the cleft on his chin. The way he enjoyed his profession and genuinely liked helping people.

But she thought of everything Sebastian and Hadley had done by the time they were twenty-five: rode llamas in Morocco and visited temples in Thailand. She and Finn never did anything more adventurous than brave the Long Island Expressway on a holiday weekend.

She always longed for a marriage like Hadley and Felix's: pleasant evenings at home with a smooth wine and warm conversation. They would go out on the weekends of course. You never ran out of things to do in Manhattan and they both loved bookstores and movies.

But maybe she didn't only want a life like Hadley and Felix's; she also wanted to be like Sebastian. He traveled to every continent and had remarkable experiences.

She suddenly had an idea. She ran down the wooden staircase to the kitchen. The sun made patterns on the tile floor and the counter was set with platters of fresh fruit and whole wheat toast.

"Good morning, you look radiant." Sebastian sprinkled salt on poached eggs. "I'm glad you're wearing a sarong over your bathing suit. My presence has been good for something."

"I just woke up." Olivia poured a cup of coffee. "Finn and I strolled on the beach after dinner and the salt air makes me sleep forever."

"Ah, the evening at La Plage." Sebastian glanced at her hand. "Did Finn propose?"

"Not yet," Olivia answered. "It wasn't the right time."

"A romantic dinner with French champagne and flaming desserts?" He raised his eyebrow. "Maybe he needs a little push."

"What do you mean?" she asked.

"Finn is a wonderful guy. I can't think of anyone I'd rather handle my last will and testament." He paused. "But he doesn't seem spontaneous. You could give him a hint." He looked at Olivia. "If you're still sure you want to marry him."

"Of course I'm sure." Olivia's cheeks flushed. "He's everything I wished for and we're in love."

"I'm glad to hear it." Sebastian buttered his toast. "Your mother thought I'd caused a disturbance. What did he say about Capri?"

"I didn't mention Capri." Olivia hesitated.

"That's a shame. I hoped you would come." He dusted crumbs from his shirt. "I wanted to show you the gardens of Villa San Michele. It's filled with exotic flowers and Egyptian artifacts."

Olivia took a deep breath. "I'm going to join you."

"That's marvelous," Sebastian beamed. "Wait until you see the rocks of Faraglioni. I'll have to paint you! Sitting in the piazza, wearing oversize sunglasses and sipping Campari and soda."

"Actually, I was wondering if I could spend the whole summer with you." Olivia looked at him.

"The whole summer?" Sebastian dropped his toast. "Doing what?"

"Anything you're going to do," Olivia suggested. "Visit mosques in Istanbul or go cliff diving in Croatia. Hadley would give me the summer off to be with you, and I've hardly been anywhere. Wouldn't it be wonderful to go where the wind takes us?"

"I'm too old for cliff diving and plane tickets are expensive." Sebastian said nervously. "Besides, wouldn't Finn be furious if you left him alone to eat Chinese takeout?"

"I have some money saved up. I could pay for our whole holiday." Olivia stopped and her lips trembled. "Unless you don't want to. You probably have other people to see."

"There's no one I'd rather be with than you." He squeezed her hand. "Finn was upset that you went scuba diving without him. What is he going to say if you purchase a one-way airline ticket?"

"Of course I'd book a return flight," she protested. "You're the one who said I should see the world before I settle down. I'll be twenty-five tomorrow; when am I going to travel to other countries?"

Sebastian ate a bite of eggs and his face broke into a smile. "It's a wonderful plan! From Capri we'll take a ferry to Casablanca. We'll sip dried apricots in cognac at Rick's Café and feel like Humphrey Bogart and Ingrid Bergman."

"I'm so excited!" Olivia clapped her hands. "I can't wait to tell Hadley."

"Maybe you should keep it our secret for now," he suggested.

"Why would I do that?" she asked.

"Hadley might think I persuaded you. It's better if you tell her after I'm gone," he explained. "What will you say to Finn?"

"He might be hesitant but I'll make him understand." She paused. "Isn't that what love is, wanting the person you love to be happy?"

"That's why love never works," Sebastian sighed. "It's almost impossible to be happy without making the other person miserable."

Olivia parked her car on Rue de la République and grabbed her purse. It was almost noon and the sidewalk teemed with men and women wearing bright swimwear and designer sunglasses. Yachts bobbed in the harbor and the air smelled of frangipani and perfume.

Olivia leaned against the sidewalk's railing and thought Gustavia really was beautiful. Palm trees lined the promenade and there were elegant boutiques and dazzling jewelry stores.

She entered Les Case aux Livres and drifted through the shelves. She was going to buy books about Africa and Australia. There was a glossy atlas and she thought it would be fun to trace their route, like a geography assignment in high school.

"Olivia!" a male voice exclaimed. "What are you doing here?"

Olivia turned and saw Finn clutching a paper bag. He wore tennis whites and his hair was damp with sweat.

"I was looking for a present for Hadley," she gulped, stuffing the atlas back on the shelf. "It is her birthday too. I thought I'd buy a hardback book or box of stationery."

"Felix and I finished our match early," Finn explained. "Why don't we get some fish and chips and sit by the water."

Olivia paid for a coffee table book and followed Finn onto the sidewalk. She adjusted her sunglasses and felt slightly guilty. They never kept anything from each other and she'd planned her summer without consulting him.

They bought mahimahi dumplings and conch fritters and sat on a red wooden bench.

"These are delicious," Olivia mused. It was heavenly sitting in the warm sun and watching sailboats skim over the waves. Finn's arm brushed her shoulder and she wondered if she was making a mistake.

"I've been wanting to ask you something since we arrived in St. Barts," he began, wiping tartar sauce from his chin. "But the first night Sebastian joined us at the Pipiri Palace and the second evening I thought he might come home early, and last night I was afraid he would appear while we were eating banana flambé."

"Ask me what?" Olivia brushed crumbs from her sarong.

"Do you remember when we met at the gallery in Chelsea?" he said. "I came inside to escape the heat and you helped me deliver a letter. I asked you to get gelato and you said you didn't date strangers," he grinned, "I might be an international spy.

"I looked at you in that red linen dress with your blond hair tucked behind your ears and you were so beautiful. Magazines make you believe love is more grueling than studying for the law review. But every day with you is better than the one before." He reached into his pocket and drew out a black velvet box. "I love you more than anything and can't imagine life without you. Olivia Miller, will you marry me?"

"You're asking me to marry you here?" Olivia glanced at tourists carrying plastic buckets and children playing in the sand.

"I wanted to propose somewhere more romantic but I didn't want to take any more chances." Finn smiled. "I saw Sebastian board a sailboat and unless he jumps overboard, he's somewhere near the horizon."

Olivia blinked back sudden tears. She always imagined Finn would propose at an intimate restaurant. They'd eat baked snapper and kiss over chocolate soufflé for dessert.

But she was being silly. It didn't matter where he proposed; the important thing was he wanted to marry her.

"I haven't shown you the ring." He snapped open the box. "I designed it with Kenneth Lane."

Olivia studied the square-cut diamond on a platinum band and gasped. Finn had exquisite taste and they were going to be so happy.

"Oh, Finn," she breathed. "It's the most beautiful ring I've ever seen."

"I asked Felix and Hadley for their permission, of course. They offered to hold the wedding in St. Barts at Christmas."

"At Christmas?" She looked up.

She pictured all the things she would have to do this summer— pick out her wedding dress, choose a caterer—and thought she couldn't possibly go away with Sebastian.

"I knew you'd want to get married in St. Barts, and we don't want to wait a whole year." He kissed her. "We'll have the ceremony at St. Bartholomew's and the reception at the villa."

"It's just a little soon," Olivia said and her stomach turned over.

"Soon for what?" Finn inquired.

"Sebastian invited us to Capri for a week in July. I know how busy you are, so I thought I'd go alone. Then I had the idea of going away with my father for the summer. You work such long hours, I almost never see you at all."

"You want to go away with Sebastian alone?" Finn's voice was tight.

"Ever since I was five years old I've kept a box of letters from Sebastian. I used to tuck them under my pillow and dream of going with him to China and the South Pacific." She fiddled with her sarong. "There's so much I haven't seen and Sebastian is willing to show me. But if we get married in December, we'll be so busy I won't be able to go away at all."

"How could you make plans without asking me?" he demanded.

"I didn't mean to, I only thought of it this morning. I was going to tell you as soon as you arrived home. I understand if you're upset but you know how important it is for me to spend time with Sebastian. When would I ever get to do it again?"

"Ever since Sebastian arrived I've tried to stay out of the way," he said slowly. "I want you to have a relationship with your father. But I've made a mistake."

"What are you saying?" she asked.

"Maybe this isn't just about being with Sebastian. Maybe it's something more. You're not sure if I'm what you want. If you truly loved me you couldn't bear the thought of being apart when we are about to get married."

"That's ridiculous, I love you and I can't wait to be your wife!

What's a couple of months when we have decades ahead of us?"
She looked at Finn. "I thought you'd be glad I get to realize one of
my dreams."

"I won't stand in your way if that's what you want." Finn
shrugged. "But you should get it out of your system before we make
any plans."

"I don't understand." Olivia's skin felt icy and she couldn't
breathe.

"Spend the summer with your father. If we're still in love when
you come back, we can get engaged."

"Of course we'll be in love!" she stammered. "Nothing is going
to change the way I feel. I just want to spend some time with Sebastian before it's too late."

"That's the problem, I don't believe you know how you feel about
us right now. If you did, we wouldn't be having this conversation."
He stood. "I'm going for a walk. I'll see you later."

Olivia looked down at her naked hand and realized Finn had
put the engagement ring back in his pocket. The tropical breeze
caressed her shoulders and she let the tears stream down her cheeks.

Olivia raced up the steps of the villa and entered the hallway. Hadley sat in the living room, arranging books on the coffee table.

Hadley looked up. "Darling, it's lovely to see you. Tell me everything about your evening. Did Finn propose?"

"He didn't propose last night but this morning I ran into him
in Gustavia," Olivia began. "We sat on a bench and ate fish and
chips and he pulled a ring out of his pocket. He said I was so beautiful and he couldn't imagine life without me." She paused. "Then
he asked me to marry him."

"Darling, I'm so happy for you." Hadley glanced at Olivia's hand. "Where's the ring? I'm dying to see it."

"We got into a terrible fight," Olivia began to shake. "He said I needed to think about things and took it back."

She climbed the staircase to her room and flung herself on her floral bedspread. She heard footsteps and her mother sat down on the bed beside her.

"It can't be as bad as it sounds." Hadley smoothed Olivia's hair. "Tell me everything from the beginning."

"The ring was stunning and I was so happy. Then Finn said we should get married in St. Barts at Christmas," Olivia hiccupped. "Sebastian and I are going away for the summer and I said that wouldn't be enough time." '

Hadley froze. "You're going away with Sebastian for the summer?"

"He invited me to Capri and I thought why not travel for a couple of months. The gallery is slow then and Finn will be busy at the law firm." She paused. "I was so excited. We were going to visit all the places I dreamed of."

"Sebastian convinced you to go away with him for the whole summer," Hadley repeated.

"Sebastian said that's what you would say, but it was my idea," Olivia insisted. "He didn't want to go at all, it's quite expensive. I told him I had money saved up and could pay for the holiday."

"How generous of you." Hadley pursed her lips. "I'm sure Sebastian is already making hotel reservations."

"Why shouldn't I do something for him?" Olivia protested. "Lots of adult children take care of their parents and he's never asked for anything."

"You're barely twenty-five and Sebastian isn't in a nursing home,"

Hadley bristled. "He's a healthy middle-aged man capable of keeping himself in silk shirts and cigarettes."

"But think of what he's doing for me," Olivia urged. "I'm going to see palaces in India and mountain villages in Nepal. By the time you and Sebastian were my age, you'd traveled to three continents. I haven't done anything except buy cinnamon danishes at Zabar's and swimsuits in Gustavia."

"You've sold thousands of dollars' worth of paintings and matched artists with collectors," Hadley insisted. "And you've fallen in love with someone who's kind and grounded and loves you more than anything."

"Of course I love Finn," Olivia replied. "All I wanted was to spend a couple of months with my father. Is that so bad?"

"If we understood love there would be no romantic movies," Hadley sighed. "Let Finn cool off. I'm going to talk to Sebastian."

"Sebastian didn't do anything wrong." Olivia sat up. "There's nothing to say to him."

"I have plenty to say to him." Hadley opened the door. "Why don't you take a shower, you'll feel better."

Olivia wrapped herself in a robe and entered the bathroom. She imagined waterfalls in South Africa and poppy fields in China and a shiver ran down her spine. Then she pictured Finn's firm jaw and her heart turned over.

She stepped in the shower and the cool water touched her shoulders. Tears ran down her cheeks and she wondered how she was going to fix things without losing everything that mattered.

Chapter Twelve

HADLEY POLISHED THE GLASS AND held it up to the light. She knew she was being silly; Esther would load the dishwasher. But you could only get glasses spotless if you washed them by hand, and she loved the feel of smooth glass under her fingers.

How dare Sebastian agree to spend the summer with Olivia? He was lucky she didn't break the glass over his head. Olivia said it was her idea. But until Sebastian appeared, Olivia was happy working at the gallery and holidaying in St. Barts. Now she behaved like a sixties flower child who had to drop out.

She remembered Olivia's tear-stained cheeks and wondered if Finn was being harsh. Sebastian was her father. One couldn't blame Olivia for wanting to be together.

But who knew what Olivia would decide to do next? It was Hadley's fault for allowing Sebastian to stay at the villa. She should have made sure he only saw Olivia for cocktails and family dinners.

The front door opened and Sebastian appeared. His cheeks were tan and he wore board shorts and leather sandals.

"I didn't think anyone was home." He entered the kitchen. "I met a German couple and they invited me on their sailboat. The sea was a sheet of diamonds, you should have joined me."

"I was busy." Hadley reached up and placed the glass in the cabinet.

"If you hold that pose, I could paint you," he sighed, perching on a stool. "You remind me of Marilyn Monroe in *Some Like It Hot.*"

"Isn't that an old movie even for you?" Hadley raised her eyebrow.

"Classics never go out of style. You're still the most beautiful woman I know. And you're positively glowing." He studied her blond hair and high cheekbones. "It must have been our tête-à-tête last night. A smooth cognac and delightful conversation is good for the complexion."

"For your information I'm not glowing. I'm furious," Hadley snapped. "Finn proposed to Olivia this morning."

Sebastian walked to the counter and opened a bottle of vodka. He poured two shots and handed one to Hadley.

"I always thought the expression 'punched in the gut' was something out of a bad detective novel. Now I understand what it means. So he really means to take our little girl away." He looked at Hadley. "But why are you furious? Don't tell me he bought a cheap ring. She should wear at last three carats."

"I didn't see the ring because she wasn't wearing it," Hadley replied.

A smile crossed Sebastian's face and he laughed. "You're furious because Olivia turned him down. She came to her senses and realized she's too young. In a few years it will be different, but she's still a child."

"She didn't turn him down. Finn said they should get married at Christmas in St. Barts and Olivia said that wasn't enough time." Hadley glared at Sebastian. "Because she was going to travel in the summer with her father. Finn was so angry, he took back the ring and stalked off."

"How very ungentlemanly." Sebastian nodded. "Of course you're furious at him. Olivia deserves better."

"The only man I am furious with is you," Hadley seethed. "How dare you agree to spend the summer with Olivia. You knew Finn would be upset."

"To be honest, I thought it was an unlikely suggestion," he mused. "I can't afford the kind of accommodation Olivia is used to. But Olivia was insistent. How could I say no?"

"By being a good parent and making her realize she needs to put Finn first," she explained. "That might be hard for you. The only person you think about is Sebastian Miller."

"Now you are being cruel." He sipped his drink. "When Olivia was twelve, I stayed at a monastery in Tibet. From the window you could see green trellises and organic gardens.

"A few days into my stay I came down with malaria. My skin was yellow and my throat was parched and I thought I was going to die." He paused. "Do you know how I forced myself to stay alive? One of the monks gave me a notebook and every night I wrote down the places I wanted to take Olivia: Kabul and Dubai and Stockholm to see the Milky Way. I still keep it in my suitcase. How could I pass up the chance to fill it with places we've actually been?"

"Malaria! And you never told me." Hadley looked at Sebastian suspiciously. "Don't they have vaccines to protect you?"

"When the doctor finally arrived he said my skin was yellow because I was anemic." He shrugged. "Those vegetable-based diets never have quite enough iron. The point is I thought I was dying and the image of our daughter kept me alive. What's two months when she and Finn have a lifetime together?"

"They won't have any time together unless they make up," Hadley sighed. "You are going to make Olivia realize she'd have more fun this summer attending engagement parties and cake tastings. And I'm going to call the club and see if I can find Finn."

"Would it really be so bad if they didn't get back together?" Sebastian fiddled with his glass. "If their relationship can't stand a small tremor how would it survive an earthquake? Olivia is a successful career woman, why does she need to get married at all? Perhaps later, when she wants children. But these days there are more ways to have a child than ice cream flavors at the supermarket."

"Marriage is the best thing in the world," Hadley protested. "You don't know anything about it."

"I know a passionate woman who sleeps under a plaid throw on the sofa when she should be wrapped in satin sheets. She spends her time polishing glassware when she could be discussing art and music." He paused. "If you and Felix are so happy, why are you never together except during cocktail hour?"

"We both love art, how do you think we met? Just because we have some different interests doesn't mean we're not happy," Hadley bristled. "Anyway, passion is irrelevant at our age. Companionship is more important."

"You sound like an ad for a seniors cruise." Sebastian grimaced. "At least Olivia is learning life is about more than designer sunglasses and how Finn likes his shirts pressed."

"Finn wouldn't dream of asking Olivia to press his shirts, they're a modern couple." Hadley paused. "But you better talk some sense into Olivia or she's going to spend the next two weeks weeping in her bedroom. When she finally emerges she's going to blame you for ruining her relationship."

"She would never do that," Sebastian said doubtfully. "She knows I only want what's best for her."

"You must remember the passion of young love." Hadley inspected a glass. "When Olivia wakes up and discovers her Prince Charming is gone, you're going to be cast as the Wicked Witch. And all your talk of exotic locations is going to be worthless."

"You may have a point. I hadn't thought about sex." Sebastian paused and a smile played over his face. "Maybe you can remind me how it's done."

Hadley put the glass on the counter and smoothed her skirt. "I would rather pour the bottle of vodka over my head. I'm going into the study to make some phone calls."

Hadley entered the study and tried to stop shaking. She really should pack Sebastian's suitcase and toss it in the driveway. But Olivia and Finn weren't speaking and Sebastian had to fix it.

She glanced at the clock and longed for a scotch and soda. But she already drank half a vodka with Sebastian and she wasn't going to turn into a matron on a daytime soap opera.

No one knew how marriage was going to turn out, but you didn't give up before you started. She sat on the ottoman and remembered when she and Felix met. For the first time since Sebastian left, she didn't have a weight on her shoulders and life seemed full of possibilities.

Hadley climbed the steps of the Central Park duplex and rang the doorbell. She didn't know why Roberta, the owner of the gallery, insisted Hadley deliver the painting herself. But Hadley had only worked there for a few months and she didn't want to jeopardize her position.

"I was expecting a deliveryman in jeans and a T-shirt," a man said as he answered the door. He wore a white shirt and navy slacks. "Please come in, let me take that from you."

Hadley glanced at the marble entry and circular staircase and had to smile. Now she knew why Roberta insisted she drop off the painting. She was worried about Hadley and playing matchmaker.

"I'm Felix London." He held out his hand. "I think we met at the art opening the other night. You were wearing a black dress and carrying a pencil."

"You're an old friend of Roberta's." She entered the living room and saw thick Persian rugs and gleaming wood floors and a view of the park. There were plush velvet sofas and vases filled with lilacs.

· He nodded. "We were classmates at Princeton," he replied, studying Hadley's glossy blond hair and long legs. "You lugged the painting all the way uptown, the least I can do is offer you a cup of Blue Mountain coffee. I'm perfectly happy drinking Nescafé but the salesgirl at Zabar's insisted it's delicious."

"I wonder why Roberta didn't tell you who was delivering the painting?" Hadley asked, suddenly feeling like a teenager on a blind date.

"Should she have?" he inquired.

"No, of course not," she answered. "Thank you, a cup of coffee sounds lovely."

They drank dark coffee and nibbled petit fours and talked about Felix's career and Hadley's job at the gallery.

"What do you do when you're not making sure people don't eat a whole tray of canapés or walk out of the gallery with a bottle of champagne?" he asked.

"I don't have time to do anything. Artists can be demanding and collectors often decide they can't live without a piece in the middle of the night," she laughed. "But my daughter is five and loves the puppet show in Central Park."

"You're married?" Felix's face fell.

"I was married," Hadley said slowly. "It didn't work out."

"In that case I have a question."

"Yes?" Hadley replied and for some reason her heart beat faster.

"Would you go to dinner with me on Friday?" he asked. "I've known the owner of La Mirabelle for years. The French onion soup is superb and the rack of lamb melts in your mouth."

Hadley put down her coffee cup and smiled. "I'd like that very much."

Hadley sat at the walnut desk in the gallery and fiddled with a pencil. She didn't know why she agreed to go to dinner with Felix. She would have to ask her upstairs neighbor to babysit, and she already had worn her one good dress to the opening.

She was quite happy working at the gallery and taking Olivia to dance lessons. And Felix's duplex was gorgeous but she wasn't interested in his money. They managed on her salary, and she could always sell *The Miller Girls*.

But it had been lovely to sit in the sun-filled living room and talk about art and books. Felix had kind eyes and when he smiled she felt warm and secure.

Hadley looked up and saw Felix enter the gallery. He wore a navy suit and clutched a white box.

"I was hoping you worked today. I wondered if you could deliver this."

"I only make deliveries for Roberta," she said uncertainly.

"It's a personal delivery." Felix handed her the box. "It's for your daughter."

"You bought a present for Olivia?" She frowned.

"La Mirabelle is quite elegant and I thought she might like a pretty dress. I bought it at Bloomingdale's so she can exchange it." He stopped and smiled. "I promise there are no large bows or pink polka dots."

Hadley opened the box and took out a blue dress. There was a blue hair ribbon and a pair of white tights.

"It's lovely, but I didn't know the invitation was for both of us," she faltered.

"I had to invite Olivia. If she didn't approve of me, we couldn't go out again," he explained. "Besides, La Mirabelle serves a mouthwatering raspberry brûlée. We'll ask for three spoons."

Hadley covered the dress with tissue paper and took a deep breath.

"It's perfect." She smiled. "She's going to love it."

Hadley paced around the study and thought the early years of their marriage were like a carousel at Central Park. Olivia led them on a giddy round of dance recitals and concerts and birthday parties. When Olivia grew older, they were so busy with Felix's career and Hadley's work at the gallery, they barely saw each other.

Had they grown distant before Felix injured his back? She picked up the phone and thought she didn't have time to worry about herself. She had to stop Olivia from making a terrible mistake.

Hadley stepped onto the patio and inhaled the scent of hibiscus. The glass table was set with platters of coconut chicken and tuna tartare. Now that it was cocktail hour, Hadley was too nervous to drink her usual rhum vanille. She poured a glass of iced tea and took a small sip.

She hadn't been able to find Finn, and Olivia was still in her room. Hadley was tempted to knock on Sebastian's door but she was so angry, she was afraid she would say something she could never take back.

"Where is everyone?" Felix stepped outside. His silvery hair was freshly combed and he wore a collared shirt.

"It's like a house party in an Agatha Christie novel." Hadley grimaced. "Except we know who did it. Sebastian has been up to mischief and ruined everything."

"It can't be that bad," Felix chuckled, eating a jumbo shrimp. "Tell me everything from the beginning."

"That's exactly what I said to Olivia." Hadley pursed her lips. "But it was worse than I imagined."

"Finn didn't show up for our afternoon match," he replied. "I wondered what happened to him."

"Sebastian Miller happened to him." She perched on a chaise longue. "He's like a tropical disease. At first you think it's a stomachache from eating something unfamiliar. By the next morning your temperature spikes to one hundred and five. If you're lucky the fever breaks and you survive, but the side effects remain the rest of your life."

"You're not making sense."

"It's my fault for sending him birthday invitations all those years," Hadley sighed, fiddling with her diamond earrings.

"He's Olivia's father," Felix protested. "You had to make him part of her life."

"That's the problem with Sebastian, he can't do anything by halves," she fumed. "He wants to take over her whole life."

"Unless he asked Olivia to marry him himself, I can't imagine what he's done."

"Finn proposed to Olivia this morning," she began. "Olivia said the ring was gorgeous."

"That's wonderful news." He beamed.

"Finn wanted to hold the wedding in St. Barts at Christmas, and Olivia said that didn't give her enough time." She paused. "Because she was going to spend the summer with her father."

"What did you say?" Felix gasped.

"You should have heard her describing the places they would see as if they were looking for the Holy Grail. Finn was so angry, he took the ring back and walked off. No one has seen him since."

"Oh dear." Felix settled on a rattan armchair. "Poor Finn and Olivia."

"You should feel bad for Sebastian." Hadley sipped her drink. "If he doesn't fix this, he's going to be sorry he arrived in St. Barts."

"Finn is young and his pride is hurt. He'll come around." Felix rubbed the rim of his glass. "Would it be so terrible for Olivia to spend a couple of months with her father?"

"Sebastian told me he thought Olivia was too sheltered," she explained. "He thinks she should travel through India and Asia and meet grungy poets and struggling artists."

"When did Sebastian say that?" Felix asked.

"The other night in the living room." Hadley waved her hand. "He made a whole speech that she's never been anywhere that doesn't sell Prada sunglasses and Italian handbags."

"You and Sebastian talked about Olivia alone," Felix repeated. "Did you discuss anything else?"

"What do you mean?" Hadley looked up.

"I didn't know you had any intimate conversations." His voice was stiff.

"I don't know what you're implying!" Hadley exclaimed. "The only thing I'm interested in discussing with Sebastian is the date on his airline ticket."

"I just wondered," Felix said slowly. "He is your ex-husband and he can be persuasive."

"Only if you haven't been indoctrinated in his ways. I'm a seasoned pro." She paused. "If it wasn't for Olivia I would have told him to get out. But if he leaves and she thinks it's her fault, she'll never forgive herself."

"You're right," Felix sighed. "I'm sure he'll be down soon and Finn will come back. We'll sit down and work it out."

Olivia appeared on the patio, wearing a white dress and silver sandals. Her cheeks were pale and there were circles under her eyes.

"Darling." Hadley smiled. "Esther prepared a delicious stuffed crab. Felix will fix you a drink and I'll make you a plate."

"I'm not hungry, thank you." She glanced around the patio. "Is Finn here?"

"I'm sure he's on his way," Hadley replied quickly. "You know how the roads are. One egg truck overturns and traffic is tied up for hours."

"He hasn't called and his phone is off," Olivia said. "What if he doesn't come back?"

"Of course he'll come back." Hadley squeezed her hand. "Tomorrow's your birthday. We're going to swim and sail and have dinner at Maya's."

"I still don't know why he's so angry." Olivia bit her lip. "Why shouldn't I spend time with Sebastian? And we've planned the most exciting itinerary: Capri and Casablanca and the Sahara Desert."

"Have you talked to Sebastian?" Hadley asked.

"Not since this morning." Olivia shook her head. "I was too upset to leave my room."

"And Sebastian didn't come to see you?" Hadley inquired.

"His door is closed." Olivia shrugged. "He's probably taking a nap."

"I'll pay him a visit." Hadley handed Felix her glass. "Why don't you fix Sebastian a drink? He's going to need a strong scotch."

Hadley raced up the stairs and knocked on the door. How dare Sebastian not talk to Olivia? She knocked again and had an uneasy feeling, like when you know the scary part is coming in a horror movie.

She flung open the door and the room was empty. The striped bedspread was neatly made and there was a cigarette packet on the mahogany desk. Sebastian's leather carry-on was missing and an envelope was propped on the bedside table.

She grabbed the envelope and strode downstairs. Olivia and Felix were waiting on the patio.

"Sebastian isn't here and his suitcase is missing." She handed Olivia the envelope. "He left something for you."

"He can't be gone! He never said a word." She looked at Hadley. "Did you ask him to leave?"

"Of course not." Hadley poured a glass of vodka. "I wouldn't dream of spoiling your birthday. I know how much you want him there."

Olivia sat on a rattan love seat and unfolded the letter. She took a deep breath and read out loud:

> *My darling Olivia,*
>
> *I admit I came to St. Barts to see how you turned out. You answered the door and you were even lovelier than I imagined. You are bright and beautiful and you're going to be as successful as your mother.*
>
> *I wanted to stay and celebrate your twenty-fifth birthday, but it seems I've stirred up a bit of trouble. It's best if I leave now, before I make things worse.*
>
> *Finn is a great guy and you're going to have a wonderful marriage. Just remember, you can love another person, but at the end of the day, you must stay true to yourself. That might sound like strange advice from someone who is all alone. But trust me. The people who are most important to you will realize how much you love them.*
>
> *Ever since Hadley handed you to me in the hospital in Johannesburg, you captured my heart. Like any father, I wished you could have houses and diamonds and anything your heart desires. But mostly, I hoped you are happy.*
>
> *Happy twenty-fifth birthday, my darling Olivia. I love you more than you'll ever know.*

"He can't leave before my birthday!" she exclaimed, tossing the letter on the glass table.

"I'm sure he's not far." Hadley's hands trembled. "Felix will call the hotels. When we find him, I'm going to wrap one of Felix's ties around his neck. How dare he desert you again."

"He would have mentioned that he was going to stay somewhere else." Olivia's eyes were wide. "What if he went to the airport?"

"Sebastian wouldn't pass up a three-course meal of seared tuna and aubergine and passion fruit sorbet," Hadley insisted. "Things were becoming heated and he wanted to get out of the kitchen. Any minute he'll appear and ask Felix to fix a martini. He'll be lucky if I don't put hemlock in it. He spent the last three days groveling for forgiveness and now does this? It's low even for Sebastian."

"It's my fault. If I hadn't suggested we spend the summer together this never would have happened. I can't let him leave like this." Olivia walked to the door. "I'm going to stop him."

"You're going to do what?" Hadley spluttered.

"The next flight to Anguilla leaves in an hour." She glanced at her watch. "I'll drive to the airport and tell him he's making a mistake. We can't celebrate my birthday without him."

"You'll do nothing of the sort," Hadley said. "What if Finn returns while you're gone?"

"I think it's a good idea," Felix interjected. "I'll go with you."

Hadley turned to Felix. "How can it be a good idea?"

"If Finn returns and Olivia is upset, things will get worse." He smiled at Olivia. "Besides, we've hardly had any time together. It will be lovely to drive to St. Jean at sunset."

"Would you like to come?" Olivia asked Hadley.

"I'm going to stay right here." Hadley clutched her drink. "When

Sebastian walks through the front door, he's going to get a welcome he'll never forget."

Hadley sat on the chaise longue and nibbled a slice of melon. Sebastian was the only person who could interrupt cocktail hour in St. Barts.

She gazed at the pink sun dipping behind the horizon and wondered if he was really on a plane. But he couldn't do that to Olivia. It would be worse than if he never came.

God! Sebastian created a mess. Finn and Olivia were fighting, and Felix questioned if anything was going on between her and Sebastian, and Olivia was more distraught than she'd ever seen her.

The letter to Olivia lay on the glass table and she picked it up. She read it again and placed it in the envelope. The evening breeze touched her shoulders and the air was filled with pollen and she wished Sebastian had never come.

Chapter Thirteen

OLIVIA SAT IN THE PASSENGER seat of Felix's convertible and smoothed her hair. The sun set over Colombier Beach and the sky was a pastel paint box. She watched seagulls skim over the water and thought it was one of the loveliest views in St. Barts.

She remembered when she was six years old and participated in a choir concert at school. The teacher promised she could kiss her mother goodbye after the performance. But after the children finished singing, the teacher led them straight to the classroom. When Hadley picked her up at the end of the day, Olivia flung herself in her arms and burst into tears.

Olivia adjusted her sunglasses and felt exactly the same. How could Sebastian leave without saying goodbye? She and Felix combed St. Jean's airport but he wasn't in the departure area or lounging near the coffee machine. The woman behind the counter apologized and said she couldn't give out passenger information.

She was still furious at Finn for disappearing but she knew he was hurt. And Sebastian wouldn't have left unless he was miserable.

"You're very quiet." Felix maneuvered around a curve. "You can't blame yourself for Sebastian leaving."

"He came all the way to St. Barts and didn't feel welcome," Olivia said. "He's my father, I should have put him before anything."

"Your mother would strongly disagree." Felix tried to smile.

"She thinks Sebastian only worries about himself, but she's wrong," she insisted. "Sebastian wouldn't have gone if he wasn't trying to protect me."

"Do you remember when I used to take you to Tamarin for lunch every year on your birthday?" Felix asked. "We'd leave Hadley at the villa and drive to Saline Beach. The first time we walked through the gate and saw the lush palm fronds and lily pads, you thought we entered a magical kingdom."

"I always hurried with dessert because I wanted to climb the tamarind tree," Olivia laughed. "It's over a hundred years old and the biggest on the island."

"Why don't we go now? I'm sure I can get a table and they serve a delicious lobster salad."

Olivia hesitated. "Won't Hadley be upset if we don't come back for dinner?"

Felix squeezed Olivia's hand. "I'm sure she'll understand."

The gravel walkway was lit with colored lights and flickering torches. There were wooden bridges and a turquoise parrot in a silver cage. Olivia glanced at elegant couples reclining against lime-green cushions and felt warm and happy.

"This was a wonderful idea." She slipped into a booth on the teak deck. The wood table was set with enamel china and gleaming silverware. There were beige linen napkins and a vase filled with daffodils.

"Your mother and I used to eat lunch here years ago and they held a fashion show between the tables," Felix recalled, eating a jumbo prawn. "The husbands were terrified their wives would add a Hermès scarf or Diane von Furstenberg wrap to their bill."

"I adore St. Barts and I'm grateful it is our home. But is it so terrible to want to see other places?" Olivia fiddled with her fork. "Hadley blames Sebastian but maybe he has a point. If I don't see the world now, when will I?"

"You're barely twenty-five," Felix said. "You could travel later with Finn."

"Finn is so busy at the law firm, it will be years before we take a long vacation." She paused. "Sebastian wanted to show me everything and it would have been the greatest adventure."

"When your mother and I got married, she didn't let me celebrate her birthday. She said for a child, the birthday was the most important day of the year and she didn't want to spoil it," he began. "I disagreed but then I saw how much you enjoyed your day: eating Esther's strawberry pancakes for breakfast and wearing a new dress at dinner. Hadley watched you blow out the candles, and she never looked so radiant. Sometimes you don't agree with your partner, but you still do what she asks."

"Are you saying I shouldn't have suggested going with Sebastian?" Olivia looked up.

"You have to be willing to listen to each other," Felix mused. "That's what marriage is all about."

They ate crab cream soup and veal with sweetbreads. Olivia sipped a cold chardonnay and suddenly missed Finn with a physical ache.

"I do love Finn but I don't want to hurt Sebastian's feelings," Olivia said, when the waiter replaced the plates with chocolate fondant in a raspberry sauce. "If I write to Sebastian and tell him I can't go away, he'll wonder why I changed my mind."

"Have I ever told you I tried to adopt you? You were ten years old and we hadn't heard from Sebastian in ages." Felix sipped his cognac. "Three days after my attorney sent a letter, I received a telegram from Sebastian that it was out of the question. I was never so happy to read a piece of yellow paper."

"You were happy he wouldn't let you adopt me?"

"Sebastian may have been absent but he loved you more than anything," he explained. "You have to put Finn first, Sebastian will understand."

"Do you think so?" Olivia's eyes were bright.

"We may be different but we have one thing in common." He nodded. "We love you and want you to be happy."

Olivia let out her breath and suddenly the night sky was a deeper shade of black and the stars sparkled like diamonds.

"I'm so lucky." She kissed him on the cheek. "I have two wonderful fathers."

After dinner they strolled through the lush gardens with their tropical birds and bright pelicans. There were pink flamingos and giant lizards and leathery turtles.

"I know where Finn is." She suddenly turned to Felix. "Could you drive me to Grand Cul de Sac?"

"What are you going to do at the beach in the dark?" Felix frowned.

"You'll see." Olivia strode toward the car. "It's terribly important."

Olivia glanced at Finn's yellow Mini Cooper and slipped off her sandals. The cove was flanked by sharp cliffs and tall palm trees. She ran down the craggy path and tried to stop her heart from pounding.

They had spent many lazy afternoons snorkeling in the green water and admiring the neon-colored fish. But now the ocean was gray and a cool breeze touched her shoulders. She saw Finn crouched on the sand and caught her breath.

"What are you doing here?" Finn stood. His cheeks were pale and there were deep lines on his forehead.

"Felix dropped me off," she said. "We went to the airport to find Sebastian. He's gone."

"Sebastian left St. Barts?"

"He thought he caused too much trouble," she said and her eyes filled with tears. "He wanted to leave before things got worse."

"If you came to blame me, I'm sorry your father didn't feel welcome." He stuffed his hands in his pockets. "But I don't want to talk about it."

"That's not why I'm here," Olivia answered. "I came to feed the sea turtles."

"You did what?"

"Do you remember the first time we visited St. Barts? We swam at Grand Cul de Sac and spread our towels on the sand. We both fell asleep and woke up to something nibbling our toes. I was terrified until we realized it was a couple of sea turtles.

"We named them Antony and Cleopatra and fed them orange slices and bits of vegetables. We visited them every day and they seemed so content with their thick shells baking in the sun.

"I'd rather stay in this cove with you than be anywhere else," she said. "I adored having Sebastian here, he is my father. But I love you and want to spend the rest of our lives together."

Finn drew her in his arms and kissed her. She kissed him back and her heart swelled. She was right where she belonged and they were in love.

Finn reached into his pocket and pulled out the black velvet jewelry box.

"I need to do this again. I forgot the most important part." He dropped to his knee. "I didn't put the ring on your finger."

"You can do it now," she whispered.

Finn slipped the ring on her finger and stood up. He kissed her and she wrapped her arms around him. Her nerves tingled and her whole body was on fire.

He picked her up and carried her across the beach. The sky was full of stars and the sand was soft as butter. There was a cluster of palm trees and the lights of St. Jean twinkled in the distance.

"Finn! What are you doing?" she asked when he put her down.

"I'm going to make love to my new fiancée," he whispered, un- zipping her dress. His hands slid between her thighs and she felt moist and dizzy.

"God, I want you," she murmured, clinging to his shoulders.

He leaned down and kissed her between her legs. The small ache became an incredible longing and a delicious wetness formed inside her.

"I love you," Finn whispered.

He stripped off his shirt and laid it on the sand. He pulled her down and stroked her nipples. Her body arched and she couldn't wait any longer.

She opened her legs and drew him inside her. The waves lapped against the shore and she wanted it to last forever. Then Finn pulled her arms over her head and it became unbearable. Finn cried out and everything disappeared and all that was left was one glorious sensation.

Olivia lay on the white sand and waited until her breathing ebbed. Sand clung to her hair and she never felt so happy.

"I've missed this so much," Finn groaned, resting on his elbow.

"We can share a bedroom now that we're engaged," Olivia suggested. "Felix and Hadley would understand."

"Certainly not," he said and smiled. "Our daughter isn't sleeping in the same room with a guy until they exchange wedding vows."

"You're going to be a strict father," Olivia laughed.

Finn sat up and ran his hands through his hair. His chest was slick and his muscles gleamed in the moonlight.

"I thought about it all day and I understand why Sebastian came to St. Barts. I can't imagine what love is like between a father and daughter."

"But you were so angry at him," Olivia started.

"I had to fight for you." His blue eyes dimmed. "You're the most important thing and I can't live without you."

Olivia touched her lips to his and felt young and vital.

"I know what you mean." She nodded. "You're everything I want."

Olivia sat in the passenger seat of the yellow Mini Cooper and gazed out the window. Finn had gone into the market to buy hot coffee and fresh fruit and hard cheese.

It had been glorious making love on the beach and it was wonderful to stop arguing. She admired the emerald-cut diamond ring and felt light and happy.

But then she pictured Sebastian in his straw hat and silk shirt and a lump formed in her throat. A small plane flew overhead and she wondered if he was on it. He couldn't leave without saying good-bye; that was worse than anything.

She thought of everything they had done in the last couple of days: drunk rhum vanille at the Pipiri Palace and gone scuba diving at Pain du Sucre and eaten lunch at Sand Bar. Could she let him disappear when she'd waited so long for him to arrive?

And what about all the places he'd promised to show her: tea plantations in Tibet and caves in Micronesia and jungles in Africa? But if she wrote to him, Finn would be furious. And what were a few weeks of adventure when what she needed was a lifetime of memories.

She made her decision and would have to live with it. The car door opened and Finn slid into the driver's seat. He handed her a paper cup and kissed her.

"You're shivering, are you all right?" he asked.

She inhaled the scent of sand and sex and dark coffee and bit her lip.

"I'm perfect," she said and sipped her drink. "I'm just excited that tomorrow is my birthday."

Chapter Fourteen

HADLEY ENTERED THE LIVING ROOM and walked to the marble bar. She didn't feel like polishing silverware or arranging flowers in a crystal vase. She needed a large vodka.

Every time Sebastian did something—insist he stay in the guest room, invite Olivia and Finn to Costa Rica, convince Olivia to spend the summer with him—she thought it couldn't get worse. But nothing was as bad as leaving a note and disappearing. Whatever harm he caused by staying was nothing compared to how Olivia would feel if he deserted her again.

Then she pictured the way he looked at Olivia and something softened inside her. Could Sebastian have finally grown up and be acting selflessly?

Olivia and Finn would make up now that he was gone. And she and Felix could spend a quiet evening alone. They would drink Tia Maria in the library and talk about everything bottled up inside her: why they weren't sharing a bedroom and how the duplex was so quiet at night she could hear her own heartbeat.

She filled a glass with Absolut and sat on the silk sofa. Maybe it was good that Sebastian had been in St. Barts. He was like an antibiotic that doesn't seem to do anything at all. It is only a few days later when your skin is clear and your fever is gone that you realize it worked perfectly.

Olivia and Finn had to learn how to have a disagreement. And she must talk to Felix. There was nothing more important than communication in a marriage. She sipped her drink and remembered when she and Felix were first together. She and Olivia were the most important people in Felix's life and he would do anything to protect them.

"It is breathtaking." Hadley had peered out the window of Felix's Mercedes. The house had white columns and a stone porch and gray slate roof. There was a fountain and green lawns rolling down to the river.

Felix's parents had invited them to their estate on the Hudson River. Hadley thought about everything Felix had told her: that his mother insisted everyone dress for dinner and there were three sizes of salad forks. She hadn't been so frightened since she'd walked into a spiderweb in Vietnam.

"I've always loved the house." Felix reached over and squeezed her hand. "When we were children we used to pick apples in the orchard and skate in the ballroom."

"Can I skate in the ballroom?" Olivia asked, pressing her face against the glass. She wore a striped smock and her blond hair was knotted in a pigtail.

"I'll take you," Felix said and smiled. "Though don't tell my mother. She thought we were practicing our dancing."

Hadley waited for Felix to open the passenger door and gulped. It was late summer and she and Felix had been dating for three months. For the first time since Sebastian left, she didn't have a weight on her shoulders. But he described his mother, Carolyn, as a cross between Babe Paley and Eleanor Roosevelt and Hadley was terrified.

"There you are." A tall woman stood on the porch. She wore a crepe dress and leather pumps. Diamond earrings dangled in her ears and a gold Chopard watch adorned her wrist.

"You must be Hadley," she said and turned to Felix. "I understand what you see. She is quite beautiful."

"Hadley is standing right here." Felix flushed. "And this is her daughter, Olivia."

"Olivia, it's nice to meet you." She held out her hand.

"My mother bought me new sandals." Olivia twisted her hair ribbon. "I'm going to wear them to dinner."

Carolyn patted her hair and smiled. "I would love to see them another time. We don't wear sandals in the dining room."

"I'm surprised she didn't check my teeth to see if I'm suitable for breeding." Hadley placed her overnight bag on the dresser. Her room had a canopied bed and a chintz armchair and a balcony overlooking the river.

"My mother is like most well-bred New Yorkers: her bark is worse than her bite." Felix kissed her. "Wait until she discovers your warmth and kindness. She'll fall in love with you like I did."

Hadley inhaled his musk aftershave and sighed. Felix was never afraid to say he loved her and when they were together she felt perfectly safe.

"If she sees us kissing, she'll put me on the first train to Grand Central Station." She pulled away. "I'm going to make sure Olivia is settled. Her bedroom is bigger than our apartment."

"I'll meet you at dinner." Felix walked to the door. "And don't let her intimidate you. You could wear a cotton dress and belong at the table."

Hadley glanced around the dining room at the high-back velvet chairs and crystal chandeliers and the signed Degas on the wall. Damask curtains covered French doors and a cherry sideboard was set with gold candelabras.

She wore a black Donna Karan dress she'd bought at a Bloomingdale's sale but still felt underdressed. Carolyn wore a red hostess gown and ruby earrings. Felix's father sat at one end of the long mahogany table and Olivia fiddled with her hair ribbon.

"Felix told me you grew up in Connecticut," Carolyn said, eating potatoes au gratin. There were platters of baked venison and summer squash. A silver tureen held asparagus soup and there was a basket of baguettes.

"I went to Miss Porter's School." Hadley nodded, hoping Olivia's soup wouldn't end up in her lap.

"That's an excellent school." Carolyn beamed. "Close friends of ours sent their daughters there. Perhaps you know them."

"We lived on campus. My father is a history teacher and my mother works in the library," Hadley continued. "It was a magical place to grow up."

"I see." Carolyn turned pale as if the cream in the soup was slightly off. "You probably moved in different circles. You wouldn't know them after all."

"Hadley works at an art gallery in Chelsea," Felix cut in. "She's very knowledgeable about modern art."

"I love what I do." Hadley flushed. "There's nothing more exciting than pairing a collector with the right piece."

"My father is an artist, his name is Sebastian Miller," Olivia announced. "He sent me this necklace for my birthday."

"It's lovely, you're a lucky young lady." Carolyn admired the bead necklace.

"He doesn't live with us anymore," Olivia explained. "He and my mother are divorced."

Carolyn put down her fork and smoothed her hair. "We don't talk about divorce at dinner."

"When do we talk about it?" Olivia asked.

Carolyn sipped her wine and frowned. "We don't talk about it at all."

"I'm sorry for the way my mother behaved," Felix said when they were sitting on the back porch. His parents had gone to visit friends and Olivia was looking at a storybook in her bedroom. "She means well, she's just led an insular life."

"She was protecting her son." Hadley smiled. "When Olivia is older, I'll inspect every boyfriend like an army general."

"I want to ask you something," he said, taking her hand.

Hadley felt his palm on hers and gulped. They hadn't talked about their future but Felix was almost thirty and anxious to get married. But Sebastian had left only ten months ago; was she ready to try something new?

"I know your life is full with Olivia and the gallery but I've enjoyed these few months. You are beautiful and bright and everything is better when we're together." He reached into his pocket and took out a blue Tiffany box. "Hadley, will you marry me?"

Hadley gazed at the emerald-cut diamond and gasped. Felix

was kind and generous and adored Olivia. How could she say no, when he was everything she wished for?

"Yes," she whispered. "Yes, I'll marry you."

Felix slipped the ring on her finger and kissed her. Hadley kissed him back and a warmth spread through her chest.

"We have to tell Olivia," Hadley said and suddenly couldn't stop smiling. She'd found someone to love and they were going to be a family.

"I already told her," Felix admitted.

"You told Olivia we were getting married before you asked me?" Hadley stammered.

"I explained you might say no but I had to ask her permission," Felix said. "If she didn't want me as a stepfather we couldn't get married at all. I love you more than anything, but Olivia is a child. She has to come first."

Hadley gazed at Felix's light brown hair and blue eyes and wondered how she got so lucky. It didn't matter if his mother was a little icy or all his shirts were monogrammed, they were going to have a wonderful future.

She took Felix's hand and stood up. "Let's tell her together. She's going to be so excited to be a flower girl."

Now Hadley plumped the silk cushions in the living room and thought whatever was wrong between her and Felix, they had to fix it. They couldn't let their marriage falter like a sailboat without a breeze.

The doorbell rang and she jumped up. She opened the door and saw a man wearing a navy shirt and carrying a leather briefcase.

"Can I help you?" she asked.

"I'm Robert Hunter, the art appraiser." He held out his hand. "I'm here to appraise the Sebastian Miller painting."

"I beg your pardon?" Hadley frowned. "You must be mistaken. I didn't order an appraisal."

"Your husband called," he explained. "He said it's quite valuable and you're only at the villa a few weeks a year."

"That's very odd. He never suggested it before," she pondered. "But I suppose he's right. Please come in. The painting is in the library."

Hadley led him down the tile hallway and turned on the light. *The Miller Girls* really was a wonderful painting. Olivia was gorgeous with her smooth cheeks and green eyes and pale blond hair. And Sebastian had captured the magic of the African plain: color and light so rich, you felt elated and empty at the same time.

"Do you always make appointments in the evening?" Hadley perched on a leather armchair.

"I was having dinner in Gustavia." He took out a clipboard. "Your husband said he was leaving the day after tomorrow. Now was the only time he was available."

"He said he was leaving the day after tomorrow?" Hadley inquired. "Did he say anything else?"

"Only that it was an important piece." The appraiser paused. "I've read about *The Miller Girls*. The artist was offered half a million dollars for it early in his career and turned it down. It's been in a private collection ever since."

"Half a million dollars!" Hadley exclaimed. "When exactly did my husband call you?"

"About half an hour ago." Robert looked at his watch. "He said he'd meet me here."

"I'll wait in the living room." Hadley walked to the door. "I want to direct him to the library as soon as he arrives."

She entered the living room and tried to stop shaking. Of course Sebastian hadn't left, that was wishful thinking. And why was he having *The Miller Girls* appraised? She heard footsteps and turned around.

"This is a pleasant sight. I'd rather see you drinking a cocktail than ironing the drapes." Sebastian stood in the doorway. He wore his straw hat and carried a leather bag. "I didn't tell you how lovely you looked in that dress this morning. The turquoise brings out your eyes."

"I thought you were on a plane to Anguilla," she said, instinctively touching her hair.

"I went to the airport but the flight was delayed." He walked to the bar and poured a glass of vodka. "A part had to be flown in from Nassau. Those small planes are as flimsy as the toy airplanes I built as a child."

"Why didn't you wait in the departure lounge?" she asked. "You could have saved on taxi fare."

"The ticket taker said it was quarantined due to a case of chicken pox." He paused. "I never had it and you can't be too careful."

"Quarantined?" Hadley gasped. "I must call Olivia. She and Felix drove to the airport to find you."

Sebastian downed his vodka and gulped. "Olivia followed me to the airport?"

"I don't believe you! You never went to the airport at all," Hadley fumed. "How could you pretend that you were leaving? Olivia was distraught."

"I wanted to leave. The thought of Olivia being upset about Finn made me want to cut my heart out." He fiddled with his glass. "But I abandoned her once and I can't do it again."

"Are you sure you don't have a case of island fever?" Hadley seethed. "I didn't think Sebastian Miller had a decent bone in his body."

"For the last twenty years I thought life was about painting and traveling to exotic locations. God! I wouldn't have it any other way. When you climb to the top of Mount Fuji you feel like you can do anything. But being in St. Barts changed me." He looked at Hadley. "I've seen what it's like to be part of a family."

"I don't know what you mean," Hadley retorted. "All that's happened is Finn and Olivia aren't speaking and Felix is uncomfortable in his own home."

"Every family has skirmishes. But at the end of the day you all sit on the patio and sip piña coladas. You care about each other and I've never experienced that before."

"You had a wife and daughter who loved you," Hadley said sharply.

"I suppose you're right. It was so long ago," he sighed. "I know I've caused a bit of trouble, but I'd like to stay for Olivia's birthday."

"Olivia already thought you left." She frowned. "I think it's better if you went to Anguilla."

"Think about Olivia. She would want me here to help blow out the candles," he insisted. "She's been dreaming about it since she was a girl."

"Now you're playing the concerned father. It's a very convincing role," Hadley laughed. "By the way, why did you call an appraiser and why does he think *The Miller Girls* is worth half a million dollars?"

"I may have mentioned the price to a journalist years ago. It made a more interesting story." Sebastian shrugged. "And you must get the painting insured. Anyone could walk in and take it off the wall."

"It's my painting. I can do with it whatever I like." She raised her eyebrow. "You better talk to the appraiser. Felix won't be happy if he gets the bill."

"Did I hear my name?" Felix entered the living room. He glanced at Sebastian and frowned. "What are you doing here? I thought you were on a plane to Anguilla."

"The plane was delayed," Sebastian explained. "Those puddle jumpers are as reliable as the Chinese subway system. There's always some part breaking off."

"Where's Olivia?" Hadley asked.

"I dropped her off at Grand Cul de Sac." Felix smiled. "I think she and Finn are going to make up."

"Well, I'm glad to hear it, I was concerned I caused too much trouble." Sebastian sighed with relief. "Apparently young love is stronger than I thought."

"Olivia was very upset. But they are a great couple and it will take more than a few squabbles to separate them." Felix looked at Sebastian. "Olivia has been through enough. She already thought you left. I think it's best if you weren't here when she and Finn return."

"We were just discussing that." Sebastian perched on a floral love seat. "Hadley agreed that Olivia would want me to be at her birthday dinner."

Hadley jumped up. "I never said anything of the sort."

"Maybe not in so many words. But your eyes got misty and your mouth trembled," Sebastian explained. "I'm an artist. I'm good at interpreting body language."

"It's not my first choice. But if Hadley thinks it's important to Olivia, we can forgive you one last time," Felix relented. "You can attend her dinner but I don't think you should stay at the villa." He scooped up a handful of pistachio nuts. "Perhaps you can stay with Eric and his wife at their hotel suite if all the other hotels are booked."

"That's an excellent plan." Hadley gathered her keys. "I'll drive Sebastian myself."

"I'm afraid you can't get out. There's a car blocking the driveway," Felix said to Hadley. "Did we invite someone to dinner?"

"I didn't get a chance to tell you. Sebastian ordered an appraisal of *The Miller Girls*." She smoothed her skirt. "He thinks someone could steal it from under our nose."

"That is a good idea." Felix nodded. "I've been meaning to do it for years."

"The appraiser is in the library." Sebastian turned to Felix. "While he's here you should have him look at the Andrew Wyeth sketch. It could be worth the price of a small car."

"What Andrew Wyeth sketch?" Felix asked.

"Last night I ate dinner alone in the study." Sebastian paused. "I was looking for a pad and pencil and discovered it in the desk drawer. I think it's from his 'Mill' series. Didn't you know it was there?"

"I never poke around the furniture. But it's entirely possible." Felix rubbed his forehead. "My parents used to have parties with artists and writers. I remember my father mentioning Andrew Wyeth but he never said anything about a sketch."

"Andy probably brought it as a housewarming present." Sebastian took Felix's arm. "I'll introduce you to the appraiser. Afterward I'll tell you about the time I stayed at Andy's farm in Maine. He had such an affinity with the landscape. No one captured American provincial in the same way."

Hadley watched them walk down the hallway and bit her lip. She knew exactly what Sebastian was doing. By the time they finished discussing art, Felix would suggest Sebastian stay in the guest room.

She heard a car and ran to the entry. Finn stepped out of the Mini Cooper and opened Olivia's door.

"Darling," Hadley said and smiled. "I'm so glad you're both here."

"We couldn't find Sebastian. He's gone." Olivia entered the hallway. Her cheeks were flushed and her blond hair was tucked behind her ears.

"I was terribly upset but you'll never guess what happened. Finn and I made up and he gave me this." Olivia held out her hand. "We're engaged and I've never been so happy."

"It's stunning," Hadley gasped, admiring the sparkling diamond ring. "Felix will open a bottle of champagne and we'll celebrate."

"Where is Felix?" Olivia wondered. "I wanted to thank him for a wonderful evening."

Hadley walked to the bar and poured two glasses of scotch. She handed them to Finn and Olivia and waved at the sofa. "I think you better sit down."

"Did anything happen to Felix?" Olivia asked. "He had a couple of glasses of wine at dinner and the roads are so treacherous."

"Felix is perfectly safe." Hadley looked up. "He's in the library with Sebastian."

"Sebastian!" Olivia exclaimed. "But he left a note. We searched the airport and he was already gone."

"Apparently he changed his mind." Hadley paused. "He wants to stay for your birthday dinner."

"I didn't think I was going to see him again." Olivia's eyes watered. "Of course I want him to stay but . . ."

"He may be your father but he's caused you a lot of trauma," Hadley urged. "You're entitled to ask him to leave."

"I wouldn't dream of it. I want Sebastian here more than anything."

"My god! Look who's here." Sebastian appeared in the doorway. "I was getting a scotch and soda for the appraiser. You two are positively glowing. Having a small argument agrees with you."

"I'm glad you're back." Olivia kissed Sebastian on the cheek. "Felix and I combed St. Jean airport and couldn't find you."

"I'm terribly sorry. I'd stab myself in the heart if I could take back the trouble I caused. I came to make amends and instead made everything worse. I never meant to hurt you, you're the most important thing in the world." Sebastian's eyes were dark. "If you can forgive me, I'd love to stay for your birthday dinner."

"Of course you're going to stay," Olivia insisted. "Finn will take your bag upstairs."

Sebastian glanced at Olivia's hand and whistled. "Is that what I think it is? The cut is exquisite and the clarity is first class. I've never seen such an exceptional ring."

"I designed it myself," Finn admitted. "I wanted something elegant and timeless."

"You succeeded. This calls for a toast." Sebastian nodded. "Where does Felix keep his best cognac?"

"Don't you touch his Rémy Martin," Hadley warned Sebastian. "Felix is going to open a bottle of Dom Pérignon."

"That's even better." Sebastian smiled. "It's a beautiful night, why don't we sit on the patio? Felix and Olivia ate dinner but I bet the rest of us are starving. I'll rustle up some jumbo prawns and tartar sauce."

Hadley followed Sebastian into the kitchen. "You've made the last few days impossible for everyone; if it were up to me I'd insist you leave. But it is Olivia's birthday and she wants you to stay." She took a deep breath. "If you create any more mischief, I will tie you up and toss you off the side of a speedboat." She paused. "Nothing will make me happier than seeing you sink into the ocean."

They sat at the glass table on the patio and ate succulent prawns and crusty bread. There was sliced mango and caramboles. Hadley inhaled the scent of cut grass and freesia.

"I'd like to make a toast." Sebastian stood. "When I arrived in St. Barts, I congratulated Olivia on bypassing young thugs and heartless playboys and finding a prince. The last couple of days have been challenging but Finn passed with flying colors. I'm so happy that they're engaged.

"When Olivia was young, I wished for one thing: that I could put her in a bottle and stop time," he chuckled. "If I figured out how to do that, I could buy the whole island. The next best thing is to see Olivia become a poised young woman. She's exactly like her mother so I'm confident she chose the right man." He turned to Finn and Olivia. "I wish you a lifetime of happiness. Now I think I should turn the floor over to someone who really deserves it." He pointed to Felix. "The man who raised Olivia."

Felix stood up and fiddled with his glass.

"I'd be lying if I didn't admit tensions have run high the last few days. My wife's ex-husband and father of my stepdaughter makes for an unlikely house guest. I haven't been thrilled with all of Sebastian's actions since he arrived, but I can't complain because he gave me the two things I value most." He paused. "Being Hadley's husband is the high point of my life but being Olivia's father is even more. Olivia has taught me what it's like to love without needing a return. Seeing her blossom into a gracious young woman is its own reward. The best moment in a parent's life is when your child finds someone who loves her as much as you do. Olivia found that in Finn and I know they are going to be extremely happy."

Felix kissed Olivia on the cheek and Hadley blinked back sudden tears. Sebastian patted Felix on the back and turned to Olivia.

"How could I forget," Sebastian said suddenly, reaching into his leather bag. "I have a gift for the happy couple."

"How did you know we were getting engaged?" Olivia opened the parcel and took out a brightly colored woven blanket.

"It was given to me by the Basotho people in Lesotho," Sebastian explained. "It's a tiny village so high in the hills it's called the 'roof of Africa.'

"I've always believed that the bed is the most important place in a marriage. It's where you talk about your goals and imagine anything is possible." He pointed to the purple fabric. "See the ear of corn? It's the symbol of fertility and good fortune."

"They're barely engaged," Hadley murmured, twisting her necklace. "It's a little early to talk about grandchildren."

"I think it's wonderful." Olivia hugged Sebastian. "It's our first present and we'll keep it forever."

"I'll get the coffees." Hadley stood. "I told Esther she could go home early."

She crossed the patio and saw Sebastian walk to the swimming pool. The moon glinted on his hair and tears streamed down his cheeks. Hadley started toward him and then changed her mind and hurried into the kitchen.

Hadley rinsed plates in the sink and hummed "Fly Me to the Moon." Olivia and Finn had gone to Bonito for aperitifs and Felix and Sebastian were in the library.

"I haven't heard that song in thirty years," Sebastian said as he entered the kitchen. "I thought having raised a daughter you'd be into hip-hop and rap. Don't all mothers acquire their children's musical tastes because it's the only thing they hear on the radio?"

"What are you doing here?" Hadley asked.

"Felix and the appraiser were discussing Fauvism." He shrugged. "I thought I'd make myself useful."

"I don't need help." Hadley turned back to the sink. "I'm loading everything into the dishwasher."

"I love doing the dishes." He picked up a dish towel. "Don't you remember what a good team we were at the guesthouse in Cape Town?"

"You sat around reading *Ladies' Home Journal* while I did all the work," Hadley retorted. "My fingers were shriveled and yours were as smooth as a baby's."

"I made you laugh. I used to read the 'Dear Abby' column out loud and you came up with answers." His green eyes flickered. "Can you imagine being so young and thinking you know everything?"

"We didn't invent the aging process," she said sarcastically. "It's a natural progression."

"We think we get wiser when we're older but that's not true," he continued. "Most people mistake wisdom for giving up and settling for less."

"I'm not interested in your self-pitying pop psychology," she answered. "Just because your daughter is getting married doesn't mean your life is over. As soon as you arrive in Anguilla, you'll be surrounded by people admiring your talent and lapping up your stories."

"I wasn't talking about myself," Sebastian said.

"What do you mean?" she looked up.

"I was thinking about you. Things aren't going to change by themselves; if you are unhappy you have to change them."

"The only thing I want to change is the linen in the guest bedroom after you leave." She wiped her hands. "Excuse me. I'm going to see if Felix wants more coffee."

Hadley entered the study and took a deep breath. Felix had gone to bed and Sebastian had walked to Gustavia for cigarettes. She slipped off her sandals and was suddenly tired. Finn and Olivia were finally engaged and there was so much to do.

If they could get through tomorrow, Sebastian would leave and she could talk to Felix. It was impossible to discuss anything with Sebastian hovering like a firefly.

She turned off the light and noticed Olivia's new African blanket. She pulled it over her shoulders and fell asleep.

Chapter Fifteen

OLIVIA LEANED OVER THE BALCONY and felt the breeze touch her cheeks. The sky was bright blue and the sea was cut glass. Goats grazed on the hill and yachts gleamed in the harbor and she was glad to be in St. Barts on her birthday.

Last night had been magical. Making love on the beach with Finn was glorious and the emerald-cut diamond ring was everything she imagined. But then she pictured Sebastian's toast on the patio and a lump formed in her throat.

If only she and Sebastian could travel together this summer. But Finn had been so angry; she couldn't mention it again. The last thing she wanted was to start another fight when they were so happy.

She had so much to look forward to: the ceremony at St. Bartholomew's and the reception at the villa. Fairy lights would be strung across the lawn and there would be a black-and-white dance floor over the swimming pool. They'd drive off in Felix's convertible and spend the night in the honeymoon suite of Le Toiny.

She slipped on her sandals and ran down the staircase. Hadley stood at the kitchen counter, slicing peaches. She wore a blouse and capris and her blond hair loose.

"It's your birthday too." Olivia kissed her mother on the cheek. "You should be reclining against silk pillows. Felix will bring you Esther's homemade pancakes and fresh papaya juice."

"The weather is too nice to stay in bed." Hadley looked up. "I think Felix is at the flower market. He had a smile on his face and wouldn't tell me where he was going."

"Finn left early on some mysterious errand," Olivia laughed. "Aren't we lucky that our men are so romantic?"

"Everything has turned out perfectly," Hadley agreed. "In twenty-four hours Sebastian will be gone and we can relax. It will be like one of those miraculous survival stories in *People* magazine."

"You're too harsh on Sebastian," Olivia replied. "His toast was wonderful and he gave us a fabulous present."

"Sebastian was on fire last night. But I still don't trust him," Hadley mused. "I'll be happy when he's sitting on the airplane and we're waving goodbye from the terminal."

"I don't want to think about Sebastian leaving. I'd rather talk about the wedding." Olivia bit into a plum. "Finn is so excited. We drank vanilla vodka and passion fruit liqueur at Bonito and he couldn't stop looking at my ring. He can't believe we're engaged."

"When you're engaged everything is new and thrilling. Felix and I tasted lobster mousse at the Carlyle and German chocolate cake at Sylvia Weinstock," Hadley recalled. "In the evenings we pored over linen samples and it was so much fun."

"I'm going to make appointments at Vera Wang and Dior." Olivia turned away so Hadley couldn't see the tears in her eyes. "You must come with me and afterward we'll have afternoon tea at the

Plaza. We haven't done that in years and I miss their smoked salmon sandwiches."

"Darling, are you all right?" Hadley asked. "You don't look like a bride whose head is swirling with images of chiffon dresses and Tiffany favors."

"Last night when Finn proposed, everything was perfect," Olivia explained. "But then Sebastian gave his toast and I felt guilty. I'm all he has and now he's leaving."

"If that's what you're worried about you can relax," Hadley laughed. "Sebastian is like a character in a Jane Austen novel. His champagne flute will never be empty and there will always be a down-filled pillow under his head."

"Sebastian has missed dozens of birthdays. There must be another reason he came," Olivia insisted. "He's getting older and doesn't like being alone."

"I tossed and turned all night wondering why he's really here," Hadley agreed. "The Sebastian I knew would never let Finn derail his plans. But I couldn't come up with anything and all I got was a headache."

"I suppose you are right," Olivia sighed. "I feel terrible. He was going to show me so many wonderful places and I let him down."

"I'll tell you what you can do. Take him this tray of fruit salad and whole wheat toast," Hadley suggested. "I'd rather not start my birthday looking at Sebastian over a bowl of sliced peaches."

"That is a good idea." Olivia picked up the tray. "I'll ask him if he wants to go for a swim."

"Afterward go to Lilly Pulitzer and buy a dress for this evening," Hadley said and smiled. "It is your birthday and there's nothing like a new outfit to make your eyes sparkle."

Olivia knocked on Sebastian's door and smoothed her hair. She knocked again and opened the door. The bed was rumpled and a linen shirt was flung over an armchair.

She entered the room and noticed a Matisse biography on the bedside table. There was a stack of magazines and a ceramic mug. She placed the tray on the mahogany desk and an envelope dropped on the floor.

She picked it up and realized it was Sebastian's plane ticket to Anguilla. She looked more closely and her heart raced. There were two tickets wedged between the pages of his passport.

She stuffed the passport back in the envelope and gasped. He'd bought another ticket and he was going to ask her to join him.

For a moment she felt light and happy. Sebastian wanted her to go to Anguilla! But Finn wouldn't stay in St. Barts alone. And Sebastian should never have done such a thing without asking her.

The door opened and Sebastian entered. He wore his straw hat and a newspaper was folded under his arm.

"I must be dreaming. There's a glowing birthday girl in my room holding a tray of fruit salad and mango juice."

"Hadley asked me to bring it up." Olivia flushed. "She thought you'd prefer eating on your own private terrace."

"Your mother is so considerate." Sebastian took the tray from Olivia and buttered a slice of toast. "What I need is a bowl of congee. It's Chinese porridge and it's the perfect cure for a hangover. All that champagne and cognac left me with a pounding headache."

"I'm sure there's a bottle of aspirin in the bathroom," she suggested.

"I already looked. Did you know that in South Africa they eat an ostrich egg omelet to cure a hangover? And in Vietnam they believe rhinoceros horns can cure everything from hangovers to cancer." He paused. "It's a pity we won't travel together this summer. There was so much I was going to show you."

"Finn called his mother last night, and she is already planning an engagement party." Olivia hesitated. "But perhaps we can join you for a week. Capri sounds stunning and Finn loves fettuccine marinara."

"I'm not going to Capri," Sebastian answered. "I decided I'm going to spend three months at an ashram in Tibet. There's no cellphone reception or Internet and all your meals are eaten in silence."

"But I thought you had a commission in Capri."

"It didn't work out." He shrugged. "I've intruded enough in your life for the time being, it's better if I disappear. Finn will be a lot happier if he knows my number can't pop up on your phone. Don't worry, there is mail service. Though the post is delivered by yak and it takes longer in the rainy season."

"You must visit Manhattan before you go!" Olivia exclaimed. "You can stay in my apartment and I'll sleep on the sofa. We'll eat apple cinnamon pancakes at Balthazar and drink vodka gimlets at the Four Seasons and it will be a proper vacation."

"That's the best invitation since a French comte asked me to stay at his country estate." He brushed crumbs from his shirt. "But I don't have time. The ashram session starts the first week of May and they frown on late arrivals. I'm going to leave straight from Anguilla."

"You are?" Olivia felt the air leave her lungs.

"Have you been to Anguilla?" he asked. "You can ride horseback into the ocean and the spa at the Viceroy hotel gives Blue Tranquility massages. I'm going to paint and eat crayfish and sip rum punch."

"It sounds wonderful." Olivia fiddled with her earrings. "The summer will go by quickly and the fall is always busy at the gallery. December will arrive faster than we can imagine."

"December?" Sebastian rubbed his forehead.

"It will be so festive with the boat parade and colored lights in all the boutiques." She stopped and her green eyes were huge. "You *are* coming to the wedding?"

"The wedding!" Sebastian put down his glass. "It's just that . . ."

"That what?" Olivia inquired.

"Never mind," Sebastian said and smiled. "How could you even ask? Of course I wouldn't miss your and Finn's wedding."

Olivia strolled along the Rue de Roi Oscar II and shielded her eyes from the sun. Usually she loved looking in the window of Black Swan with its French bikinis and brightly colored sarongs. She could spend hours sifting through jeweled caftans at Poupette and admiring rope handbags at Lolita Jaca.

But she thought about the two tickets wedged into Sebastian's passport and her stomach turned. If Sebastian asked Olivia to go to Anguilla, Finn would be furious. And why had Sebastian hesitated when she mentioned the wedding?

She passed Calypso with its striped men's shirts and European loafers. She should be angry with Sebastian: he'd showed up after twenty years and almost ruined her engagement. But she pictured his green eyes and cocky smile and felt a pang in her chest. When he was around, the world was full of possibilities.

She entered Marina and gazed at the Chloé dresses and Calvin Klein shifts. There were Tory Burch sandals and Gucci moccasins as smooth as butter.

"Can I help you?" the saleswoman asked. "We have Façonnable wraps that are perfect for the beach and Lanvin tunics that are wonderful for lounging around the pool."

"I was looking for a cocktail dress," Olivia explained. "It's my twenty-fifth birthday and we're having dinner at Maya's."

"I adore Maya's! The grilled sole is mouthwatering and the orange sorbet is the best on the island. The last time I was there, Johnny Depp was at the next table with his wife." She glanced at Olivia's blond hair and high cheekbones. "You want something fabulous that compliments your complexion."

She handed Olivia a green Courrèges sheath and silver sandals. Olivia zipped it up and glanced in the mirror. The color brought out her eyes and the cut was elegant and sophisticated.

"You could be on the cover of *Vogue*," the woman commented. "Wear your hair in a chignon and add diamond earrings. You'll look like a French movie star."

"I do like it." Olivia turned in front of the glass. "I think I'll take it."

"What a gorgeous ring," the woman said as she glanced at her hand.

"Thank you. I just got engaged yesterday." Olivia flushed. "I'm not used to seeing it on my finger."

"It's your twenty-fifth birthday and you're engaged," she said and smiled. "People on St. Barts are so lucky. They seem to have everything."

Olivia thought the saleswoman was right; she was worrying about nothing. Sebastian hadn't mentioned Anguilla and he said he wouldn't miss their wedding. It was her birthday and they were going to have a delicious dinner.

"I do love birthdays." She took out her charge card. "Everyone spoils you and the whole day is perfect."

Olivia stepped onto the sidewalk and saw Finn leaning against the railing. His sunglasses were propped on his forehead and he clutched a bouquet of tulips.

"What are you doing in Gustavia?" Olivia asked.

"Hadley said you went shopping." He kissed her. "I wanted to give you a present."

"You already gave me a diamond ring," she laughed. "I don't need anything else."

"Come with me." He took her hand. "You're going to like it."

Finn drove along the winding roads and Olivia caught her breath. Clouds scudded across the sky and the sea was an Impressionist painting: all clear water and pastel-colored boats and white sand beaches.

The car pulled around a curve and she wondered what they were doing at Le Toiny. It was the most exclusive hotel in St. Barts, with its own coconut grove and pineapple orchard. Cottages with tin roofs climbed the hill and there were sweeping palm trees.

Finn stopped in front of the canopied entrance and turned off the engine.

"I thought about getting a suite, but we'd never get out of bed. And if we ate lunch at Le Gaiac, we wouldn't be hungry for dinner," he turned to Olivia. "We're going to spend the afternoon in the Spa Cottage."

"The Spa Cottage?" Olivia repeated.

"I read the brochure and it sounds fantastic." Finn's blue eyes sparkled. "You can have a hot shell massage or coconut rub and milk ritual wrap."

"It sounds heavenly. But what are you going to do while I'm lathered in lotions?" she said and laughed.

He tucked her blond hair behind her ear and kissed her. "I'm going to eat avocado bruschetta by the pool and wait for you to join me."

Olivia slipped on a cotton robe and knotted her hair into a pony-tail. The Spa Cottage had blond wood floors and white rattan so-fas. There were bowls of red cherries and heated hand towels.

She rarely got a massage. In New York she was too busy at the gallery to join her friends at Elizabeth Arden. And in St. Barts it didn't seem right to lie on a table when she could be snorkeling or sailing.

But the spa attendant wrapped her in a towel and coated her skin with Japanese oils. Cucumber slices covered her eyes and the air was scented with jasmine and rosemary.

Now her skin was polished and her cheeks glowed. She thought fleetingly of the places Sebastian wanted to take her and bit her lip. She didn't have to get on an airplane; everything was available in St. Barts.

"You look like a movie poster," Finn said when she walked out to the pool. "We should do this more often."

"I've never been so pampered." She lay on a chaise longue. "The hot shells come from the Philippines and the oils are extracted from flowering plants in Kyoto. It was like taking a mini-vacation."

"I've been planning it for days. I wanted your birthday to be special." Finn ate a bite of pomegranate. "You know, I was thinking about Sebastian."

"You were?" Olivia looked up.

"I'm glad he came," he continued. "We might not be able to travel the world but we're going to have wonderful experiences. And as long as we tell each other everything, nothing will come between us."

Olivia kissed him and his lips tasted of coconut and pineapple. The sun glinted on her diamond ring and she felt calm and relaxed. Everyone she loved was in St. Barts to celebrate her birthday. She crossed her fingers and hoped nothing would go wrong.

Chapter Sixteen

HADLEY RUBBED HER LIPS WITH red lipstick and glanced in the mirror. Her black dress was tighter than she usually wore and her gold sandals were quite high but they were having dinner at Maya's. It appeared casual, with its open-air tables and plain white china, but everyone knew it was the most coveted reservation in St. Barts.

Maya and her husband, Randy, personally welcomed every diner, and celebrities adored the restaurant perched on the harbor. Hadley had seen Paul McCartney sampling creole pumpkin soup, Leonardo DiCaprio eating sautéed scallops, and Marc Jacobs devouring Maya's chocolate cake.

She spritzed her wrists with Chanel No 5 and knew the real reason she'd spent an hour applying blush and mascara. She wasn't trying to impress Pierce Brosnan or become friends with Salma Hayek. She wanted to be irresistible for Felix.

Her stomach did a little flip and she wondered how she could be nervous after twenty years of marriage. It was all Sebastian's fault. Until he started poking around her relationship, she was happy sleeping on the leather sofa.

But she fiddled with her ruby necklace and thought that wasn't true. She'd stuffed her yearnings away like the library books she didn't have time to read and the Carolina Herrera dress she needed to take to the dry cleaner.

She grabbed her quilted evening bag and walked down the circular staircase. Felix stood in the living room clutching a shot glass.

"I didn't know you were downstairs," Hadley said. "Are you all right?"

"I pulled my shoulder in the shower." Felix flinched. "It hurts terribly. I washed two aspirin down with a shot of vermouth."

"We can stay home if you like," Hadley suggested. "Olivia would understand."

"I'll be fine." He glanced at his watch. "Where is everyone? I don't want to lose our table."

"Olivia is almost ready and I heard Sebastian singing in the shower." She paused. "It was very nice of you to let Sebastian come back to the villa."

"It means a lot to Olivia. But I'll be glad to see him leave tomorrow." Felix tried to smile. "My board shorts keep disappearing and Esther is tired of emptying ashtrays."

"Did I hear my name?" Sebastian entered the living room. He looked at Hadley and put his hand over his mouth. "My god, you look beautiful in that dress, like a Tintoretto painting. But I'm sure I'm repeating what Felix already told you."

"Thank you." Hadley touched her hair. "Felix is in a lot of pain. He pulled his shoulder."

"Our bodies betray us so easily at our age," Sebastian replied. "Last year I had to bow out of heli-skiing because I twisted my ankle."

Hadley looked up and saw Olivia and Finn descend the staircase.

Olivia wore a green sheath and silver sandals. Her blond hair was knotted into a bun and diamond earrings dangled in her ears.

"Darling, you look stunning," Hadley gasped. "What a gorgeous dress."

"I took your advice and went shopping." Olivia smiled.

"It's perfect. We should go; Felix is anxious to get to the restaurant." Hadley put her hand to her ears. "Oh dear, I lost a ruby earring."

"We'll all look for it," Olivia said.

"You mustn't be late." Hadley shook her head. "I'll find it and be right behind you."

"If you're sure," Felix said and kissed her. "But please hurry. I called ahead and Randy is chilling a bottle of 1982 Château Margaux."

Hadley crouched down and examined the floral rug. She heard footsteps and turned around. Sebastian stood in the doorway. His pin-striped blazer was folded over his arm and he wore his straw hat.

"What are you doing here?" she asked. "I thought you went with Finn and Olivia."

"I didn't want you to drive alone," Sebastian explained. "The roads are terrible at night."

"That wasn't necessary. I'm perfectly capable of driving by myself."

"Didn't Olivia look beautiful?" Sebastian sighed, pouring a glass of vermouth. "Being in love is more flattering than any blush or lipstick. Do you know why the *Mona Lisa* is the most beautiful woman in history and no one has ever replicated Botticelli's *Birth Of Venus*? Because the artist was in love with his subject and it shows on the canvas."

"This is hardly the time to discuss art history," Hadley replied.

"If you want to make yourself useful, help me search for my earring. Felix gave it to me last year and it's very special."

Sebastian walked to the side table and picked up Hadley's purse. He opened it and handed her the ruby earring. "Then you'll be happy to know it's right here."

"Why is it in my purse?" she gasped. "Don't tell me you hid it. Even you wouldn't stoop that low."

"That's ridiculous. Of course I didn't hide it," he scoffed. "I noticed it when you placed your purse on the table."

"And you didn't say anything?"

"Felix seemed out of sorts and those little cars are terribly cramped." Sebastian shrugged. "I didn't want to end up sitting in his lap."

"Thank you for finding it. There better not be any surprises tonight." Hadley fastened the earring in her ear. "We're going to eat banana flambé and sing 'Happy Birthday' to Olivia. Tomorrow you're going to thank Felix for his hospitality and leave Esther a little something, and drive to the airport."

"You have my word." He hesitated. "There is another reason I waited. I wanted to ask you a question."

"What is it?" Hadley inquired.

He opened his mouth and then stopped. He drained his glass and looked at Hadley. "I want to request a special dessert. Does Olivia like hazelnut or pistachio ice cream?"

Hadley walked to the door and turned around. "Olivia loves pistachio."

Hadley gazed at the white picket fence and bright yellow sign and thought Maya's was still her favorite restaurant in St. Barts. It might not have sea-foam silk cushions like La Plage or smooth teak booths like Le Carre, but the tables were covered with checkered tablecloths and vases were filled with purple daisies and waiters could spend hours going over the menu. And the food! Grilled mahimahi that melted in your mouth and curries with just the right amount of spices and desserts that were light and fluffy.

They started with wahoo tuna in yogurt and creole sauce. Sebastian said the brothy soup was the best he ever tasted and Finn complimented Felix's choice in wine and everyone chatted and smiled.

Now Hadley cradled her glass and was glad Sebastian had stayed. Olivia's green eyes sparkled and she was like Alice in Wonderland. She couldn't stop exclaiming about the flickering candles and fresh fish and spring vegetables.

"I want to thank everyone for coming." Olivia sipped her wine. "Having Sebastian here means so much to me and being engaged to Finn is everything I wished for. And I must thank Felix and Hadley. I had the most wonderful childhood with ice skating in Central Park and weekends at the Guggenheim." She smiled. "No child could have felt more loved and I am truly grateful."

"You've been a joy since I wrapped you in your first baby blanket." Hadley kissed her. "Now you're a grown woman with a brilliant career and bright future. We're all so proud of you."

"I'd like to add something." Sebastian stood. "Olivia mentioned the wedding earlier and I hesitated. I think she wondered if I was going to attend and with my track record I can't blame her. But I wanted to ask an important question and I was afraid of the answer." He turned to Olivia. "I wonder if Felix and I could share the honor of giving you away."

Olivia flew out of her seat and hugged Sebastian.

"Of course you and Felix must give me away," she urged. "I wouldn't have it any other way."

"Well, then," Sebastian beamed, "I couldn't be happier."

Hadley ate the last bite of shrimp fricassee and pursed her lips. Only Sebastian could make Olivia's birthday dinner about himself. But she mustn't be hard on him. What father wouldn't want to give away his daughter?

Olivia and Finn stepped onto the dance floor and Hadley swayed to the music. The air smelled of vanilla and hibiscus and she felt relaxed and happy.

"It's the perfect night for being outdoors," Sebastian mused. "You and Felix should dance."

"I'm afraid I can't." Felix winced. "My shoulder still hurts and we're playing in the finals tomorrow."

"What a pity . . . They're playing Frank Sinatra instead of that hideous rap music." Sebastian stood. "How about if I take Hadley for a spin?"

"No, thank you," Hadley said. "I'm happy watching Finn and Olivia."

"You're tapping your toes under the table," Sebastian insisted. "You're dying to get on the dance floor."

"Go on," Felix urged. "You shouldn't sit out the whole evening because I have a bad shoulder."

Sebastian took Hadley's hand and escorted her onto the wooden dance floor. The band played a fast jazz number and Sebastian twirled her around. Her cheeks were flushed and her heart beat faster.

"That's enough," she laughed. "I'm exhausted."

"They're playing 'What a Wonderful World.' We have to dance, it's our song."

"We haven't danced in over twenty years and we never had a song," Hadley retorted. "I'm going back to the table."

"Perhaps it played on Olivia's baby mobile but it still brings back memories." Sebastian touched her elbow. "Please, just one more song."

Hadley inhaled the scent of musk cologne and closed her eyes. The breeze touched her cheeks and she remembered the trout farm outside Johannesburg. She and Sebastian danced under a giant willow tree and he had to keep running inside to wind up Olivia's mobile.

Suddenly Sebastian pulled her close and kissed her. His lips were warm and for a moment she kissed him back. Then she pushed him away and her blue eyes flashed.

"What do you think you're doing?" she spluttered.

"I was seeing if you were still a woman," he answered. "You kiss wonderfully and you smell exactly the same: like lavender and fresh-cut flowers."

"How dare you?" she spat. "I'm a happily married woman."

"If you're happily married, why isn't Felix on the dance floor?"

"Felix has to rest his shoulder. He has a match tomorrow."

"Do you ever wonder why tennis is the most important thing in Felix's life?" Sebastian mused. "If my wife wore that black dress, I wouldn't let her out of my sight."

"Felix needs a physical outlet because he works hard," Hadley snapped. "You had a wife. But that didn't stop you from leaving."

"So that's it. You're still bitter that I left."

"Why should I be bitter?" Hadley seethed. "I have a wonderful daughter and caring husband and successful career."

"Do you remember when we discovered the bonobo chimpanzees in Africa? The female seemed like she couldn't stand the male but it was actually the opposite. There's only one explanation as to why you're so cold." Sebastian's green eyes flickered in the moonlight. "You're still in love with me."

"You haven't changed a bit. You think the whole world is in love with Sebastian Miller." Hadley turned away. "It was so long ago. I can't remember why I fell in love with you in the first place."

Hadley stood in front of the mirror in the powder room and fixed her makeup. She couldn't go back to the table until her heart stopped pounding. How dare Sebastian kiss her? He acted like the high school quarterback who flexed his muscles and could have any girl he wanted.

The only reason she'd kissed him back was that she'd been remembering the farm outside Johannesburg. But she stopped being in love with him years ago. She was lucky to have found Felix and they really were happy.

Hadley walked back to the table and pulled out a chair.

"Are you feeling all right?" Felix asked. "You look a little pale."

"You do look peaked," Sebastian chimed in. "Perhaps you'd like to return to the villa. I'd be happy to drive you. I did plan a special dessert but everyone can eat it without us."

"I've never felt better," Hadley said and turned to Felix. "They're playing 'It Had to Be You.' Would you dance with me?"

"I suppose I could manage one dance; it was our favorite song." Felix stood and took Hadley's hand. "Shall we?"

Hadley stood at the sink and poured a cup of coffee. She knew she shouldn't drink coffee at night but she was so angry with Sebastian, she couldn't possibly sleep.

A car pulled into the driveway and she peered out the window. Felix hopped out, carrying a brown paper bag.

"I stopped at the pharmacy and bought some more aspirin." He joined her. "That coffee smells delicious."

"Would you like some?" she asked. "I brewed a fresh pot."

"No, thank you." He unbuttoned his collar. "I'd never fall asleep and my shoulder is killing me."

"It was a lovely evening." Hadley perched on a stool. "The banana flambé was perfect and everyone had a wonderful time."

"Even Sebastian behaved himself. Except for the extra glass of Hennessey he put on the bill," Felix laughed. "Should I get up early and drive him to the airport?"

"His flight leaves at six a.m. and you need a good night's sleep." Hadley shook her head. "Olivia could take him but that might upset her."

"Are you going to take him?" Felix asked.

"We'll call a taxi," she decided. "Don't worry. I'll tell the driver to not let Sebastian out of his sight until he boards the plane."

Felix leaned forward and kissed her.

"What's that for?" she asked.

"It hasn't been easy for you dealing with Sebastian. I can tell by the tension in your shoulders," he explained. "But you did it for Olivia and she never looked more radiant."

Hadley fiddled with her cup and thought it was nice to sit

opposite her husband. His silvery hair was brushed over his fore-head and he had a warm smile.

"I want to talk to you about something." She hesitated. "It's quite important."

"Could it wait until tomorrow?" Felix asked and stood. "If I don't go to bed before the aspirin wears off, I'll be in pain all night."

Hadley gulped the coffee and tried to smile. "Of course. We'll talk in the morning."

Hadley sat in the library and flipped through a magazine. It was almost midnight and the villa was quiet. She should have said a proper goodbye to Sebastian but she couldn't face him. She'd have Esther leave some peach muffins for him to take to the airport.

Her phone rang and she picked it up.

"Hadley?" a female voice said. "It's Phyllis Irvine. I hope I'm not calling too late."

Phyllis was one of her best clients. She had a ten-room apartment on the Upper East Side and an unlimited art budget.

"Of course not. It's lovely to hear from you," Hadley answered. "Is anything wrong?"

"I'm in Monaco and it's seven in the morning." Phyllis paused. "I heard a rumor and wondered if you could help me."

"What kind of rumor?" Hadley asked.

"Years ago, I read a piece in *The New Yorker* about a very spe-cial painting. The artist was offered half a million dollars for it and turned it down," she began. "It's called *The Miller Girls* and it's been in a private collection ever since. I heard it's finally going on the market."

"*The Miller Girls!*" Hadley exclaimed. "Are you sure?"

"The price could go as high as three-quarters of a million dollars. I'd like to scoop it up before the news becomes public," Phyllis said. "I remember you were somehow involved with the artist and thought you might know something."

"Oh yes. I know the artist." Hadley felt the rage build inside her. "But I never heard it was for sale."

"It's hush-hush, of course," Phyllis explained. "But you know how word leaks out. Art collectors rub shoulders at the roulette table and say things they wouldn't tell their mistresses."

"What a fascinating story. I'll do some investigating." Hadley pursed her lips. "If you don't mind me asking, where did you get the information?"

"I can't reveal my source or I'll never get another inside tip," Phyllis laughed. "But trust me, it was quite reliable."

"Give me a few days," Hadley said. "I'll get back to you as soon as I can."

"I hope you can track it down," Phyllis replied. "It sounds like a fabulous piece and I have to have it."

Hadley hung up and walked to the bar. It didn't matter that she'd had two glasses of champagne at Maya's; she needed a very tall scotch.

So that's what Sebastian was up to! He didn't come to St. Barts to celebrate Olivia's birthday and he had no interest in taking Olivia to Capri. Even their kiss on the dance floor was a decoy. Sebastian was here because he'd run out of money and decided to sell *The Miller Girls*.

Not that it was his to sell. He had given it to her as a gift, even if they never put it in writing. What if he disappeared with it in the middle of the night like a character in a Le Carré novel?

She downed her scotch and thought she was being ridiculous. If he was desperate for money, he could have asked for help.

But Sebastian was too proud to admit he couldn't keep himself in Italian loafers. And Felix was unlikely to give a handout to her ex-husband. Selling *The Miller Girls* might be the only option he had.

Three-quarters of a million dollars! Where had Phyllis gotten such an absurd amount? Sebastian's paintings hadn't sold for more than five figures in years. But the art world was full of outrageous prices. All it took was for someone to whisper that a piece was difficult to acquire, and it became as valuable as Van Gogh's *Sunflowers.*

She put down her glass and thought she'd go upstairs and confront Sebastian. But she remembered the kiss on the dance floor and shuddered. What if Sebastian told Felix or Olivia? The kiss hadn't meant anything but it would be so difficult to explain.

She would lock the door and sleep on the sofa. Sebastian wouldn't be able to sneak down and take the painting and he would have to leave without it. Perhaps she'd send him a small check; after all, he was Olivia's father. And Olivia would be heartbroken if he couldn't afford to attend the wedding.

She curled up on the leather sofa and glanced at the painting. It really was a magnificent piece: the colors were bright and the brushstrokes were confident and it reeked of youthful egoism and ambition.

She pulled the cashmere blanket over her shoulders and closed her eyes. It would be satisfying to stop Sebastian from carrying out his plan. He had taken so much; he couldn't have *The Miller Girls,* too.

Chapter Seventeen

OLIVIA STOOD AT THE BALCONY and inhaled the scent of wet grass. It was 5:00 a.m. and the villa was completely silent. The sky was pale pink and the swimming pool was liquid silver.

She never woke up this early but something had disturbed her, like a mosquito bite that begins to itch in the middle of the night. She tossed and turned for hours, and finally gave up and got dressed.

Maybe she was disappointed that her birthday was over. She remembered when she was a child and all the excitement—opening her presents, blowing out the candles, eating too much chocolate cake—left her tired and fidgety.

The afternoon at Le Toiny with Finn had been magical and dinner at Maya's was everything she imagined. Sebastian was going to give her away at her wedding! Her heart lifted and she had never been so happy.

But ever since they'd returned to the villa, she had an ache in the pit of her stomach. She'd expected to sit up with Sebastian, sipping cognac and talking about scuba diving and snorkeling. Instead he'd kissed her on the cheek and hurried upstairs to his bedroom.

And he never mentioned Anguilla; she almost thought she'd

imagined the extra plane ticket. Maybe he was afraid Olivia would turn him down. But why did he buy it in the first place?

Suddenly she remembered her mother returning from the dance floor and gasped. Hadley's cheeks had been flushed and her hair tousled and her lipstick smeared. Could something have happened between them? Had they rekindled old feelings?

Hadley was still beautiful with her blond hair and high cheekbones. Sebastian could have realized what he had been missing and begged Hadley to take him back.

Olivia's eyes were wide and she realized she'd got it all wrong. Sebastian never intended to take her to Anguilla. The extra ticket was for Hadley. Sebastian had asked Hadley to run away with him while they were dancing. And she said yes!

But how could Hadley do such a thing? She'd be giving up Felix and the gallery and the villa in St. Barts. Olivia remembered Sebastian saying he thought Hadley seemed skittish and unsettled. Maybe Hadley had been unhappy. And Sebastian could be so compelling with his descriptions of South Pacific islands and mountains in Tibet.

It was all her fault. If Sebastian hadn't come to St. Barts to celebrate her birthday none of this would have happened. Olivia's knees buckled and she sat on the floral bedspread.

Felix was the best stepfather; she loved him so much and couldn't bear to see him hurt. And it would never work out between Hadley and Sebastian. They had been so in love and Sebastian still walked out.

She crossed the hall and opened Hadley and Felix's bedroom door. Felix was asleep but Hadley's side of the bed was empty. The silk pillow was smooth and her purse was missing.

Olivia closed the door and hurried down the hallway. She

opened Sebastian's door and peered inside. The cotton sheets were rumpled and his suitcase and straw hat were gone.

She raced down the staircase and checked the driveway. The cars were there but that didn't mean anything. They could have taken a taxi to the airport. She had to reach Hadley before she boarded the plane, and convince her she was making a terrible mistake.

She grabbed the keys from the side table and hesitated. She could ask Finn to come with her. But Finn and Felix were terribly close and Finn would feel obligated to tell Felix what happened. If she went by herself, Hadley would be home before Felix was awake.

For a moment she thought of everything her mother had done for her: listened to her recite her lines when she was Little Red Riding Hood in the school play, picked her up from the cinema after a horrible date. What if Hadley had longed for Sebastian to return and Olivia was ruining her dreams?

But she had watched Hadley and Felix host gorgeous dinner parties and curl up in the den with the Sunday *New York Times*. Every relationship had dry spells, but she was certain they loved each other.

She slid into the driver's seat and backed out of the driveway. An egg truck honked and she wished she were lying in bed, dreaming of Esther's strawberry pancakes. But the plane left in less than an hour and she couldn't be late. She put the car in drive and pressed on the accelerator.

A light fog settled over St. Jean airport and she pulled into the parking lot. She remembered when she arrived in St. Barts and had been looking forward to swimming at Shell Beach and sipping lime daiquiris at Pink Parrot. Now she was trying to save Hadley and Felix's marriage.

She entered the terminal and crossed the linoleum floor. A ticket taker stared at a flickering computer screen and clutched a Styrofoam cup.

"I wonder if you can help me," Olivia began. "I need to know if two passengers are booked on the flight to Anguilla."

"The flight is in the final boarding stages." The woman looked up. "All the passengers are on the plane."

"It's very important. Could you see if Hadley London has a reservation?" Olivia pleaded. "It might be under the name Sebastian Miller."

"I'm sorry," the woman shook her head, "I'm not allowed to give out that information."

"You don't understand. If my mother leaves on that plane her whole life might be ruined." Olivia's eyes watered. "Couldn't you possibly make an exception?"

"If I gave out the names of every wife who decided to take a day trip with her private chef or husband who was running away with the nanny, I'd be fired." The woman clicked on her screen. "I'm afraid I can't help you."

"There must be something I can do," Olivia insisted.

"The only way you're going to find out who's on that flight is to buy a ticket." The woman glanced at her watch. "You better do it quickly. It leaves in fifteen minutes."

Olivia gazed out the window at the planes lining the runway. There were sleek private jets and tiny propeller planes painted in bright colors. Could she really confront Hadley and Sebastian in public? And what would Finn say if she disappeared to Anguilla without telling him?

But she couldn't let her mother do something she would regret. She would send Finn a text saying she went to Anguilla with Sebastian. There was nothing to worry about and she would explain everything.

"One ticket, please." She opened her purse and took out her charge card.

The woman handed her the red and blue boarding pass and smiled. "You are all set for your trip. Have a wonderful time in Anguilla."

Olivia slipped her credit card back in her purse and opened the gray metal door. The warm breeze touched her cheeks and St. Barts had never looked more beautiful. The ocean was a shimmering turquoise and the green hills were filled with tropical plants and lush flowers.

She slipped on her sunglasses and took a deep breath. The morning sun made patterns on the runway and she ran to the plane.

Chapter Eighteen

THE LIGHT STREAMED THROUGH THE gauze curtains and Hadley shifted on the sofa. She reached for her phone but the screen was dark. She pressed the button and realized the battery was dead.

She remembered everything about the night before—Sebastian's kiss on the dance floor and Phyllis's late-night phone call—and shivered. Then she looked up and saw the sun glinting on *The Miller Girls* and the air left her lungs. Sebastian hadn't taken the painting!

The clock above the marble fireplace chimed and she jumped up. How could she have slept until 10:00 a.m.? Felix must have gone to the club without his usual dark coffee and fruit salad.

She smoothed her hair and hurried up the circular staircase. Sebastian's door was open and she peered inside. A towel was flung over a chair and his leather bag was missing.

She walked downstairs and felt like Grace Kelly in *To Catch a Thief.* She wanted to leap over the waves in a speedboat or roar down the hill in a convertible. Sebastian was gone and she could finally enjoy her vacation.

There was a platter of whole wheat toast and cut fruit on the kitchen counter. She didn't have to worry about Felix missing breakfast; he was perfectly capable of feeding himself. He even left a pot of coffee and a pitcher filled with whole cream.

She ate a slice of papaya and saw Finn's phone on the table. She never read private texts but she noticed Sebastian's name and suddenly had an uneasy feeling. She picked up the phone and read out loud:

"'I had to go to Anguilla with Sebastian. There's nothing to worry about and I'll explain everything. Love, Olivia.'"

The phone dropped on the wood floor and she started. What was Olivia doing in Anguilla and why hadn't she said anything to Hadley?

"Oh, that would be incredibly low," she gasped. "Sebastian wouldn't dare."

She tried to put the pieces together, like the jigsaw puzzles she'd done with Olivia as a child. Perhaps Sebastian told Olivia he'd wanted to spend more time together but couldn't put off his commission. He begged her to accompany him to Anguilla and she agreed. But Anguilla was a fifteen-minute flight from St. Barts. If Olivia planned on going for the day she would have mentioned it.

Sebastian must be up to something. He still believed Olivia and Finn were too young to get married and was trying to separate them. He was going to tell Olivia he'd decided not to go to the ashram and they should spend the summer traveling. Finn would be furious and break off the engagement.

It was too underhanded even for Sebastian. And what did it have to do with *The Miller Girls*? But nothing else made sense. Olivia was young and impressionable and loved her father. And Sebastian was like an Indian snake charmer: he could make anyone do what he wanted with a few carefully chosen words.

If she called Sebastian and demanded that he put Olivia on a plane, he could say he tried but failed. She would have to talk to him in person.

"It's not going to work this time, Sebastian Miller," she said out loud. She entered the library and took *The Miller Girls* off the wall. Then she walked out to the driveway, climbed into her yellow Fiat, and put the car in reverse.

Hadley walked up the gravel path and rang the doorbell. The house had floor-to-ceiling windows and twelve-foot double front doors and a pond filled with calla lilies. There was a bronze statue and a circular driveway lined with brightly colored sports cars.

A man in a white uniform answered the door. "Can I help you?"

"I'm looking for Sebastian Miller." Hadley smoothed her skirt. "He's a guest of James Oliver."

"Please follow me. Mr. Miller is staying in the pool house."

Hadley walked through rooms with ash-blond floors and low white furniture and glass coffee tables. Abstract paintings hung in silver frames and huge vases were filled with purple orchids. A white grand piano stood by the window and the view was all pink hibiscus and white sand beach and sparkling ocean.

"The guesthouse is on the other side of the pool." The man pointed to a rectangular pool flanked by chaise longues.

Hadley walked to the guesthouse and knocked on the door and tried to stop her heart from racing. She knocked again and opened the door. The pool house had a gold and white marble floor and blue linen sofas. There was a teak dining room table and a telescope next to the window.

"My god! This day is getting stranger every minute." Sebastian appeared wearing a patterned shirt and linen shorts. "Who's going to show up at my door next? Jasper Johns or Angelina Jolie? What are you doing in Anguilla?"

"I'm sure you know exactly why I'm here," Hadley snapped. "I came to see Olivia."

"Well, that didn't take long," Sebastian said and smiled. "We only arrived a few hours ago. Apparently she didn't sleep well last night and she's taking a nap. Sit down; you must be frazzled from your flight. Fifteen minutes on those tiny planes can be an eternity. I was certain the pilot was going to miss the runway and land in the ocean.

"James has his own personal chef and there's a platter of shrimp kebobs and aubergine on the terrace," he continued. "Can you believe this place? Two acres of oceanfront property and a collection of European motorcars. Anguilla is a favored tax haven and James has done exceptionally well in organic supermarkets."

"I didn't come for brunch," Hadley seethed. "I'm here to collect my daughter."

"You have to let me explain." Sebastian walked to the bar and poured two glasses of bourbon. "But first we need a stiff drink. I couldn't live in the Caribbean full-time. All the humidity makes me thirsty."

"You're not going to twist your words like the warm pretzels they sell in Central Park. I'm going to tell you exactly what you've done and you're going to listen," Hadley said. "Last night I got a call from one of my best clients. She heard a rumor that *The Miller Girls* was going on the market and was going to fetch three-quarters of a million dollars. I realized you weren't in St. Barts to celebrate Olivia's birthday. You came because you ran out of money and the only way you could keep yourself in scotch and cigarettes was to sell the painting. I locked the door and slept in the library. This morning you were gone and I finally relaxed. But then I discovered Finn's cell phone and Olivia left a message saying she went to Anguilla.

"I tried to put the pieces together. Why did you take Olivia to Anguilla and what did it have to do with selling the painting? It's quite simple. You're getting older and you're afraid of not having anyone to listen to your stories. What better audience than your own daughter?

"Somehow you convinced Olivia to come to Anguilla and then you were going to beg her to travel with you this summer. You were worried she would say no so you were going to use the proceeds of the painting to fund a spectacular adventure: palaces in India and castles in Scotland. You'd take her to the finest restaurants and buy fabulous jewelry. It would be the summer every girl dreamed of.

"The best part was Finn would be furious and break off the engagement. You never liked Finn and you think Olivia is too young to get married. You would have everything you wanted and Olivia's heart would be broken."

Sebastian let out a low whistle and refilled his glass. "Are you quite finished? You should have been a trial attorney. You're more convincing than Gregory Peck in *To Kill a Mockingbird*." He paused and his green eyes flickered. "But you're wrong."

The sun streamed through the floor-to-ceiling windows and the ocean looked so inviting. Hadley longed to slip off her dress and run into the waves. She turned to Sebastian and took a deep breath. "I don't believe you."

"Of course I came to St. Barts for Olivia's birthday. I used to gather the invitations like a squirrel collecting nuts. But something always got in the way: a new commission or the exorbitant price of plane tickets. The few times I could have come, I was terrified of living up to her expectations. A young girl's imagination can turn an absent father into some dashing war hero and I was nothing but an itinerant artist.

"Then I received the invitation and I was already on my way to Anguilla. I couldn't skip St. Barts when it was a fifteen-minute plane trip. And seeing Olivia was worth the bottles of TUMS I swallowed to knock on the door. God! She was beautiful with her blond hair and long legs.

"You can't imagine how wonderful it was to spend time together: scuba diving and snorkeling and sipping piña coladas. She's smart and inquisitive and I could listen to her for hours.

"But I'm not the monster you think I am. I want Olivia to be happy. Of course I think she's too young to get married and I'm not convinced Finn is the right guy. But does any father think differently?"

"Why should I listen to a word you're saying?" Hadley interjected. "If you loved Olivia you wouldn't have brought her to Anguilla."

"I haven't finished. Olivia isn't the only reason I came to St. Barts." He looked up. "I came to see you."

"Me?" Hadley repeated.

"I walked out all those years ago because if I was unable to paint, I couldn't breathe. What I didn't realize was that without you, breathing seemed irrelevant. Every day the pain of missing you grew greater, like a lump that becomes an inoperable tumor. But then I saw the article in *Town & Country* about your and Felix's wedding. How could I compete with a Central Park duplex and your own gallery and villa in St. Barts. And look at everything Olivia had:

the finest schools and dance lessons and year-round passes to the Guggenheim.

"I wasn't being altruistic by staying away. If I had a chance I would have taken it. But I kept tabs and you looked so happy: attending charity galas and the ballet.

"Then I arrived in St. Barts and you were more beautiful than I remembered. I still would have left you alone, I had no desire to become a marriage wrecker. But then I learned you slept on the sofa and spent more time cleaning than a Portuguese maid." He sipped his drink.

"I fell in love with you all over again. I wanted to buy up every boutique on the island: pretty dresses and silk robes and handbags as soft as butter. And flowers! Every time I passed a bed of roses, I wanted to make them into a bouquet. But I was your husband's houseguest. I could hardly woo his wife over Esther's deviled eggs.

"Then last night on the dance floor, I held you in my arms and we were back on the farm in Johannesburg. You were so familiar but brand-new. I wanted to kiss you forever.

"I know you felt it too; your whole body was on fire. But you were afraid and I couldn't blame you. What was to stop me from hurting you again?

"But this morning a vision appeared on my doorstep. Don't you see that we've been given another chance? Olivia is all grown up. And Felix would only notice you were gone when he ran out of cocktail olives." He ran his hands through his hair.

"A buddy wants to sell his art gallery in Crete. We can sell *The Miller Girls* and buy it. Don't you remember the month we spent in the Greek Islands? Waking up every morning to a sky the color of topaz and buildings so white, we were blinded."

He placed his glass on the teak sideboard and walked to the sofa. He pulled her up and kissed her. Hadley kissed him back and inhaled citrus aftershave. A warmth spread through her chest and she longed to wrap her arms around him. It had been so long since she felt warm lips and muscular shoulders.

"I left the risotto simmering on the stove." Sebastian gasped and pulled away. "James won't forgive me if I burn the house down."

Sebastian disappeared into the kitchen and Hadley walked to the window. Her knees were wobbly and her eyes burned and she felt like she'd come down with a sudden flu.

The garden was filled with pink hibiscus and she remembered the guesthouse in Cape Town. The rain didn't stop for weeks and she and Sebastian played checkers and ate boerewors and malva pudding. They were like two kittens with a warm bowl of milk.

It was so long ago; did she really feel that way again? Or was she intoxicated by the idea of someone wanting her so badly he couldn't eat or sleep?

But Sebastian was right; he only left because he had to paint. Now Olivia was engaged and they had no other responsibilities. They could cruise on a yacht and kiss under the moonlight.

Sebastian's leather overnight bag stood in the corner and suddenly a chill ran down her spine. She couldn't leave Felix. Then she would be just as bad as Sebastian.

If someone in the marriage was unhappy, you tried to fix it. And even if you couldn't entirely, that didn't mean you gave up. The only guarantee in a marriage was that you stayed together. And she did love Felix. He was kind and considerate and they shared so many wonderful moments.

She sipped the bourbon and felt like she'd woken up from a

terrible dream. Sebastian entered the living room and she held up her hand.

"Please don't come any closer."

"But you just kissed me," Sebastian replied. "You're in love with me."

"I was in love with you at the guesthouse in Cape Town and the trout farm in Johannesburg and the resort in Chiang Mai. I loved you when you walked out of our Morningside Heights apartment and I was probably still in love with you when I met Felix.

"But that was a long time ago. I'm not in love with you now." She looked at Sebastian. "I love my life and couldn't possibly give it up."

"You're acting like a character in a Thomas Hardy novel!" Sebastian exclaimed. "You think a curse will be put on you or Olivia if you follow your heart. You're supposed to be happy, that's why God invented love. If you ignore it, you're going against everything life is about."

Sebastian's eyes glistened and for a moment he was the young man in Cape Town who insisted she could sell his paintings. Handsome and cocky and not afraid of anything.

"I really have to go." She rubbed her lips. "Where is Olivia?"

"The bedroom is down the hall on the right," Sebastian replied. His shoulders sagged and there were new lines on his forehead.

"Why don't you make lunch while I talk to her," Hadley said and smiled. "I'm sure she'll be hungry."

Hadley knocked on the door and opened it. The bedroom had high ceilings and a white four-poster bed and sliding glass doors opening onto the sand. There was a geometric rug and love seat littered with pastel-colored cushions.

"Darling!" Hadley exclaimed. "It's so good to see you."

Olivia looked up from her iPhone and gasped. "What are you doing in Anguilla?"

"I came to ask you to return to St. Barts." Hadley perched on the bed. "You can't just run off and leave Finn. Your engagement is one of the best times of your life; you have to enjoy it. And Sebastian has been alone for years. He doesn't need a travel companion."

"You think I came to Anguilla to be with Sebastian?" Olivia asked.

"Why else would you be here?" Hadley wondered.

"When I took Sebastian's breakfast to his room yesterday, I discovered two plane tickets to Anguilla. I thought he was going to ask me to accompany him, but he never mentioned it," Olivia began. "Then at dinner, you seemed flustered when you returned from the dance floor. I couldn't sleep all night." She fiddled with her earrings. "I finally realized what was bothering me. The extra plane ticket was for you! I was sure Sebastian was still in love with you and asked you to run away." She paused and looked at the ocean.

"I checked Sebastian's room and he'd already left. Then I peered in your room and your side of the bed was empty. I had to stop you from making a terrible mistake."

"So you came to Anguilla?" Hadley frowned.

"I was just going to drive to the airport, but the plane had already boarded," Olivia continued. "The ticket taker said the only way I could find out who was on the flight was to buy a ticket. It was only when I got on the plane that I realized you weren't on it." Olivia smiled thinly. "Sebastian suggested I come to the house and have a good breakfast before I fly back. I must have fallen asleep, because now it's almost noon."

"Why didn't you ask Finn to go to the airport with you?" Hadley inquired.

"Finn is so close to Felix. I was afraid he would tell Felix what happened." She looked up and her eyes watered. "I texted Finn from the airport to explain and he never replied. I've been calling his phone, but there's no answer."

"Finn isn't answering because he left his phone in the kitchen," Hadley said. "I saw your text to him and that's how I knew you were in Anguilla."

"What if he's angry that I left without telling him?" Olivia asked.

"Finn will understand." Hadley paused. "You were only trying to help me and Felix."

"You and Felix have been there my whole life." Olivia bit her lip. "I couldn't do anything else."

"Why don't we join Sebastian for lunch and then go to the airport." Hadley stood and hugged her.

"That sounds wonderful. I haven't eaten all day and I'm starving." Olivia hesitated. "I did want to ask you something."

"What is it?" Hadley asked.

"Are you still in love with Sebastian?"

"Good heavens, no." Hadley shook her head. "Felix and I are very happy. Even good marriages have ups and downs. But the important thing is you know you'll always be there for each other," she said and smiled. "It's the best feeling in the world."

They sat at the teak dining room table and ate shrimp kabobs and avocado salad. There was a bowl of fresh fruit and coconut sorbet.

Olivia's phone buzzed and she picked it up. "It's Finn." She stood. "Excuse me, I'll be right back."

"She's so beautiful," Sebastian sighed. "Finn is a lucky guy."

"They are going to be a wonderful couple."

"I supposed you are right," Sebastian admitted. "As long as they don't have children for a while."

"You'll be a terrific grandfather when the time comes." She paused and looked at Sebastian. "The shrimp is delicious but there's no risotto."

"I beg your pardon?"

"When you kissed me, you pulled away and said you had to take the risotto off the stove," Hadley said slowly. "But we're eating lunch and there's no risotto."

Sebastian put down his fork and rubbed his forehead.

"I couldn't let you throw your life away because of one kiss," he answered. "You needed time to make sure that was what you wanted. So I invented a simmering pot of risotto. It was the honorable thing to do."

"You're a better man than you think." Hadley said and then laughed. "It wasn't that great a kiss."

Sebastian looked at Hadley and his eyes were bright. "Yes, it was."

They walked to the driveway and Hadley opened the door of the rental car.

"I forgot something." She took a painting out of the backseat. "This is for you."

"You're giving me *The Miller Girls*?" he gasped.

"I brought it to bribe you into convincing Olivia to come home,"

Hadley explained. "But it has always belonged to you. We were just storing it for you."

"If you're sure." Sebastian took the painting. "I promise I'll take good care of it."

"I know you will." Hadley slid into the driver's seat.

"One more thing. About Olivia's wedding." Sebastian poked his head in the window. "Hotel rooms in St. Barts are so expensive at Christmas. Could I stay at the villa?"

Hadley waited while Olivia ran down the driveway to join them. Olivia kissed Sebastian on the cheek and climbed into the passenger seat.

Hadley turned on the ignition and said to Sebastian, "I'll ask Felix."

Chapter Nineteen

HADLEY OPENED THE FRONT DOOR of the villa and entered the living room. It was late afternoon and the air smelled of lemon polish. A crystal vase was filled with pink roses and there was a stack of magazines on the coffee table.

"There you are." Felix looked up. He wore a collared shirt and pressed slacks. "I came down from taking a shower and the villa was quiet. Olivia isn't here and Finn took the car."

"He is meeting Olivia at Hotel Eden Rock," Hadley explained. "I booked them a suite as an engagement present. I thought it would be nice for them to have time alone."

"That's an excellent idea." Felix beamed. "I'll tell Esther it will be just two for dinner."

"I'd like to talk to you about something," Hadley said. "Could we go into the library?"

"Is anything wrong?" He frowned. "Are you sick?"

"It's nothing like that." Hadley shook her head. "Let's discuss it over martinis."

They entered the library and Felix glanced at the wall above the fireplace.

"Good god! *The Miller Girls* has been stolen!" he gasped.

"No, it hasn't. I gave it to Sebastian. I'm sorry, I should have asked you first." She paused. "He always loved the painting and I thought he should have it."

"It must be worth a fortune." Felix rubbed his brow. "I thought you wanted to give it to Olivia and Finn."

"I doubt it's that valuable. A Sebastian Miller hasn't gone for more than five figures in years." She smiled. "Anyway, Sebastian will never sell it. Eventually he will pass it down to Olivia."

"To be honest, I don't mind seeing it go. I always thought you were more beautiful than the woman in the painting." Felix filled two glasses with vermouth and handed one to Hadley. "What did you want to talk about?"

Hadley sipped her drink and took a deep breath.

"When you injured your back it made sense to sleep in separate rooms. And it took months to recuperate," she began. "But now you play tennis every day and we're still sleeping apart. I wonder if there's another reason. Perhaps you don't find me desirable."

Felix gulped his drink and ran his hands through his hair.

"You think I want separate bedrooms?" he spluttered.

"Well, yes." Hadley nodded. "You never tried to change things."

"The worst thing about injuring my back wasn't the hot compresses or hours missed on the tennis court. It was not holding you in my arms at night," Felix said. "But then I got better and you never moved back into our bedroom. I thought you weren't interested. When my mother was your age I overheard her talking to a friend about 'the change.' She said a woman's needs become different and she and my father never slept in the same bed again. I assumed—"

"You thought I didn't want to make love because of menopause?" Hadley interrupted.

"I don't know much about the subject." Felix flushed. "But yes, I suppose so."

"Why didn't you say something?" she asked.

"I didn't know how," he admitted. "I hoped you would bring it up first."

"I can imagine Carolyn saying something like that but it would never occur to me." Hadley fiddled with her glass. "We have decades ahead of us and I don't want to become one of those couples who only meet over breakfast. I'm forty-eight years old and I want to make love to my husband."

Felix leaned over and kissed her. His lips were warm and he ran one hand over her breast. Hadley gasped and something wonderful stirred inside her.

"It's not too late," Felix murmured. "We can make up for lost time."

"We have to promise to never let it happen again," Hadley urged. "We should be able to talk about anything."

"I promise as long as you do something for me," Felix agreed.

"What?" Hadley looked up.

Felix stood and took her hand. "Come upstairs to the bedroom."

Hadley put her glass on the marble bar and glanced at the empty space over the fireplace. She must get a new painting. Something lush and tropical with all the colors of St. Barts.

Chapter Twenty

OLIVIA UNWRAPPED A CHOCOLATE TRUFFLE and glanced around the hotel suite. It had a white-canopied bed and mahogany floor and bright orange furniture. There was a stand-alone bathtub in the bathroom and a window seat littered with silk cushions. From the moment Finn insisted on carrying her through the door, she felt almost giddy.

They swam in the ocean and strolled along the white sand beach. They showered in the outdoor shower and kissed under the palm trees. Then they dressed for dinner and walked to the hotel's dining room.

And the food! Platters of crispy egg and seared foie gras and lobster medallions. There was red snapper and Caribbean chocolate cake. They sipped a French chardonnay and talked about snorkeling at Saline Beach and feeding the sea turtles at Grand Cul de Sac.

Now the sun slid behind the horizon and St. Jean's Bay was a sheet of glass. Torches flickered on the lawn and soft jazz filtered through the sound system.

"You look so beautiful." Finn stepped out of the bathroom. A towel was wrapped around his waist and his hair was freshly washed.

"I was looking at wedding dresses." Olivia flipped through the magazine. "I've always pictured an ivory sheath with a long white train. I'll borrow Hadley's diamond and sapphire earrings and carry a bouquet of purple freesias."

"I don't care what you wear as long as I can undress you," Finn said and kissed her.

"It's going to be wonderful to get married in St. Barts at Christmas," Olivia mused. "The garden will be strung with fairy lights and pastel-colored sofas will be scattered over the lawn. Round tables will be set with pink tablecloths and gold candelabras and it will be like a movie set."

"I'll leave the décor to you and Hadley." Finn grinned. "I wanted to talk to you about something."

"I hope it's not the size of the guest list," Olivia laughed. "All the bedrooms in the villa are already spoken for and I will have to reserve every room at Le Toiny."

"I spoke with my father today." Finn fiddled with his towel. "The firm is opening a London office and he wants me to be in charge. It would only be for a year but it would be a great experience."

"London!" Olivia exclaimed.

"He's been wanting to expand the firm for ages and it's a tremendous opportunity. You could work at a gallery in Mayfair or Piccadilly." He touched Olivia's hand. "I know how close you are to Hadley and Felix. We won't go, if you don't want to. But it might be fun to live somewhere new. We could explore some of the places you wanted to see with Sebastian: the Great Wall of China and the fjords in Scandinavia. Or we could just relax on a beach in Majorca or the South of France."

Olivia imagined a garden flat in Notting Hill or a terrace house in Belgravia. She could visit the British History Museum and spend hours at the Tate Gallery. They'd shop in the food hall at Harrods and take the boat train to Paris.

"I think it's a wonderful plan! The London art scene is one of the most dynamic in the world," Olivia said excitedly. "I'm sure Hadley and Felix would love to visit. We could even ask Sebastian. We'll check out photography exhibits at the Gagosian and see the Old Masters at the National Gallery."

"We should celebrate." Finn opened a bottle of champagne. He poured two glasses and handed one to Olivia. "We have so much to look forward to: the wedding and a fabulous honeymoon and a whole new adventure."

Olivia placed her champagne flute on the side table and a smile lit up her face. She took Finn's hand and led him to the bed.

"I have a better way to celebrate," she said and kissed him.

He kissed her back and she inhaled the scent of coconut shampoo. The lights twinkled on the harbor and a tropical breeze wafted through the sliding glass doors and she had never been so happy.

Acknowledgments

Thank you to Melissa Flashman for being a tremendous agent and to Lauren Jablonski for being such a generous and wise editor. I am grateful for the whole team at St. Martin's Press. Staci Burt, my publicist, never fails to amaze me, and Karen Masnica in marketing does a fantastic job. Thank you to Danielle Fiorella for her gorgeous covers and to Karen Richardson, Emily Walters, and Laura Clark. And always a huge thank-you to Jennifer Weiss and Jennifer Enderlin.

I'm lucky to have great friends: Andrea Katz, Christina Adams, Traci Whitney, and Pat Hazelton. And I am most grateful for my family: my husband, Thomas, and my children, Alex, Andrew, Heather, Madeleine, and Thomas Jr.

1. In the very first scene, Olivia's father, Sebastian, appears after a twenty-year absence. How would you receive a long-absent parent if this happened to you?

2. Describe Hadley. Do you think she is a strong woman? In what ways is she strong and in what ways might she be weak?

3. Olivia is put in a position where she has to choose between Sebastian and Finn in various instances. Do you agree with her actions, and why or why not?

4. Much of the flashbacks are set in South Africa and Thailand. Are these places you have visited or are interested in visiting? What are your feelings about them from the descriptions in the book?

5. Describe Hadley's relationship with her husband, Felix. Do you think it is a good marriage? Why or why not?

6. Do you think Olivia and Finn are right for each other? What makes them a good couple and what instances might give you doubts about their future?

7. Most of the action takes place on St. Barts. If you had a vacation home you visited every year, where would you like it to be?

8. Describe Sebastian. What are his redeeming qualities and what are his faults?

9. How do the relationships between the different characters change and develop throughout the novel?

10. Are you satisfied with the ending? Could you see a different ending for any of the characters?

St. Martin's
Griffin